The Darkness Rises

STACY STOKES

VIKING

VIKING
An imprint of Penguin Random House LLC, New York

First published in the United States of America by Viking,
an imprint of Penguin Random House LLC, 2024

Visit us online at PenguinRandomHouse.com.

Library of Congress Cataloging-in-Publication Data is available.

ISBN 9780593327692

1st Printing

Printed in the United States of America

LSCH

Edited by Kelsey Murphy
Design by Lucia Baez

Text set in American Garamond

For Jay, my light in the darkness

1

THE NIGHT WAS A SWEATY PALM CLAMPED OVER MY mouth. Still, I took a grateful gulp of air. Anything was better than the mass of sweat, bodies, and chaos inside the house.

Marissa pulled the sliding glass door shut, muffling the noise inside.

"Better?" she asked, fluffing her dark curls. They immediately started to wilt from the humidity. I could tell she wanted to be back in the center of the living room with the rest of the dance team, shouting song lyrics and performing snippets of the choreography they'd learned at dance camp. Things had probably been easier this summer without me.

"Better." I tried smiling. Her real question was written all over her face: *What's wrong with you? What aren't you telling me?*

I jerked my head skyward, pretending I hadn't noticed. Pretending the freckled sky and finger of clouds passing over the moon were the reasons I came outside.

"I just needed some air," I said, like that would explain everything. "Why don't you go back inside? I'll meet you in a few."

"Nice try, Whit." She arched an eyebrow and thumped my shoulder with hers. "You're stuck with me."

I smiled and thumped her back. More like she was the one stuck with me.

The back door slid open, belching music and several people onto the yard. Beau Gunter marched toward us, balancing a pitcher of his infamous punch in one hand and a stack of cups in the other.

"Ladies," he drawled, "don't tell me y'all are leaving. It's early! The Beau hasn't even had a chance to hang out with you."

He grinned like he expected us to be grateful for *the Beau*'s presence. If it wasn't for his height, he might have been cute, but his lanky build made him look too much like a praying mantis. That, and he had a penchant for referring to himself in the third person and making innuendo-laden puns out of his name, which for obvious reasons made me hate him.

"Haven't seen you all summer, Supergirl. Where you been?"

My fingers curled into fists at the sound of my old nickname.

I am not super. I am a monster.

I squeezed my eyes shut, trying to stop the onslaught of images. Trying to keep Dwight's face from surfacing. I pictured Gams's dance studio, remembering the way the wood felt against my feet and the resin crunched against my pointe shoe. I tried to disappear inside that feeling.

For an attitude turn, begin in a wide fourth position, croisé devant arms in third position, right leg in plié . . .

"Whit?" Marissa's voice came to me like an echo down a hallway.

"What'd I say?" Beau asked. "Supergirl, you all right?"

I opened my eyes, cheeks flaring with heat.

"Stop calling her Supergirl," Marissa snapped. She may not know why I hated that nickname, but Marissa had my back.

"It's fine," I told her, even though it made me want to shove my way through the crowd inside and run straight out the front door. "I'm fine. I just—I have a headache."

"I have just the cure for that!" Beau shook the pitcher of punch at us, sending the pink liquid sloshing onto the ground.

"That stuff is liquid headache." Marissa cocked her head and perched a hand on her hip, making her look like a teapot on the verge of exploding. Although if she knew I was comparing her to something a song called *short and stout*, her exploding would be the least of my worries. If you valued your life, you did not refer to Marissa's diminutive size.

"Calm down. I'm just playing around," Beau said.

She glared up at him. He grinned.

The group hovering on the porch let out a loud *whoop* as Beau gave up on us and moved to refill their cups.

Marissa sighed and gave a huff of defeat, sending dark curls dancing around her face. "You wanna go?"

"Why don't you stay? There's no reason for me to ruin your night."

"No way." She looped her arm through mine. "I haven't seen you in almost two months. You owe me major catch-up time. Plus I'm going to get pregnant if I stand on that dance floor any longer."

She gave me a wry grin and pulled me toward the side yard, where we could make our escape unnoticed. I thought she was going to let me off the hook, but when we got to the street, she tugged me to a stop. "Are you going to tell me what that was back there?"

"What do you mean?" I dug through my purse for my keys, feigning innocence.

Marissa bit her lip and looked away, and I felt the familiar knife of guilt slice through me. Lying to Marissa was a skill I'd acquired out of necessity. She would hate me if I told her the truth. Everyone would.

"You never minded when people called you Supergirl before. What gives?"

"I'm just over it, that's all." I searched the street to avoid eye contact, trying to remember how far down I parked. "People shouldn't make me out to be some hero just because I happened to be in the right place at the right time."

Marissa pressed her lips together. She knew it was more than that. She'd been with me when I darted across the cafeteria to give that kid the Heimlich maneuver, which may have seemed *right place, right time* to anyone else watching. Except she'd also been with me when I'd pulled Janell Barbers out of the deep end, at Nordstrom Rack when I'd told the woman working the register not to take her lunch break, and standing next to me when I'd told Mr. Franklin to go to the doctor. He ended up getting triple bypass surgery two days later. There were way too many *right place, right time*s to explain away as a coincidence. Marissa was too smart for that.

Still, she didn't know the truth. And I was grateful.

I clicked my key fob, avoiding her stare. As the lights on my Accord flashed, I caught sight of a figure fumbling with the driver's-side door.

"Hey!" I called. The figure yanked on the door handle. I shouted again, this time jogging ahead with Marissa close at my heels. "Hey, what are you doing to my car?"

A guy looked up and staggered back, squinting. There was a pink stain around his lips. He was one of Beau's punch-chugging minions.

"Your car?" He put a hand on the doorframe to steady himself. "This is my car."

I clicked the remote again and my headlights flared to life. "Nope, my car."

"Well, it looks like my car. Where's my car?"

The boy scratched his head, stumbling slightly. Strands of sandy hair clung to his forehead. In the muted glare of the streetlights it was difficult to tell exactly what color his eyes were—blue or green. Maybe both. Either way, they looked unsteady. *He* looked unsteady, like he'd been riding a Tilt-A-Whirl and his feet were still adjusting to stable ground.

"Looks like your car?" Marissa crossed her arms and glared at him. "That's exactly what a car thief would say."

He held up his hands. "I swear! I'm sorry, I thought it was mine. Where *is* my car?"

"Whatever." Marissa moved to the passenger side. "Find someone else's car to vandalize."

He opened his mouth like he wanted to say something, but closed it quickly, looking to me for help. I offered him a shrug and reached for the door handle. "You probably just parked farther down the street. But you don't look like you should be driving."

"I'm fine. I didn't drink that much." The alcohol wafting off him told a different story.

He went back to scanning the street. Hopefully he was smart enough not to drive home. Not that it was any of my business.

I slid into the front seat and closed the door but couldn't resist glancing once more toward the boy. There was a small smudge of a black cloud forming over his head that hadn't been there a moment ago.

Oh no. Not tonight. Please, not tonight.

Through the rearview mirror I saw him ambling down the street inspecting vehicles. With each step the cloud grew in size, roiling larger and larger. It pulsed above his head like a black tuft of living sky, sliding over his hairline and down his cheeks. It was growing too quickly.

"What's wrong?" Marissa turned around to look at him, trying to figure out what caught my attention.

I shook my head. It wasn't my job to save him. If he wanted to get behind the wheel drunk, that was his problem.

Except it was my problem, wasn't it? I couldn't tear my eyes away from the churning darkness swelling around his head or stop the what-ifs from squelching the finely tuned logic that told me to ignore him.

What if he hurts someone else? What about his family? He's just a kid.

And then the other thoughts crept in—the ones that kept my mind racing in the middle of the night.

You don't know if he's a good guy. What if you save him and he goes on to do something horrible?

I squeezed my eyes shut. It was an impossible choice. It was always an impossible choice. But it was my choice to make, and my consequences to live with.

I let out a growl and slammed my palms against the steering wheel. "Stay here." I jumped out before Marissa could argue. Then I marched down the street to catch up with him, cursing myself the whole way. Why was I doing this again? What was wrong with me?

The boy turned at the sound of my shoes clapping against

the pavement. I could barely see his face through the cloud thrumming around his head. The wisps of smoke had already begun to lick at his shoulders, curling around him like a hungry shadow.

"Hey, wait up!" I called, jogging to close the distance.

"I told your friend I'm not a thief." He slurred when he said the word *thief*. "I have keys, see?" His fingers displayed a car remote with a Texas Longhorns key chain dangling from it.

"Yeah, I know. I just thought that maybe I could drop you off somewhere. Or call you an Uber?"

"Thanks, but I don't need a ride. I just need to find where I parked." He ran a hand through his hair, squinting as he scanned the street.

"I really don't think you should be driving. Why don't you let me drop you off?"

I couldn't read his expression through the blackness swirling around him, but I thought his shoulders slumped with relief.

"I can't leave my car here. My mom will kill me."

"Your mom can't kill you if you're already dead. And if you need me to, I'll bring you back here in the morning. I'll even give you my number so you can call me if you need to. Come on, let me take you home."

He stood there for a minute like he was weighing his options, but I already knew he'd made up his mind. The cloud had begun to curl in on itself, the tendrils of smoke sliding up his cheeks until it finally shrank to a tiny puff of gray above his head and vanished altogether.

He nodded once and shoved the lump of keys back into his pocket. "Thanks."

Marissa's right eyebrow arched when he climbed into the back seat.

"We're making a pit stop," I said in a voice that removed any possibility of discussion. Marissa shrugged and fiddled with the radio until music filled the small space, but there was a smug smile on her face, like she knew all along I wouldn't be able to stop myself from driving him home.

This is the last time, I thought as I eased onto the road. *No more saving people after this.*

Because there are consequences to saving people.

Because enough people have already died from my choices.

2

I WAS SEVEN THE FIRST TIME I SAW THE DARKNESS.
My numb fingers wriggled inside my mother's hand as we
bumped along the rush hour–packed sidewalk, weaving in and
out of bodies with the frustration that only a last-minute can-
cellation from the nanny could bring. I kept looking at the
glistening giants that made up the Dallas skyline. I imagined
them coming to life and reaching with metal fingers to pluck
me from the crowd.

"Whitney, *please*," my mother begged after I smacked into
another pedestrian. "You can stare at the buildings from my
office." She squeezed my hand, making her intention clear:
walk faster.

That's when the man lumbered into view. He was taller than
nearly everyone on the sidewalk, with a thick tuft of brown
hair that only added to his height. A phone was pressed to his
ear while he screamed words my mother would never let me
say out loud.

"Sorry's not good enough!" he shouted, his cheeks flaming
red to match his neck. I gaped, first at the enormous butterfly
of sweat soaking through his dress shirt, then at the matching
tuft of shadowy blackness taking shape above his head.

"Look, Mommy."

"Don't point, Whitney. It's rude." She smacked my hand
down. Had I not been so enthralled in the growing fingers of

smoke swirling around the man's head I might have thought to cry out, but my mind was elsewhere. I couldn't understand why no one else gaped at the shifting, stretching cloud.

Then I remembered something my Gams had told me only a few weeks before.

"Someday you may see a dark cloud hovering over a stranger's head. It's important that you tell me as soon as it happens. Tell no one else."

She had refused to answer my questions but told me that I would know it when I saw it, *if* I saw it. She made me promise I wouldn't tell anyone but her.

Now I gaped at the cloud, a giddy sense of excitement swirling in my tummy. This must have been what she was talking about.

The man was yelling louder, swears flying out of his mouth like spit. He was so busy yelling that he didn't notice the light had changed. He didn't realize that everyone else had stopped on the sidewalk to let the traffic through.

For one brief second I had a ridiculous thought—that I could *save* him. But then the cloud above his head swelled. His foot lifted off the curb and onto the crosswalk. A car barreled around the corner.

The car smacked into him. His body rolled onto the windshield and landed on the crosswalk in a heap, thudding to the ground like a felled tree.

People shouted. Horns blared. Phones fumbled out of pockets.

The blackness crept up the length of his body until it encased him. He was a blacked-out smudge on the ground.

My mother clamped an arm around me and dragged me away from the gathering crowd, but not before I saw the cloud start to recede from the man's body, licking back down his sides the way it had come.

The man was dead. I knew it the way I knew the buildings were tall and the sky was blue. Why else would Gams have warned me?

Mom knelt down so she was eye level to me. She smiled, but her eyes didn't crinkle at the corners the way they usually did.

"Don't worry, sweetheart. He's going to be just fine. All those nice people will help him."

"Don't lie, Mommy," I said, using the same tone I might use to ask for a glass of juice. "He's dead. The rain cloud killed him."

"The—rain cloud?" she asked, voice hesitant.

I nodded, assuming she'd seen it. Assuming everyone had grandmothers who whispered warnings about black clouds.

"What rain cloud are you talking about, sweetheart?"

"The one that was floating above his head. It gobbled him up."

"Honey, there wasn't a . . . rain cloud." She stumbled over the last two words. "The man's just in shock. He probably fainted, that's all."

"No, he didn't. He's dead."

She flinched, her smile wobbling as something passed across her face. Gams's warning flashed inside my head: *Tell no one else.*

"We should get going." Mom studied my face for a beat longer, brows pushed together, then she grabbed my hand.

We began to walk again, but I didn't feel like staring at the buildings anymore. Mom kept glancing down at me, her expression dark and unfamiliar. She touched my forehead like I might have a fever.

It took several months and many more rain cloud sightings before I finally understood why Gams had been so adamant that I tell no one, or why Mom had looked at me that way— like there was something wrong with me. Fear became an easy thing to spot once I knew what to look for.

Even now, all these years later.

I tightened my grip on the steering wheel, frowning as Marissa flipped to yet another song, unable to settle on one for more than a few seconds.

I felt the heat of staring eyes. When I glanced at the rear-view mirror, the boy's gaze darted away, but not before I caught that familiar flicker of fear. Had I done something to scare him?

I thought of Beau tossing around my old nickname like it was a toy. Maybe someone had told this guy about me—the girl who saved a kid's life last year. The girl who always seemed to be in the right place at the right time, saving people. And here I was, at it again.

Would they call me Supergirl if they knew about Dwight? If they knew I saved the kid who shot all those people at the football game?

The car thumped as it went over a pothole. Marissa let out a squeal and grabbed on to the dashboard.

"Hey, NASCAR. Slow down. Are you trying to kill me and drunko back there?"

I let out a snort—I was the reason he *wasn't* going to die tonight—then squinted at the reflection of the darkened back seat in the rearview mirror. The boy's head remained blissfully cloud-free.

"You okay?" I asked him. His previously flushed cheeks looked pallid, his eyes glassy. He nodded once, then turned his head to the window, like the trees outside were more interesting than whatever he'd seen when glaring at me. The knot in my stomach unwound just the teeniest bit.

"What's your name?" Marissa asked, spinning to face him. She wrapped her arms around the headrest and leaned her chin against the faux leather. "And why haven't I seen you at Beau's before? Are you new? Visiting from out of town? What's your story?"

He shrank back and stole another glance at me. There it was again—that flicker of uncertainty. Someone had definitely told him about me.

"Isaac," he croaked. "My name's Isaac." Then he pressed his forehead against the glass and closed his eyes. A sheen of sweat glistened on the back of his neck despite the blasting air conditioner.

Maybe I was overreacting. Maybe he just needed to puke.

"Do you want me to pull over?" I asked, suddenly less concerned with his knowledge of my past than my pristine car's interior.

"You don't look so hot," Marissa added, still facing him. "Just how much of Beau's punch did you drink, anyway? You must be new. Rookie mistake, dude."

"Turn right," Isaac said at the same moment my phone's navigation spat out an identical instruction. He cracked the window and leaned out, gulping down night air.

Yup, definitely on his way to Vomit Town.

I turned onto a wide tree-lined street with tidy houses peppering well-manicured lawns. Marissa went back to her fight to find the perfect song.

"There," Isaac said. "It's that one." The car hadn't even come to a complete stop before he wrenched the back door open and launched himself onto the grass.

"Hey!" I called, pulling to a stop. "Hey, wait!"

Marissa shot me a quizzical look as I leaned over to grab a pen and a piece of paper from the glove compartment, scribbled my number, then hopped out and followed Isaac's unsteady trajectory toward his house.

"Good luck," she quipped.

I hopped out of the car, caught up to the boy, and held out the piece of paper. Isaac wobbled unsteadily, eyes narrowing at my outstretched hand like it held a gun.

"It's my phone number," I explained. "In case you need someone to take you to get your car tomorrow. I said I'd take you in the morning?"

He looked at me blankly. When he didn't take my number, I pressed it into his palm.

"Take it, just in case. My name's Whitney."

He turned without so much as an acknowledging head nod and continued his zigzagging shamble toward the house.

"You're welcome!" I called after him, reminding myself that thank-yous didn't come with the job. Plus I shouldn't have even saved him in the first place. If there's one thing the universe has taught me, it's that no good deed goes unpunished.

3

THE SCHOOL HALLWAY ON MONDAY MORNING WAS A sea of chaos. Marissa pulled me back against a row of lockers so we could avoid a swarm of students pushing their way through to look at the decorations.

"Watch it!" she called, deftly avoiding an elbow as another person wedged their way into the crowd.

"We're going to get crushed." I eyed the packed horseshoe-shaped hallway that made up the senior class balcony. "Do all these people even go here?"

Some clubs, like the dance team and cheerleading squad, treated the tradition of having freshmen decorate senior lockers on the first day of school like a competitive sport. A mosh pit of gawkers crowded the senior corridor to look at everything before it fell down—but at this rate I wouldn't make it to class before the bell.

"Maybe we should come back after first period?" I suggested, readjusting the bag on my shoulder as another person bumped into me.

"Are you kidding? I've waited three years for this." Marissa lifted her chin like she was a member of some royal court, then motioned for me to lead the way. "After you, madam."

I glanced behind me, debating if I should make up some excuse about having to pee. But then I spotted Mrs. Bower at the opposite end of the hallway, hovering just outside the bathroom. Our eyes met and her hand rose in a wave. I quickly looked away, trying to make it seem like I hadn't seen her. Trying to make it look like everything was fine and my stomach didn't just plummet to my feet.

Before Gams got sick, Mrs. B was a regular fixture in our lives. Gams was her mentor and once Mrs. B moved back to town, she assisted at Gams's dance studio. The two of them were so close she was practically family. Now looking at her was a knife to my gut, a walking reminder of every horrible mistake I made last year. Or, I supposed, a limping reminder, considering the boot still encasing her foot. The boot that was there because of me.

I grabbed Marissa's hand and pulled her forward, and suddenly we were ping-ponging our way down the hallway, straight into the chaos.

It looked like a craft store exploded, sending yellow streamers, black ribbon, and gold glitter onto every visible surface. Gold and silver letters screamed from wrapping-paper-covered locker doors: GO HORNETS! Clusters of flowers dangled from handles and spelled out graduation years. Fake pom-poms constructed from multicolored ribbons were mounted to doors. The football team had outdone themselves, erecting tinfoil stingers the size of my head with the words HUNG LIKE A HORNET! shouting from a hand-painted sign.

To the left end of the hallway, there was a row of four lockers covered in all white, the words IN LOVING MEMORY written in silver ribbon across the middle. People had piled cards, flowers, and stuffed bears underneath. There were no names on the lockers, not that I needed reminding. I saw their faces every night before I went to sleep.

A few students hovered in front of them, hands clasped. One of them was Alexia Mendel, Atticus Dunburt's girlfriend. He'd died on the way to the hospital the night of the shooting. Another was Raphael Greer. He'd been shot in the leg while trying to flee the stands. Now he placed a folded piece of paper on top of the gift pile, his lower lip quivering.

There were only four lockers, which meant they hadn't included the kids from Collin Creek High who'd died that night. If they'd included them, the total would be eight. Eight dead. Countless others injured.

And then, of course, there was Dwight. No one put up a memorial locker for him.

My breath left my body. Of course they would have a memorial. Of course. I squeezed my eyes shut and looked away, trying to focus on the other decorations. Trying not to look at the tears staining Alexia's cheeks.

Your fault your fault your fault.

Marissa tugged gently on my arm and motioned toward the white lockers. "It's nice, right? The memorial?"

I nodded numbly. "Yeah. Nice."

There was a debate about whether to decorate lockers at all this year. Everything was a debate now—as if settling into the normal rhythms of life would tarnish the memory of those we'd lost. As if forgetting was an option.

The general response, it seemed, was some combination of adding a tribute and increasing security. Cancel the decorations? No, add a tribute and a security guard. Cancel the football games? No, add a memorial and a metal detector. The world had to keep turning, and apparently sporting events and all associated activities were essential to making that happen.

"Come on." Marissa tugged my sleeve away from the haunted corner. Her somber face told me she didn't want to look at it any more than I did. "The dance team lockers are this way."

She pulled me through a cluster of students taking in the rest of the decorations.

"Not bad," Marissa shouted over the drone. "I mean, we did a better job when we were freshmen, but I'd give it a close second. Oh, there's mine!"

She squealed when she spotted her locker nestled between the rest of the dance team officers' lockers. Mine was a few down and impossible to miss—it was the only one without decorations.

I'd made Marissa promise that no one from the team would put up pity decorations for me, but still. Seeing it bare made my stomach squeeze.

It's just a locker. It doesn't matter anymore.

I almost had myself convinced when I heard Penny Ansel's voice knife through the crowd and my bravado shriveled.

"Do you see any roses? Because I sure as hell don't."

Penny marched up to the row of lockers with **HORNETTES** spelled out in silver ribbon and pointed at the one with **CAPTAIN** subscript. Mia Collins followed behind, eyes wide and glistening as she followed Penny's finger.

I remembered Mia from last year's dance team tryouts. She performed the choreography well, but fell out of her triple pirouette. Still, we'd voted to let her on the team. I wondered if she'd learned how to perfect her turns over the summer.

"Your roses were there this morning, I swear," the girl said, chin wobbling. "I helped tape them up."

"Well, they're not there now, are they?" Penny's voice dripped with venom as she motioned toward the line of gold-wrapped lockers. Christmas lights lined the edges, winking on and off behind a layer of glittery tissue paper halos. Despite the gaudiness, there was a conspicuously empty space in the center of each one where the roses must have been. "Are you trying to ruin my first day? Does tradition mean nothing to y'all?"

Mia's eyes brimmed and she looked down at her hands. Her long braids swung when she shook her head.

"What's going on?" Marissa asked, putting herself between Penny and Mia. I pressed myself closer to the wall, digging in my bag to find the slip of paper I'd written my locker combo on.

"There aren't any flowers on our lockers. *Supposedly* they were there this morning, but now they've magically disappeared. *Poof.*" Penny snapped her fingers to illustrate her point. Mia jumped.

"If Mia says they were there, then I'm sure they were there." Marissa placed a hand on Mia's shoulder and gave her a reassuring smile. "Someone probably took them as a joke or something. Jeez, Penny, give it a rest. They're just flowers. They'd probably be dead by lunch."

"It's a tradition," Penny said, her cheeks flaring pink. "And the cheer captains all have white roses, for Christ's sake. White roses are supposed to be *our* thing."

"Our lockers are tacky enough without them."

I had to agree with Marissa. Plus, there was something morbid about the white roses—like funeral flowers placed on top of a casket. Or the white *In Loving Memory* lockers at the other end of the hallway.

"Something tells me we'll find a way to persevere, roses or not." Marissa turned the girl away from Penny's shotgun stare. "Don't worry about it, hon. Tell the other newbies that our lockers look great. Y'all did a really good job."

Mia nodded and scurried away before Penny could yell again.

"Great." Penny worked the combination on her locker like it was to blame for the missing flowers. "Now I look like the jerk. Thanks a lot, Marissa."

"That poor girl looked like she was about to burst into tears. She obviously had nothing to do with it."

Before Penny could retort, Marissa bounced over and pulled me into a tight hug.

"Isn't it great? Our lockers are practically next to each other!" She clapped her hands and pointed toward the flashing door three down from my bare one. "I'm so glad they didn't move you to another hallway when you, you know, quit." She whispered the last word, as if my undecorated locker wasn't a glaring neon sign announcing to the world that I was no longer a Hornette.

Penny slammed her locker door shut and turned to face me with a tight-lipped smile. We were roughly the same height and shared the same light hair and eyes, so everyone called us the Twins, but the similarities ended there. Penny was all sharp angles and edges, with thick hair and cold, demanding eyes. She moved the same way she danced—every action a well-calculated slice.

"Hey, Whitney. Great to see you. How was your summer?"

"Great. Really great." I mirrored Penny's empty grin. The

polite thing would have been to ask Penny about her summer, but I already knew all the gory details thanks to Marissa. That, and being polite to Penny was at the bottom of my to-do list, right after full body waxing and getting a leg chopped off. It was hard to imagine that we'd once been friends.

"I'm so glad I bumped into you." Penny's voice dropped an octave and she leaned toward me. "I wanted to talk to you about the Kevin thing."

Ah, so now it was a *thing*. I shook my head. I didn't want to have this conversation, especially if it was officially *thing* status. But mostly I didn't want to hear Penny say his name again. There was something overly familiar in the way it hung on her lips, like she'd become too accustomed to using it.

"Don't worry about it. I broke up with him, remember? He's free to date whoever he wants." *Except you*, I thought with a clenched smile, hoping my voice held up the masquerade.

"Right, I know. I just wanted a chance to explain. I don't want things to be weird between us." There was an earnestness to her voice that made me wonder if she actually cared how I felt. But then Marissa stepped between us, breaking the do-si-do of politeness.

"How can things be any weirder than they already are?" Marissa asked. "But I suppose it's true what they say: one person's trash is another person's treasure."

I stifled a laugh and turned my attention to the combination on my lock so I could avoid the flames that were no doubt flying from Penny's eyes.

I eased the door open, then frowned when I saw that my locker wasn't empty.

A broken bouquet of green stems filled the interior. White

flower heads were ripped off and scattered along the bottom shelf. Petals were mashed into pieces and smeared against the metal walls.

And on the inside of the locker door, someone had taped Dwight Hacken's yearbook photo. Above his head they'd squiggled a round, black, inky blob. It almost looked like the darkness I'd seen hovering over Dwight's head the day I'd saved him. Except that wasn't possible.

Because nobody knew about that day—and nobody knew about the darkness.

4

THE HALLWAY TUNNELED IN AND OUT OF FOCUS.
I stepped back, my mouth hanging open. Dwight's picture
glared at me like an angry ghost. The dark cloud-shaped
squiggle over his head seemed to pulse.

"What's wrong?" Marissa moved to stand behind me.

My shaking hand ripped down the photo, but it was too
late—Marissa had seen it.

She sucked in a sharp breath, catching Penny's attention.
I shoved the crumpled photo in my pocket before anyone
else saw. Marissa tried to block Penny's view but wasn't fast
enough.

"You've got to be kidding me." Penny grabbed the locker
door and opened it wider, then reached inside and plucked out
one of the mashed petals. "You really had to take it there?"

"I didn't—I wouldn't—" I couldn't seem to get my tongue
to work right.

"Come on, Penny. It's obviously a prank," Marissa said.
"Why would Whitney do something like this?"

"Because she can't stand that I'm captain now. Or that Kevin
and I are together." Penny crossed her arms and glared at me.
A few petals fell to the floor.

"The only reason you're captain is because Whitney *chose* not
to be on the team anymore. It's not her fault you keep lapping
up her sloppy seconds."

I wanted to tell them to stop, but my lungs couldn't find enough air. I squeezed my eyes shut and pictured Gams's studio, forcing myself to see the familiar wooden floors and full-length mirrors that ran along the wall instead of Dwight's face.

To execute an axel, start with a châiné turn and, without stopping, pull your right leg into passé followed by the left.

"I bet you think this is funny." Penny's voice was a knife in my thoughts.

"Don't be ridiculous. They were my flowers, too," Marissa said.

I leaned against the wall to steady myself. The black squiggle of marker on my locker door writhed against the tan metal like a living thing.

Maybe it wasn't a cloud. Maybe they were trying to write something but scribbled it out.

But why was his picture taped inside your locker?

"Are you okay?" Marissa's hand was on my arm. "Whitney?"

It had to be a mistake. No one knew what happened on that rooftop. And no one knew that I had any connection to what happened at the football game. This was all just one big, horrible mistake.

I shook my head, my insides twisting like the pile of ruined flowers.

When I turned around, Principal O'Connell stood between Penny and Marissa with his nostrils flaring.

I didn't hear Penny and Marissa's explanation of what happened; everything sounded garbled, like it was underwater. When Principal O'Connell asked me to follow him to his office I moved on gelatin legs.

"Something needs to be done about this, Mr. O'Connell," Penny said, walking quickly to keep pace with him. "We can't just let people run around vandalizing decorations. It's an affront to our high school's traditions."

"Oh, please," Marissa countered. "This has nothing to do with tradition, or you for that matter. The only person who's been *affronted* is Whitney." She used air quotes when she said the word *affronted*. "Obviously, someone's trying to frame her."

"Obviously, Whitney did it to get back at me," Penny said.

"Ladies, I appreciate your input, but I think Whitney and I can take it from here." Principal O'Connell raised a hand to silence them. "If I need anything else I'll be sure to let y'all know."

Penny gave him a curt nod before heading back down the hallway. Marissa hesitated, concern etched in her brow, but finally slunk off as well.

Mr. O'Connell was a caricature of a high school administrator, with an egg for a head and two tufts of hair where his ears should have been. His infamous glare made me squirm, like his eyes could hollow me out and find the broken bits. I followed him into the stuffy confines of his office, ducking under his arm as he held the door open for me.

He motioned for me to sit. The chair creaked beneath me.

"Miss Lancaster, I'm going to ask this plainly and I expect a straight answer. Did you remove the roses from the dance team lockers?"

I swallowed hard. "No, sir."

I pressed my back against the chair, eyes flicking over plants and dusty books. A fan in the corner barely coughed air into the room, which felt ten degrees hotter than the hallway.

He leaned back and steepled his fingers, examining me over the rim of his glasses. The clock on the wall ticked down the seconds. Silence stretched like the arms of a dancer widening to second position. Suddenly I understood why he had such a reputation. I had nothing to do with the roses in my locker and yet I was tempted to confess just to fill the space with something other than his stare and the ticking clock.

"Okay," he said finally, enunciating each syllable with more force than necessary. "Do you have any thoughts on how the flowers may have gotten inside your locker?"

My eyes bounced around the room to avoid his glare, settling on a brown, dehydrated plant. Mr. O'Connell's gaze probably sucked the green right out of the leaves.

"No, sir."

He frowned and scratched his chin. "I understand from Mrs. Bower that you quit the dance team."

Guilt fanned over me at the sound of Mrs. B's name. Then I felt guilty for feeling guilty, because Mrs. B made me promise I wouldn't feel sorry for her. These days I was a Russian nesting doll of guilt.

I nodded.

"That seems surprising given that you were an officer last year and a shoo-in as captain this year. I understand the officer auditions are quite grueling."

I nodded again, not sure what he was getting at. It *had* been grueling. They didn't call it Nightmare Week for no reason. In addition to learning three new pieces of choreography in five days, all the prospective officers had to choreograph three of their own routines. It was a tradition for the outgoing officers to make everything as hellish as possible, keeping us late after rehearsals and making us start the routines over if so much as a fingernail was out of place.

"And yet you quit the team," Principal O'Connell said, like he could see inside my brain.

I glanced toward the window that overlooked the parking lot. Rows of cars glinted in the September heat. A few students scurried between them, trying to make it inside before the bell.

"I need to focus on my college applications." I met his gaze, reciting the lie I'd been telling everyone since I quit last year. "And I decided to focus my dance training at the studio—it's better for my technique, and I need to improve if I'm going to dance in college. I don't have time for the team anymore."

I tried to keep my face neutral even though the truth had claws and teeth as it squirmed inside me: *I couldn't bear to look at Mrs. B and remember the choices I made that put her in that cast.*

Mr. O'Connell's chair squeaked as he leaned back, studying me.

The clock ticked.

The silence stretched.

"This school has been through a lot this past year, as you no doubt are very aware, Miss Lancaster. It's important to me that the students have a positive environment that enables them to move beyond last year's tragedy. And that means upholding our traditions, however inconsequential they may seem to others."

I nodded so he'd get to the point. He didn't really think I tore down the flowers, did he?

"I'll be speaking with the club members in charge of this morning's decorations to see if we can get to the bottom of who did this to your locker. And if it turns out that you had something to do with it, then rest assured that there will be consequences. Do I make myself clear?"

I opened my mouth to say something, but the first period bell rang and he stood sharply.

"You should get to class, Miss Lancaster. Let's hope this is the last time I see you in my office." A smile that looked more like a grimace stretched across his face as he motioned for me to leave the room.

I felt the weight of his glare all the way to first period.

5

"SHE'S CLEARLY TRYING TO TAKE OVER YOUR LIFE."
Marissa leaned against my car, her face turned toward the
edge of the football field where Penny was currently attached
to my ex-boyfriend's face. "It's like she doesn't just want to
look like you, she wants to become you. Make sure you check
under your bed before you go to sleep. She might be waiting
to skin you and turn you into a Whitney coat."

"Don't be weird." I threw my bag into the front seat and
slammed the door, willing my eyes not to look at the Penny-
Kevin horror show. It took every ounce of strength not to
scream, while Marissa seemed one popcorn tub short of enjoy-
ing the spectacle.

"They have to come up for air sometime soon."

"Stop talking about it."

"Look at that death grip she's got on him! Is she trying to
eat his face?"

"Stop *talking* about it."

"Fine. Elephant in the room, but sure, we'll ignore it."

I fiddled with a button on my sleeve, pressing it like I could
somehow turn the whole scene off. The last thing I wanted to
think about was Kevin.

"He asked about you a lot this summer." Marissa looked
down at her feet, like she felt guilty for having spoken to him.
"I think he missed you."

"Doubt it," I said, thinking about the many texts he'd sent

me throughout the summer. He tried to play it off like he was checking up on me, but it felt like each text was laced with an ulterior motive—to make sure I kept his secret. Even at our last face-to-face conversation, he'd seemed more concerned that I would tell someone about what he'd done to Dwight than about the fact that I was breaking up with him. Which, in hindsight, was typical Kevin—he always put himself first. I don't know why it took last year's tragedy to make me see him for what he was. But then again, assessing people's character was clearly not one of my strengths.

"Any word from Principal Asshat about what happened to your locker?"

I shook my head and scanned the emptying parking lot. It felt strange leaving school so early. I'd spent every afternoon the last three years at dance practice with Marissa and the rest of the team. And before that, at my grandma's dance studio. What did people without extracurricular activities do with their free time?

"I saw Penny go into his office after lunch," Marissa said. "I only caught a little bit of their conversation, but I think she was trying to pin it all on you."

"Figures." I glanced back at the make-out scene, then quickly looked away.

"Penny's reaction to the whole thing was *way* too extra. I bet she's trying to get you in trouble so you don't change your mind about quitting the team. The captain thing has already gone to her head." Marissa brushed her hair back, surveying the line of cars making its way toward the white clapboard security station.

I rolled my eyes. "Please, Penny would never destroy her own property, even to make me look bad."

"Maybe." She pressed her mouth into a line. "And the picture . . . that was pretty messed up."

I bit my lip. I'd seen Marissa's face when she saw the photo, but still. A part of me had hoped it hadn't registered.

"Whitney." Marissa's tone was somber. She only ever called me by my full name when she was serious about something. "Why would someone put a picture of Dwight Hacken in your locker?"

"I don't know," I answered truthfully. I thought of his face and the scribbled black ink above his head. It had to be a coincidence.

"It's a sick thing to do," Marissa said. Her voice had the same edge as last year, when she kept asking me about the photo that was plastered all over the news.

"Do you think it's someone from our school?" she had asked in a way that told me she saw the similarities between me and the blurry image—the height and build, the time stamp on the photo that matched the time I'd been over two hours late to pick her up.

The photo was taken a few days before the shooting. In it, a girl stood next to Dwight—in the midst of a heated discussion with him. No one knew who she was. And it was that blurred-out photo that made everyone suspect Dwight might have had an accomplice—or at least someone who knew about his plan. Pleas were made. Rewards were offered. And still, after all these months, no one had figured out who was in the picture.

"Really sick," I responded with a grimace.

Marissa studied me. "I wish you'd tell me what's going on with you."

I swallowed and feigned a smile. "I told you, I'm fine. I swear. There's nothing going on. It's just weird not being at practice with you guys. I miss it more than I thought I would."

It wasn't a lie. Not exactly. And even if it was, what other choice did I have?

A muscle twitched in Marissa's jaw as she watched me, like she could see the lies and half-truths etched across my skin. Avoiding her gaze, I looked back toward the school and saw Beau Gunter walking toward the parking lot with someone who looked a lot like Isaac.

"Isn't that the guy we drove home Saturday?" I pointed, grateful for the distraction. I was even more grateful when Marissa took the bait.

"Yeah, I think so." She shielded her eyes to get a better look. "I guess that solves the riddle of what he was doing at the party. He must be new here."

His hair was lighter than I remembered, a few highlights catching the afternoon sun as it flopped against his forehead. He started to laugh, his already-pink cheeks turning bright red. He was flushed on Saturday, at least until he got in my car, but I assumed it was from the alcohol. Now I wondered if he always looked like he'd just gotten back from a run.

"He's cute when he's not wasted." Marissa smirked. "Did he ever call about getting a ride to pick up his car?"

"Are you serious? He looked at me like I was trying to kid-nap him."

"That's because you made him nervous. He's in luuurve with you. He kept giving you Cookie Monster eyes in the rearview mirror." She opened her eyes wide and hungrily smacked her lips at me to illustrate her point.

"Don't be weird. He probably just had to puke."

"Or he thinks you're a snack."

I gave her shoulder a playful shove.

"Uh-oh." Marissa's eyes flicked back toward the Penny-Kevin make-out session. "Looks like they came up for air. I should run so I can beat her to practice. It's fine for Penny to be late because she's sucking face in the parking lot, but God forbid anyone else not be there *exactly* on time. Have I mentioned how much the team wishes you were captain instead?" She gave me a wan smile. "How long will you be at the studio tonight?"

"I don't have class today." I wondered what Marissa would say if she knew I hadn't taken a dance class in months, that I couldn't stand looking at myself in the full-length mirrors and thinking about what I'd done. "I'm going to visit Gams instead."

Marissa's face lit up at the mention of my grandmother. "Aw, how is she? I miss her."

"She's doing okay," I said, hoping that it would be one of her good days. I still couldn't believe I hadn't seen her in person in almost two months. "I'll tell her you said hello. Text me later tonight?" I jingled my keys, anxious to get as far away from school as possible.

"Of course. I'll give you a full report. I bet we don't even make it through practice before there's a mutiny attempt. Did you know she makes us do twenty high kicks for every demerit we get? I swear, I'm going to murder that girl before football season even starts."

"At least your high kicks will look good."

"Don't even pretend to take her side." Marissa gave me a glare that quickly melted into a grin as she turned and walked toward the gym, her dark curls bouncing. Inside, Mrs. B and the rest of the team would be gathering to start warm-ups.

By some miracle of the cosmos I'd managed to escape the day without running into Mrs. B, not counting the brief sighting I'd had this morning. I'd have to see her at some point, but the longer it could be avoided, the better.

The afternoon sun was warm and bright, beating onto my car like it was the middle of the summer rather than the end of it. Early September always felt like the inside of someone's armpit. Except for last year, when the cold came early.

I shivered and tried to shake the memory off. I climbed into my car, flipped the knob on the AC, and gave the vent a few cursory bangs with my palm to get the air flowing. Damned thing never worked right. I'd have to talk to my brother about fixing it the next time he was in town.

I merged into the line of cars inching toward the main road. Across the street from the school, a small cluster of protesters was gathered. I was too far away to read the signs, but it was probably more of the same from last year—pleas for gun control regulation and pictures of shooting victims. I swallowed and tried not to look. It seemed like every corner of the school held some reminder about last year.

Then a car horn honked and I turned to see Jenny Chan, my old Chem partner, leaning out of the passenger side of an ancient-looking truck. Her brother's, I realized as my heart dropped to my feet. Luke used to drive her to school every morning. I wondered if Jenny helped decorate one of the four

In Loving Memory lockers for him this morning.

She tucked a strand of shoulder-length black hair behind her ear and motioned for me to roll down my window. A thin gray cloud hovered over her head, like someone exhaled a plume of smoke. Except it wasn't cigarette smoke.

I winced. She must be sick again. As if her family hadn't already been through enough.

"Whitney Lancaster, out in the wild," she said, smirking as my window slid down. "Why aren't you inside with all of the other bunheads?"

"I'm not—" I cleared my throat. "I quit the team."

The cloud was small—just a tiny puff of gray dancing over her head like a question mark. Which meant the danger wasn't imminent and there was still something she could do to stop it. Or really, something *I* could do to stop it. The darkness only appeared when there was an action I could take that would save someone. Which meant it was my job to tell her, otherwise . . .

I thought of her brother. How much loss could one family take?

Loss that you could have prevented.

Jenny whistled, looking impressed. "Wow, I thought you were the queen bunhead." She motioned toward the main road. "We're going to the Holy Donut. Wanna come?"

I liked Jenny. Everyone liked Jenny. Last year, when I was struggling in chemistry, she took extra time to help me with the labs and my homework. And she was one of those people who always had a joke and a smile. Even now, surrounded by memories of her murdered brother, she couldn't help but smile. I couldn't let her go without saying something. She couldn't be like Dwight. If I saved her, surely nothing bad would happen. Right?

Plus, I owed her. I owed her entire family.

I squeezed my eyes shut, the potential butterfly effect of my actions spinning wildly inside my head. There was simply no way of knowing. It was always an impossible decision. Save them, risk something worse happening. Don't save them, live knowing I let them die.

"Hey, listen—" I looked up at the ceiling of my car, trying to find the words. This was always the uncomfortable part—the part that made people think there was something wrong with me. "You should go see your doctor. For a checkup."

The smile fell from her face and her brows pinched. "I should go see my doctor?"

Ahead, the line of cars started to move. Someone behind us honked.

I nodded. "Yes. It's important. Please, just do it. As soon as you can."

Jenny's expression darkened. I was pretty sure this would be my last invite to the Holy Donut. Most people steered clear of me after I creeped them out with one of my warnings. She opened her mouth to say something else, but I rolled my window up and pulled the car forward before she could speak.

When I got to the street I turned right, averting my gaze from the protesters. Jenny turned the same direction a few seconds later. In the rearview mirror, I could just make out the sliver of gray still ghosting above her head.

This time really would be the last.

6

WHEN I WAS IN SECOND GRADE I WANTED TO BRING Gams to school for share time. I couldn't think of anything more amazing to tell my classmates about than my grandmother—she'd been a principal ballerina at the New York City Ballet and owned a dance studio, and when there wasn't a dance class in session, she'd let me slide around on the studio floor in my socks, pretending to be a prima ballerina from one of the many ballets she'd taken me to see over the years.

"Surely you can find something more interesting to share with your class than me," she'd said when I'd asked her to come. Her hair was up in its usual bun, always the proper ballerina.

"But there's nothing more interesting than you, Gams."

She laughed, her hands pausing over the recent shipment of leotards she'd been sorting. Then she motioned for me to come closer, her expression turning serious.

"We need to talk about the rain clouds you keep seeing. I told you not to tell anybody about them."

I looked down at my hands, guilty. "I know. It's just . . . why do I have to keep it a secret? And why doesn't Mom believe that I can see them?"

That week I'd heard my parents yelling at each other through the wall of my bedroom. Words like *psychosis* and *hallucination* were lobbed back and forth like tennis balls. I knew they were arguing about me. Mom wanted me to try yet another psychologist. Dad thought they should leave me alone, that I'd grow out of it. I just wanted them to stop fighting. And I wanted my brother to stop looking at me like I was something that needed to be fixed.

"It's not that she doesn't believe you." Gams's lips pursed as she considered our reflections in the mirrors lining the studio walls. "But you have to realize it's not easy for people to digest. People are scared of things they don't understand. And I'm afraid, dear, that this is one of those things that people are never going to understand. Even your parents and brother. I know you don't like to keep secrets from them, but I need you to trust me, Whitney. Do you trust me?"

I nodded. There was no one I trusted more.

"Good. Then I need you to listen. You have to stop telling people about the things you can see. I need you to promise that from now on the only person you'll talk to about it is me." She touched my chin gently. "No one can know about the rain clouds but us, do you understand?"

"But Mom and Dad and Will already know."

"Yes, but that's because you keep telling them. If you stopped talking about it, they'd think you were no longer seeing things. They'd stop making you go to those doctors. And people would stop being so nervous around you."

"You mean like Mr. Maynard." I looked down at my hands again. Little red half-moons dotted my palms where I'd clenched my fists.

"Yes," she said. "Like Mr. Maynard."

I'd seen him on his front porch a few weeks earlier grumbling while he furiously worked a broom back and forth, like autumn shook the leaves from his trees just to tick him off. I didn't really like Mr. Maynard. His face looked like melted Play-Doh, and he constantly muttered under his breath about one unpleasant thing or another—those goddamn kids who kept ringing his doorbell, that goddamn dog that wouldn't stop yapping, that goddamn paper boy who wouldn't know a front door from a hole in his ass. But when I saw the squiggle of gray ghosting above his head, I couldn't *not* tell him.

"You're the devil's child, you know that?" he'd said, stopping his assault on the front porch to point a gnarled finger at me. "The goddamn devil's child." Then he gave me the kind of look I reserved for pickles and brussels sprouts, and I ran back to my house crying.

One week later, Mr. Maynard died. A few days after that, my mom sent me to see Dr. Nessbaumer. Then Dr. Adams. Then Dr. Fritz. I hated the way all of them watched me, like they wanted to scoop out my broken parts to see how they worked.

Still, a knot twisted in my stomach.

"If I ignore the clouds, who will tell people that something bad is going to happen?"

Gams pressed her red lips into a line and looked me directly in my eyes. "Sometimes people shouldn't be warned, honey. Trust me, I learned that the hard way."

"What do you mean?"

She shook her head and looked away, eyes tracing the length of the barre running along the far wall. When she finally met my gaze, her face was as hard as the wooden floor, and suddenly it clicked into place—the way she'd known to warn me about the clouds before that day at the crosswalk, the way she didn't look at me like Mom and Dad or Will did when I talked about the darkness. My grandma and I were alike in so many ways, sometimes Mom joked that I was a carbon copy. It made sense that we'd share this, too.

"People are afraid of the things they don't understand, Whitney. And people do mean things when they're afraid. Scary things. I wish you'd just ignore it, but if you can't then you at least need to be more careful." She lifted my chin so that I had to look at her. "There are rules you need to follow. Things you need to do to keep yourself safe."

She reached underneath the stack of leotards and handed me a pink notebook with tiny ballerinas all over it. On the inside cover, four rules were written in her tidy, slanted handwriting.

Rule One: Don't tell anyone what you see.
Rule Two: Don't attract attention. Make the rescue look like an accident or a coincidence.
Rule Three: If you have to break rules one and two to save someone, you can't save them.
Rule Four: Keep this journal hidden at all times.

The journal, she said, was for me to write down the details of my rescues so that I wouldn't feel compelled to talk about them.

"You have to follow the rules at all times, do you understand? Never, ever break the rules. No matter what."

"You see them, too, don't you?" I said.

Gams nodded once. A sharp, awkward movement that made me wonder how long she'd been holding on to her secret.

"But I've never seen you save anybody." I looked at the ballerina-covered book in my hands. Was that her trick—follow the rules and no one noticed?

She looked away, but not before I saw her eyes fill with moisture. She was quiet for a long time before speaking.

"I'm just trying to keep you safe, Whitney. I'm just trying to protect you. There are consequences to saving people. I don't want you to have to learn that lesson the hard way, like I did."

"Will doesn't see them," I said, thinking of the way my brother had looked at me when I'd told him about the rain cloud I'd seen hovering over Mr. Maynard's head. The way his eyes had widened just before he'd run out of the room to tell Mom.

"No, he doesn't. For some reason only the women in the family seem to get it."

"But not Mom."

"No." Gams sighed. "Not your mom. Not my mom either. And I'd hoped so very much that you wouldn't have it. But from the moment you took your first steps, I knew you would. There's something about the way your body moves, like you're floating. The same way you move when you're dancing. The same way I move, and my grandmother moved. She was also a dancer."

"We move like the rain clouds." I thought about the way the darkness curled and undulated, swirling around heads almost like it, too, was dancing. Like the videos I'd seen of Gams's old performances. Like I felt when the music started and movement took over.

"Yes, I suppose we do." Gams's voice was sad.

"Are there other people who see the clouds?"

"I don't know. I suppose it's possible. There are other people in the world who can do things that aren't easily explained. Like mediums who can see the future or receive messages from people who've passed. I suppose we aren't that different from them."

"Are people afraid of them, too?"

Gams's lips pressed into a thin line. "Yes."

As I got older, Gams told me about her own experience with doctors. About the medications they'd made her take and the hospital she'd been sent to because of the rain clouds. A place where there were no dance classes or ballet barres. A place where the worst thing you could do was see something that no one else could.

People were afraid of the things they didn't understand, and Gams didn't want the same fate for me.

Most of the time I followed Gams's rules without issue. It became easier once I understood how to read the darkness.

The thick clouds were the easiest. They came suddenly, a blink of gray that quickly swelled into a deadly storm cloud when someone made a split-second choice that meant the difference between life and death. I usually just needed to stall them long enough for the danger to pass.

But it was harder to be discreet with the small, lingering gray clouds that meant the danger was inside them. Sometimes I tried writing a note or sending an anonymous email. But occasionally I had to tell them outright. It broke Gams's rules, but how could I just let someone go when I was the only one who could prevent their death? I couldn't live with that, no matter what Gams said. And secretly, I liked the way it made me feel—like I was a hero in a story. Despite Gams's concerns, outside of odd looks and annoyed glances, most of my rescues went off without much fanfare.

Until last year, when I followed Dwight Hacken to a downtown roof and convinced him not to jump. Now eight people were dead. Eight people who might still be alive if I'd listened to my grandmother.

Because she'd been right all along. There are consequences to saving people.

7

THE OUTSIDE OF LONE STAR ASSISTED LIVING WAS BUILT
to look like a colonial house, with white pillared columns,
dark red bricks, and white shutters. It wasn't until you walked
through the main entrance that you realized what the building
really was—a glorified hospital dressed as a home. No matter how many floral arrangements, overstuffed couches, and
brightly colored window treatments, nothing camouflaged the
scent of antiseptic, the railing-lined walls, or the nurses sta-
tions peppered around the residential floors.

"Whitney, is that you?" The spray-tanned woman behind
the reception desk grinned warmly as I pushed through the
entryway doors. Her voice was thick with Texas twang, and
her bright red blouse was the exact same shade as her lipstick,
fingernails, and the large plastic hoop earrings dangling from
her earlobes. "I heard a rumor you might be stoppin' by this
week. How was your summer? Did you go to that dance camp
you went to last year?" She drew out the word *camp* so that it
sounded more like "cay-yamp."

"No, I went to visit my dad in California. How've you been,
Mindy?" I leaned down to sign the guest log she'd slid in my
direction and saw a neon red rhinestoned purse wedged underneath the desk. Clearly Mindy's flair for the gaudy and monochromatic hadn't waned since I last saw her.

"Oh, you know me." She tapped her fingernails on the table.

Each one had a red sequin glued to the tip. "I've been thinking about you kids a lot, what with school starting back. Must be hard being back on campus. I mean, at least it didn't happen at *your* school. It's terrible to say, but thank God it was an away game, right? Can you imagine those kids at Collin Creek High having to go back to the place where it happened? It makes me sick to think about."

I nodded and avoided her gaze. My throat suddenly had a fist inside it.

Mindy bit her lip, waiting for me to say something, then changed the subject once she realized I wasn't going to take the bait.

"Say, what's that brother of yours up to these days? He hasn't been to visit me in months." Her cheeks flushed. Will was a charmer, but when it came to the employees of Lone Star Assisted Living, he was a Hemsworth in a Speedo.

"He spent the summer in Austin," I answered. "He got an internship."

"Such a smart one, that Will." Mindy smiled wistfully, patting her large mound of heavily sprayed hair as her red plastic hoops jingled. "Your grandma will be so happy to see you. She's been in such a good mood. She hasn't had an episode in days."

She whispered the last sentence like it was a secret. The words filled me with relief. It was impossible to predict the good days from the bad, and I was glad that I'd get to see Gams on a day when she was feeling more herself.

The doctors thought Gams had some form of dementia, though they weren't entirely sure. There was so much about the human brain they didn't understand, they said. It manifested differently in people, they said. But I knew it wasn't the same kind of dementia the other patients in Lone Star Assisted Living suffered from. I knew that what lived inside Gams was something else—the same something else that had come for Gams's grandmother, squeezing her from the inside until there was less of her than there was of it. The same thing, I could only assume, that would one day come for me.

Maybe the darkness was punishing us for the tidal waves we created when we interfered with fate. Or maybe that was just the way of our curse. Maybe the darkness that appeared above strangers' heads eventually found its way inside us and made a home. And maybe there just wasn't room for both of us.

"Tell Will hi from me," Mindy called longingly as I made my way to the elevator. I hid my laugh behind my hand, then pulled out my phone.

Your girlfriend Mindy said to tell you hi, I texted, adding a kissy emoji for effect.

Will's response was immediate. Isn't she Mom's age? And married?!

She's in luuurve with you, I typed, stealing Marissa's line from earlier. I could practically hear Will's groan through the phone.

On the way to Gams's room, I popped my head into a few rooms to say hello, feeling ashamed that it had been so long since I'd visited. I tried not to linger over the fact that several rooms held new faces. At least here there wasn't any darkness to worry about—no choices for me to make. The darkness only appeared when there was something I could do to stop death from taking hold, and for most of the residents at Lone

Star Assisted Living the time for help had passed. Eventually, death comes for all of us.

"Come in," a voice cheered after I knocked and pushed the cracked door the rest of the way open. Even though she hadn't performed in years, Gams's voice had the rich sound of someone at the center of a spotlighted stage. "Is that my Whitney? Oh, come over here and let me see you!"

I crossed the room in two quick steps and folded her into my arms. She smelled exactly as I remembered: a mix of coconut lotion and rosewater soap.

The walls were covered in playbills and photos of Gams from her time with the New York City Ballet, many capturing her in some form of jewel-encrusted costume midway through a pas de deux.

She squeezed me with surprising force, then pushed me back so she could get a good look at my face. Once satisfied, she motioned for me to sit in the armchair next to her.

"How are you feeling?" I asked. Her eyes were bright and alert, as if nothing had changed—as if everything was normal. It made my heart swell with hope.

"Oh, I'm fine." She patted her bun, smoothing away the flyaways. "It's so good to finally see you, my dear! You look beautiful, as always." She folded her hands in her lap to hide their tremor, but I noticed. "Tell me about your first day of school."

The picture of Dwight with the black squiggle drawn over his head flashed red inside my mind.

Someone knows, Gams.

But no, they couldn't. It had to be a coincidence.

In another time, I wouldn't have hesitated to tell Gams

about the flowers or the photo, but her face was so hopeful and her smile so warm. The words stuck inside my throat.

"It was fine. A little somber, but overall good. What about you? What's the hot gossip?" I asked before she could probe further, reaching out to cover her hands with mine. "Tell me everything I missed."

She huffed out a laugh and looked out the window. "You know nothing interesting ever happens here. Except"—she turned to look at me, a mischievous grin splitting her face—"I met a boy. A cute one."

It was my turn to laugh. "You have a *boyfriend*?"

"Oh God no. You know I don't like to be tied down. He's for you. He comes by to read to me sometimes when he's here visiting his grandfather. I can't wait for you to meet him!"

I rolled my eyes. All I needed was for Gams to start setting me up with the rotating cast of Lone Star grandsons.

"Thanks, Gams, but I don't need you to play matchmaker."

"Whatever you say," she said with another sly grin. "Tell me about you, dear. Tell me about California."

I clutched her hand and leaned back. I'd already told her everything over the phone, but it was hard to know how much she remembered. The doctors said it would happen faster and faster—the good days would be fewer and fewer. It felt like a gift that I got to see her on a day when her blue eyes were bright and her smile was the same as I remembered from our many afternoons spent inside her studio. So I told her again about San Francisco and how beautiful it was, how the fog rolled in from the Golden Gate Bridge and bathed the city in clouds. Then she told me about her own visits to San Francisco when she'd been touring with a dance company. I listened like it was the first time, just glad to be close to her again.

When she finished, she motioned toward her kitchenette.

"Why don't you make us some tea, dear. All this talking has me parched."

I stood, then noticed her journal sitting out in the open where anyone could see it. The floral cover was faded from use, the edges slightly worn. She'd shown it to me the day she'd given me my own pink journal with her rules written on the inside cover, making me promise I'd keep it hidden.

"You shouldn't leave this out in the open," I said, showing her the book. "You don't want one of the volunteers to think it's a book and start reading it."

Gams frowned. "What's that doing there? I thought I put it back . . ." She looked back toward her bed and shook her head. "I could swear I put it back."

"Just be more careful," I said, walking the journal to her bed and sliding it into its usual spot under the mattress. If someone was to read it they'd probably just think it was filled with the confused thoughts of a woman with dementia, but still. It was a risk she taught me never to take. It was unsettling watching the woman who'd been so adamant about her rules now forgetting to follow them.

The teakettle started to scream. I dropped a bag of Earl Grey into a cup, filled it with hot water, and brought it over to Gams. She set it on the table, then gripped my hand tightly and looked me square in the eye, her expression serious.

"And what about you, dear? Tell me you've stopped punishing yourself. Tell me that you're dancing again."

I looked down at the floor. There was a splatter of something brown on the floral rug, and I traced the outline of the stain with my toe. It was Gams's idea for me to go to Dad's. She thought the change of scenery would do me good, that it might help me move past what happened last year.

Gams sighed in response to my silence.

"What happened was horrible, and I don't blame you for leaving the dance team. I can understand how hard it would have been to face Mrs. Bower and the team day in and day out. But that doesn't mean you *stop* dancing. You have a gift, dear. And I'm not just saying that because I'm your grandmother. You can't keep punishing yourself. You need to be brave."

Somehow Gams always knew how to get to the heart of the bruise—the part that still aches even after the outside heals. I looked down at my hands.

"I just can't right now. I don't know how to explain it."

Her lips puckered and the tiny lines around her mouth deepened. "You were always better than me. I spent my life trying to ignore the darkness, but you—your heart was too big to look away."

"You mean my ego," I whispered, thinking of the way I'd felt after I'd saved someone—like I was important. I'd been so wrapped up in my Supergirl routine that I'd never stopped to think about the consequences. I'd never really understood that they weren't my choices to make.

"All those times you told me to leave it alone, you were right. I should have listened. I should have—"

"No," she said, her voice firm. "It's not your fault. It's my fault."

I shook my head and laughed. "It's not your fault—"

"It *is*. It's my fault because I never told you the whole truth. I told you why you couldn't tell anyone about it, but I never told you why I was so adamant that you *ignore* it. It was my own shame that kept me from telling you. Maybe if I'd told you everything, history wouldn't be repeating itself."

Something squirmed inside my stomach. Gams and I didn't have secrets from each other. At least I thought we didn't.

"What are you talking about?"

There was a slight tremor in Gams's hand. When she spoke next, her voice sounded far away.

"I saved a man once. Years ago, when you were much younger. Back then I was a little more like you. As long as I could do it without anyone noticing, I'd help people when I could. So when I saw this man sitting alone in his car with the darkness overhead, I thought, *I have to do something to help him*. He looked like a nice, normal man. I couldn't just let him leave without doing something."

Gams's lower lip quivered. Her eyes filled with moisture. My heart squeezed, realizing where this story was headed. Realizing how naive I'd been all these years when I'd assumed Gams was just being overprotective. Now, her warnings flashed red in my mind.

There are consequences to saving people.

"What happened?" I asked, wanting to know but not wanting to know at the same time.

Gams's whole body was shaking now. My fingers twisted under her grip and her nails dug into my skin.

"He didn't look like the kind of man who would hurt anybody. He just looked sad. How was I supposed to know he'd hurt that little girl?"

A tear slid down Gams's cheek. I tried to pull my hand free, but she squeezed tighter. She was looking at me, but her eyes were unfocused. The hand gripping mine began to shake with more fervor.

"Gams, are you okay?" I tried again to stand, but she clung too tightly. Her mouth opened and closed. This wasn't normal. "Gams?"

A low moan came from deep in her throat. Her eyes found mine, but she wasn't seeing me anymore.

"I should have told you . . ." she said, her voice raising. "I should have told you . . . history repeats itself . . ."

She sat up straight. Her free hand clawed at the couch while the other one squeezed mine until finally I cried out. The teacup clattered to the floor, sending a stream of Earl Grey onto the floral rug.

"Gams, you're hurting me—"

"If I hadn't saved him . . . if I'd just ignored the darkness, she would still be alive." Another moan escaped her lips. "Her poor family . . . I tried to help them . . . I tried to make it right . . ."

Tears sprang to my eyes and I stood, finally wrenching my hand free.

Gams fell backward onto the couch, her mouth slack.

"Maybe I should get one of the nurses?"

She didn't look at me when I spoke. I reached for her arm and gave it a gentle pat, but she jerked it away, shouting like I'd hurt her. Then she put both hands over her ears and squeezed her eyes shut.

"I should have told you . . ." She spoke more quietly now, but she was still trembling, her whole body seeming to vibrate with agitation. Something was wrong with her. She was having an episode. Only this one was . . . different.

"I shouldn't have saved him . . . I tried to make it right . . . too late . . ." Her chin lolled.

"I'll go get a nurse." My stomach clenched as I stepped toward the door, but it sprang open before I got to it.

A boy stepped into the room, his expression serious. Then I remembered something Gams had said earlier, when she told me about the cute boy she wanted to introduce me to.

He comes by to read to me sometimes when he's here visiting his grandfather. I can't wait for you to meet him!

I recognized the sandy hair and red cheeks immediately.

It was Isaac.

8

"I'LL GO GET HELP," ISAAC SAID, EYES ON GAMS.
Then before I could ask him what he was doing there, he
turned and left the room. A few moments later a nurse came
in, brushing past me.

"Constance," she said, flashing a light into Gams's eyes.
"Constance, can you hear me?"

"Is she going to be okay?" I wiped at the tears stinging my
eyes. She'd been fine when I arrived. And Mindy said she
hadn't had an episode in days . . .

The nurse glanced at me, finally acknowledging my presence. I recognized her from the last time I visited Gams. Nurse
Sandra, one of Gams's favorites.

"She'll be fine, Whitney. Can you go downstairs to the waiting area? I'll come find you in a little bit."

"I don't think I should leave her—"

"I'll come find you," she said more firmly, not giving me a
choice.

A warm hand touched my arm and I realized Isaac was still
standing there.

"Why don't we go down to the dining area?" he offered.

He tugged me toward the door. I looked back at Gams's
unfocused eyes and trembling form. It took everything not to
run back to her side. Her words echoed inside my head.

I should have told you.

If I'd just ignored the darkness, she would still be alive.

"Come on," he said more gently, squeezing my fingers. An electric shock shot up my arm. This time I followed, feet heavy as I made my way toward the elevator.

"Are you okay?" Isaac asked. His hair looked lighter under the fluorescent hallway lights. His eyes reminded me of the view I'd had from my father's house, overlooking the ocean and the hills of Marin County. He released my hand and pressed the elevator button.

"What are you doing here?" I asked, avoiding his question. Because clearly I was *not* okay.

"I come by to read to your grandmother sometimes when I'm visiting my grandpa. She asked me to stop by today."

I bit back an irrational laugh. *Of course* Gams was trying to set me up with the guy I'd rescued Saturday night. It was like the universe wanted to remind me why I couldn't keep saving people.

"Something funny?" he asked. The elevator doors slid open. We stepped inside.

I shook my head, trying to control my emotions. They were all over the place. "It's just a bit odd that we keep bumping into each other, don't you think?"

He shrugged. "I didn't know you'd be here. Although I should have been suspicious. She was *very* specific about when she wanted me to meet her. And she told me to wear something nice."

"That sounds like Gams," I said, my voice cracking. I looked away so he couldn't see the tears threatening to break free.

Was it my fault she'd had the attack? Had talking about the

past agitated her? Or was this what she'd been like all summer?

"She's going to be okay," Isaac said, his face sympathetic. "Was that your first time seeing her like that?"

"Kind of," I answered honestly. I'd been with her a few times when she couldn't remember certain things or when she'd been confused. But never anything like what I'd just witnessed, with the trembling, her empty eyes, and the fear in her voice.

And then there was the confession.

If I'd just ignored the darkness, she would still be alive.

I squeezed my eyes shut. I had no idea she'd dealt with something like that. Although now that I thought about it, the clues were there. She'd been so adamant I not tell anyone that I was the girl in the photo that kept appearing on the news. And she'd encouraged me to leave for the summer, assuring me that a break from everything was exactly what I needed. It's like she *knew* what I was going through firsthand.

History repeats itself.

We reached the ground floor and the elevator pinged. I led the way to the dining room, my feet heavy on the carpeted floor.

A few people looked up when we entered the room. A man in a wheelchair sat motionless by the window, staring blankly at the parking lot beyond. A few more people sat scattered in chairs around a television, eyes fixed on an episode of *Judge Judy*.

"Do you want anything to eat?" Isaac asked, motioning toward the back wall where the snacks were laid out.

I shook my head. My stomach was in knots—even if I was hungry, I didn't think I could eat.

He sat down at an empty table, motioning for me to do the same.

I hesitated, trying to gauge his motivation. On Saturday he'd looked at me like he couldn't wait to get as far away from me as possible. Why was he suddenly being so nice?

"She's going to be okay," he repeated, like he was an authority on the subject. "I'm sure that must have been really scary for you if you haven't seen it happen before."

"And you have?" I asked with more bite behind my words than I'd intended.

He nodded. "A few times, when I was reading to her."

I swallowed, thinking about the memory she was sharing when she started trembling uncontrollably. Had she shared similar memories with Isaac? With the staff? The mashed-up roses and photo of Dwight flashed inside my mind again. Could Gams have accidentally told someone what happened?

"Can we change the subject?" I asked, studying my nails. I didn't want to talk about Gams with this stranger. Or near-stranger. It made me feel guilty that he seemed to have a better grasp on Gams's health than I did.

"Okay," he started. When he smiled a small dimple folded into his right cheek. "How come this is the first time I'm seeing you here?"

"I was visiting my dad in San Francisco for the summer," I said. "How come I never saw you before I left?"

"We moved my grandpa here at the start of the summer. He lived alone before that." He looked down at his hands, like the admission pained him.

"I'm sorry. Is he okay?" I felt a sympathetic pang.

Isaac shrugged and looked away.

"He's all right. He wasn't happy about having to move out of his house, but he's adjusting. We couldn't leave him on his own anymore, and both of my parents work, so this seemed like the best solution."

"That must be really hard for you and your family." I pressed my lips together, remembering the day Gams announced her decision to sell her house and move into Lone Star. By that time she'd already sold her dance studio; letting go of her house felt like we were shredding the last vestige of the unbreakable prima ballerina from my childhood. She said it was because she didn't want us fussing over her all the time, but I knew the truth—she didn't want us to watch her deteriorate. And she wanted it to be her decision to leave.

"Is your grandpa the reason you moved here?" I asked.

He gave me a bemused look and shook his head. "We didn't move."

I waited for him to elaborate, but he didn't.

"So you just decided to start a new high school for funsies?"

"No, not for *funsies*." His dimple escaped again. "We moved to our house when I was in eighth grade, but my parents had me use my grandpa's address so I wouldn't have to change schools. When we sold his house I couldn't use that address anymore and the school board said I had to switch schools." He shrugged again, like it was no big deal.

"That sucks. What school were you at before?"

He hesitated. "Collin Creek."

I felt the color drain from my face.

"I wasn't at the game last year, if that's what you're thinking," he said, reading my forlorn expression. "None of my friends were. I mean I knew people who were there, obviously. But that's not why I switched schools. Although it made switching much easier. It was hard to be there after what happened. The whole place felt haunted."

I nodded, hoping he couldn't tell that my stomach had turned inside out. These days it seemed impossible to meet someone who hadn't been affected by last year's tragedy. By me.

He must have seen something in my expression, because he continued. "I mean, I know your school was affected, too. It's terrible for everyone. It's just that it's harder to be in the place where it all went down, you know? There's no way to escape it."

"Right," I said numbly, thinking of the *In Loving Memory* lockers. It may not have happened at our school, but our hallways were just as haunted.

Isaac cleared his throat. "Anyway, I'm glad I bumped into you. I wanted to say thank you for giving me a ride home on Saturday. Sorry if I was kind of a dick."

I snorted. "You looked a little green, so I just figured you had to puke."

"Yeah, I barely made it into the house. I don't usually drink." He cleared his throat, glancing down at the table. "And if I seemed a little weird, it was because I recognized you. It started to become a thing for me to stop by your grandma's room when my grandpa was napping, and there are all those pictures of her all over the walls. You look just like her when she was young." He shrugged, looking sheepish. "You probably thought I was a total weirdo for staring."

I smiled. And here I'd thought he was staring at me for some sinister reason. These days I always assumed the worst.

"How'd your mom take it when you came home without your car?"

"She was surprisingly cool, but mostly because she blamed my cousin. He's the one who kept forcing his quote, unquote *infamous* punch down my throat all night."

"Wait. Your cousin is *Beau Gunter*?"

"Isaac Gunter." He pointed a finger at himself. "You say his name like it's a disease. He's not *that* bad."

"He calls himself *the Beau* and makes all these gross puns with his name. I'm pretty sure I once heard him ask a girl if she wanted a Beau job."

Isaac snorted, then covered his mouth like he was trying to hold in the laugh. "Sorry. He can be a douche sometimes, but I promise he's harmless."

I took stock of his dimple and flushed cheeks, marveling at the mysteries of genetics. Isaac was tall like Beau, but the resemblance stopped there. Isaac's shoulders were broader, his chin more confident, and his eyes bluer. And then there was the matter of that dimple.

"Why do you call your grandma 'Gams'?" He changed the subject. "Could you not say your *R*'s when you were a kid or something?"

"No, Gams was her nickname long before I came along. I think because of her long legs and the whole ballerina thing."

I felt my cheeks flush as Isaac's eyes flicked over my face. I wondered if he was comparing me to her photos. Then just as quickly he glanced over my head and jumped to his feet.

"Grandpa Jack, what are you doing down here? I thought you wanted to nap."

I turned to see an old gentleman shuffling into the dining room with a walker, his jowls jiggling under a frown. He wore a gray three-piece suit despite the heat outside, and his thick wire-framed glasses had slipped dangerously close to the tip of his nose. A frustrated-looking nurse followed behind him, hands on the hips of her blue-and-white scrubs.

"I told him I'd come get you," the woman said, pushing a dark plait of hair over her shoulder.

"ISAAC, I NEED YOU TO TIE MY TIE." The old man's voice boomed and I noticed the large plastic hearing aids in both his ears. "SHE WAS DOING IT ALL WRONG. SHE ALWAYS DOES IT WRONG." His cheeks were red with agitation.

The nurse rolled her eyes at Isaac, giving me the impression this wasn't the first time they'd had this exchange.

"I got it, Gramps." Isaac jogged toward the old man. He took the loose tie ends dangling from his grandpa's neck and expertly wove them together. "Better?"

The old man nodded and patted Isaac's shoulder. "SHE WAS DOING IT ALL WRONG. NOT LIKE YOU. YOU'RE A GOOD BOY, ISAAC."

Isaac turned toward the nurse and gave her an apologetic smile. "Thanks for bringing him to me. I can stay with him until dinner."

"Thank God." She rolled her eyes toward the ceiling, shaking her head as she left the room.

Isaac gently took his grandfather by the arm and helped him

shuffle toward a nearby table. I looked away, feeling like I'd peered inside a private window to Isaac's life.

"Can you give me a sec to say bye to my friend?" Isaac glanced in my direction. I felt a surprising pang of disappointment.

When he got back to our table, he took my hand and gave it a formal shake. My skin tingled underneath the weight of his palm. "Nice officially meeting you, Whitney. And thanks again for the ride on Saturday. I'd say see you around, but at the rate we're going it probably goes without saying."

He brushed the hair back from his eyes. I noticed again how blue they were.

"Thanks for your help with Gams."

He smiled and shoved his hands into his pockets. "I'm glad I could help. Constance—er, *Gams*—is a really special person."

I swallowed the lump in my throat at the same moment Nurse Sandra entered the dining room. I practically launched myself at her.

"Your grandmother's resting now, but you can come see her if you'd like."

I sighed in relief. "Thank you so much."

When I turned back to say bye to Isaac, he was seated with his grandfather, a deck of cards in his hand and a smile on his face. He saw me and waved, and something in my heart squeezed.

Gams certainly knew how to pick them.

9

VISITING HOURS ENDED LONG BEFORE I FINALLY MADE
my way down to the nursing home lobby and into the dark
parking lot. I searched my bag for my car keys, footsteps echo-
ing against the pavement as I walked toward the back of the
lot. A cloud passed over the moon, causing even deeper shadows to pool around the few remaining cars. The two streetlights edging the back row of trees hadn't yet turned on, or
maybe they weren't working. It made the back of the building eerily black, like the darkness I saw had settled across the
night. I shivered and quickened my pace.

When I climbed into the front seat, the interior of my car
seemed different—opaque. I blinked to adjust my eyes, figuring it was just the busted streetlights and overcast sky. It
wasn't until my headlights flared to life that I saw the red
streaked across my windshield.

I let out a sharp gasp and jumped back.

Rust-colored smears covered most of the glass, blocking my
view of the street. In the few gaps between the scarlet streaks,
the meager moonlight cast silvery slants onto the dash.

Paint, I thought, trying to calm my thudding pulse. *Someone
threw paint on my windshield.*

But no. The drops sliding down the glass were too thick to
be paint.

It looked like blood.

I pressed my back against the seat. Between the drips and rivulets running down the glass, I saw the streaks weren't haphazard—they formed a shape. Then I noticed the piece of paper tucked under the windshield wiper.

I climbed back out of the car, heart beating fast as I took in the painted image.

To anyone else, it might have looked random. But I noticed the scalloped edges, the care that was taken to make the rounded borders.

It was a cloud.

I swallowed and looked around the parking lot to see if someone was watching. It was too dark. Too quiet.

My shaking fingers plucked the paper from the windshield. Whoever had placed it there had done it carefully, making sure that none of the paint got onto the page. I unfolded it.

My lunch threatened to crawl back up my throat.

It was the grainy picture of me and Dwight standing together on the roof. The same picture that news outlets had posted in the days following the tragedy. The same photo that made everyone believe Dwight had an accomplice. Why else would the person in the photo have remained quiet all this time, if they didn't have something to hide?

Because I'm a coward. Because I didn't tell the police what he told me that day and now it's too late. Because I could have stopped him and I didn't. Because people are afraid of the things they don't understand.

In the photo a winter hat and scarf covered most of my face. What was visible was grainy and unrecognizable. No one knew that it was me.

At least I thought no one knew.

How? Who?

Just like the photo left in my locker, this one had a thick black cloud drawn over Dwight's head, matching the bloody cloud painted on my windshield.

I flipped the photo over, looking for a clue about who might have left it. But there was nothing.

It had to be from the same person who vandalized my locker. Someone wanted to send me a message. But who?

I crumpled the note and chucked it into the front seat. Then I jumped back in my car and wrenched on the wipers. The horrible shape smeared into a solid block of red, covering the glass.

I pressed my fists into my eyelids until blue and black pinwheels twirled into view.

When executing any leap, make sure to point and stretch your feet the instant they leave the ground. Elongate the neck to give the illusion of more height.

A knock on the window jolted me back to reality.

"Whitney?" Isaac peered into the window, brows pinching in concern. "What are you still doing here?"

My fingers shook as I rolled down the window.

"What happened? Are you hurt?" He looked from the windshield to me. The wipers screeched across the red-stained glass. "Did someone throw something at you?"

"I don't know. It was there when I got in. It looks like blood—" I swallowed to stamp down the scream threatening to burst through.

Isaac stepped to the front of my car and scraped off some

of the muck. He rolled it between his thumb and forefinger, sniffing.

"It's syrup. Totally harmless. Someone added food coloring or something."

He must have expected me to be relieved, because his smile crumbled when he saw the horror still fixed on my face.

Because it didn't matter. Someone wanted me to *think* it was blood. Someone *knew*.

"People are such assholes," Isaac started, face twisting in disgust. "A few weeks ago someone keyed one of the nurses' cars. And earlier this summer they found graffiti on the side of the building. Who spray-paints an old folks home?" He shook his head, like I was just the victim of a random act of vandalism.

"I can go inside and find something to clean that stuff off your windshield."

"No." I shook myself out of my stupor and climbed out of the car. "I have some wipes in the trunk."

I needed to get out of there. What if the person who vandalized my car was there now, watching? I shivered and pulled out a canister of Clorox wipes from the depths of my trunk. Isaac took one and soundlessly began helping me clean the gunk off my window. I could feel his eyes on me but kept my gaze glued to the muck on the glass, trying to make it go away as quickly as possible.

Whoever vandalized my locker did this to me. They followed me—otherwise how would they have known I'd be here? I glanced around the parking lot, but all I could see were shadows and the inky black of the unlit street.

Are they just trying to scare me? What do they want?

Isaac's hand bumped against mine as he reached to wipe off the last of the red. He gave a nervous laugh, then stepped back to admire our work.

"All clean," he said. "Like nothing ever happened."

My face must have betrayed my thoughts because he touched my arm. A ripple of warmth shot through me.

"Hey, you okay? I know it looked bad, but I promise, your car is fine."

"I know," I said. "I guess I'm just rattled. Thanks for your help."

I hoped he didn't catch the struggle in my smile. I *was* grateful, but in that moment I just wanted to disappear and pretend the whole thing never happened. I reached for the door handle, hoping he might take the hint.

"Don't worry. Whoever did this will get caught eventually. What goes around comes around, right?"

I almost laughed. He had no idea.

Someone has been watching me. Someone knows about the darkness. Someone knows it's me in the photo.

Isaac glanced in the direction of where his car must have been parked, then back at me. His fingers plucked at a loose thread on his shirt. His toe tapped the ground. He looked like I felt right before I went onstage to dance a solo at competition—a big ball of jittery nerves. Was he stalling?

"Would it be weird if I texted you?" he finally asked, cheeks turning to matching rose-colored inkblots.

"I—uh—" I stumbled over my words, trying to make sense of what he was saying. "Like to check on me?"

"Sure," he said. "And to, like, talk. If you wanted. It's okay if you don't. Sorry, I didn't mean to put you on the spot. I guess it's been a weird night." He ran his hand through his sand-colored hair and looked down at the ground.

"Oh," I said, realizing what was happening. Of course the universe would choose right now for someone like Isaac to show interest in me. If he had any idea about the crumpled picture of me and Dwight Hacken sitting on the passenger seat, he'd run as fast as his legs could carry him.

"Sure," I said, because I couldn't think of anything else to say. Because I just wanted to get as far away from the parking lot as possible.

But also because the way he was looking at me made my pulse speed up.

"Do you need me to give you my number again?" I asked, remembering the way he'd looked when I'd forced him to take it on Saturday.

He looked down at his feet, embarrassed. "I may have already saved it in my phone."

Heat flared in my cheeks.

"I'll text you," he said, making it sound official. Then he gave the side of my car a light thump before stepping back so I could get in. I waved, then turned my eyes to the dark road ahead.

Tomorrow, I'd come back to ask Gams if she'd told someone about Dwight, even though it made no sense. Gams was clear about two things—always point your feet, and never, ever tell anyone about the clouds we saw.

I drove home like someone was chasing me.

Because maybe someone was.

﹏ ﹏

Mom was in the office when I arrived home, the bluish light from her computer casting eerie shadows across her face. When I flicked on the overhead light, her head snapped up in alarm.

"Oh, you're home," she said, rubbing her eyes. "I didn't hear you come in."

I swallowed at the idea that anyone could have marched inside the house and Mom wouldn't have noticed.

Just like someone followed me tonight and I had no idea . . .

"Why are you working in the dark?" I stepped into the room and flipped on the lamp next to her desk. At least the blinds were closed.

She rubbed her eyes again. "The slides for this presentation tomorrow are a complete mess. The new analyst on our team can barely string together a sentence, so I have to fix everything before our meeting." She let out an exasperated huff and a few pieces of blond hair escaped the loose bun at the top of her head.

On the computer, words like *margin expansion* and *forecast* glowed from a PowerPoint slide. Sometimes I wondered if she made up her own work drama just to give herself an excuse to keep working.

"How about I make you a sandwich?" I picked up the empty mug from her desk. She always forgot to eat when she was busy.

"I'm almost finished. I'll fix myself something then. How was school? First day go okay?"

For one brief second, I thought about telling her the truth— about my locker, the note, and the fake blood that was probably still stuck to my wiper blades. But then her eyes flicked back to the computer, and I could tell her mind was on work. Not that it mattered. It's not like she could do anything about it. And more specifically, when it came to the things I saw, it was better not to involve Mom unless I wanted her to think there was something inside me that was broken.

People are afraid of the things they don't understand.

"Everything was great." I plastered on a smile that probably looked as fake as it felt, but she didn't notice. "I'm going to get ready for bed. You sure you don't need anything?"

"No thanks, sweetheart. I'll come in to say good night as soon as I'm done here."

I nodded, but we both knew I would be asleep long before that happened.

I walked down the hallway to my room, flicking lights on as I went. It was too dark. How could Mom not be creeped out being alone in a pitch-dark house? My bedroom was equally dark. The blinds were raised, and I could see the sliver of moon and anemic glow of the streetlight beyond. When I turned on my overhead light, the bare window suddenly felt like a spotlight shining right into the house. Anyone walking down the street could see straight inside my bedroom. Anyone could be watching.

The hairs on my arms rose.

I crossed the room in three quick steps and wrenched the blinds down, then pulled the curtains shut for good measure.

Someone had followed me from school to the nursing home. Either that, or whoever left the note on my car already knew I was planning to visit Gams.

If their goal was to scare me, mission accomplished. But why leave photos instead of confronting me directly? Or worse— why not take the information straight to the police? There was probably still a reward being offered for information about the girl in the photo.

Which begged the bigger question—what did they want? There hadn't been any threats or blackmail messages written on the pictures—just that ominous cloudlike squiggle. So what then? Was I just supposed to bumble around in a terrified stupor while I waited for them to confront me?

I reached under my mattress and pulled out my notebook. The pink ballerina cover was bent at the corners, worn from years of sliding it in and out of its hiding spot. I climbed into bed, then flipped to the first page and traced my finger down the list of names and the notes I'd made about what I'd done to save them. Once, the list was a thing of pride. I'd started keeping a record not long after Gams gave the book to me, back when I believed that everyone should be saved. Now I understood that choices were like pebbles tossed into an ocean, the impact rippling outward until eventually it became a crushing wave.

I didn't have names for everyone—only vague descriptions, like *mail delivery guy* or *hot dog vendor*—but for those I did have, I'd spent the summer researching them. I wanted to see if they were good people, or if they were like Dwight, if the darkness I'd seen over their heads matched the darkness inside of them. I needed to know that not every decision I'd made led to tragedy. I needed to believe there was good inside the people I'd saved. There had to be.

I flipped to the last entry—Isaac's. In the empty space below, I wrote Jenny Chan's name and the details about our encounter. Then I slid the notebook back into its hiding spot and closed my eyes.

I heard the door click open a while later when Mom came to check on me. I pretended to be asleep, but it was hours before sleep finally found me.

10

"MRS. B JUST WANTS TO MAKE SURE YOU'RE OKAY, that's all. Just go and talk to her. You can't avoid her for the entire school year." Marissa pressed a napkin to her pizza, letting oil seep into the thin white paper.

I picked up my slice and took a bite, avoiding Marissa's quizzical stare. The note from Mrs. B sat open on the table next to me, her familiar swirly handwriting covering the page. I wanted to throw it in the trash, but I knew that wasn't an option. Not with Marissa watching.

> Whitney,
> Please stop by my office when you have a minute. It feels like I haven't seen you in forever! I hope the school year is off to a good start. We miss you at practice.
>
> XO,
> Mrs. B

"It's a note, not a tumor. Stop looking at it like it's going to kill you." Marissa's words were garbled against a mouthful of food. "I'm pretty sure she's over the whole you quitting thing by now. I doubt she's going to lecture you if that's what you're worried about."

I pressed my lips together, thinking of the way she'd winced when I'd told her that I wanted to spend more time working on my technique. When I was growing up, Mrs. B had practically lived at Gams's studio. Not only was she a former student and protégé of Gams's, but she was one of Gams's favorite people in the world. She'd been Gams's guest at Thanksgivings and birthday parties and had even asked Gams to be the matron of honor at her wedding. She'd also been my dance coach long before I'd joined the Hornettes. Telling her that I was quitting her team to focus on my technique was basically the same thing as calling her a shitty dance teacher, which probably cut even more deeply given how close she was to my grandma.

Still, it had to be done.

"Just go see her and stop making things weird," Marissa said. "She misses you."

"Okay," I said, the guilt-knife cutting deeper. I pressed my temples, trying to drown out the cafeteria noise. It was making my already pounding headache worse. I'd spent half the night tossing and turning, trying to figure out who could have vandalized my car. Maybe it was someone who worked at Lone Star? Maybe they'd read Gams's journal after she'd left it out and now they were trying to scare me. Except that didn't explain the flowers in my locker. It had to be the same person, which meant it was someone who probably went to my school. But who?

My phone buzzed, making me jump. But when I flipped the screen over and saw the message, I couldn't help but smile.

Isaac had been texting me all morning. The first message was there when I woke up—a simple hi, it's Isaac. Hope you got home okay. Then when I got out of the shower, I found the second: Before we go any further, I have some important questions to ask you.

I assumed he was kidding, but then the questions started to arrive, each more ridiculous than the last. Even though I was sleep-deprived and completely on edge after last night, he made me laugh.

> Would you rather fight one hundred duck-sized horses or one horse-sized duck?

> Would you rather have a butt for a nose or a nose for a butt?

> Would you rather have hands for feet or feet for hands?

My responses took me way longer to craft than they should have, and every time I hit send my stomach flipped with excitement. It was an odd sensation considering how tense everything else felt.

In answer to the most recent question, I typed: Hands for feet. Imagine how easy it would be to pick up socks?

Marissa poked me with her fork, bringing me back to the present.

"Hello? Earth to Whitney?" She poked me again. "Why are you grinning like an idiot? Wait, is it another text from Isaac? Let me see!"

I angled my phone so she could look, and she nodded her head in approval.

"Good call, although that was a softball question. Can you imagine having to type with your toes? Or clap with your feet? Gross." Then her eyes widened and she pointed across the cafeteria, where Isaac was making his way toward us balancing an overcrowded lunch tray.

"Is he coming over here?" Marissa leaned closer to me and

75

lowered her voice. "Oh my God, he's coming over here. Shit, he sees me looking. I bet he knows we're talking about him. Pretend I said something funny. Act natural." She let out a fake bark of laughter, fluffed her hair, arched an eyebrow, and perched her hand on her hip, looking anything but natural.

An irrepressible grin split his face when he got to the table. Some winged creature inside my chest fluttered to life.

"Mind if we join y'all?" He slid into the empty seat before either of us could respond, then motioned to a cluster of guys loitering by the vending machines to join us.

A thought flashed through my head. *Would you rather sit with a girl who sees death clouds over people's heads, or sit with a normal girl who doesn't know about the darkness that comes for us in the end?* But I shook it away.

"Just make yourself at home why don't you," Marissa said, sweeping an arm out to the rest of the empty table. "Never mind that we might be saving these seats for our friends."

"What, we aren't friends?" Isaac flashed Marissa a warm dimple-exposing smile before turning to me.

Marissa gave me a sharp kick under the table. *He luurves you,* she mouthed. I kicked her back.

"'Sup ladies?" Beau slammed his tray down next to Marissa, sloshing water onto the table. "If I knew my cousin was so popular, I would have convinced him to transfer sooner."

"Your *cousin?*" Marissa looked back and forth between Beau and Isaac like she was working a math problem. "I don't believe it."

"Believe it, baby." Beau clapped Isaac proudly on the shoulder. "This handsome devil is one of the blessed members of the Gunter clan."

Marissa snorted. "*Blessed* is hardly the word for it."

"Trust me, babe. I am a very *blessed* man. Where do you think they got the phrase 'everything's bigger in Texas'?" Beau winked. "They don't call me Beau-meo for nothing."

"You're disgusting. And no one calls you that."

Isaac flicked a fry at his cousin. "Try to reel in the charm."

Beau leaned back in his chair and gave Marissa a slow smile. "Whatever you say, cuz." Marissa glared.

"What's with the love note?" Beau turned his attention to me, pointing at Mrs. Bower's letter.

"It's not a *love* note." I folded it in half and tucked it under my tray. "And it's none of your business."

I didn't mean to give my words teeth, but they snared out of my mouth anyway. Sleeplessness made me cranky. Beau shrugged and lifted a powdered donut to his lips. Isaac watched me, curious.

More of Beau's friends joined us, clapping Isaac on the shoulder and acknowledging us with juts of their chins. The rest of our friends were relegated to the opposite end of the table, which didn't seem to bother Marissa in the slightest. She looked pleased with the variety of boys suddenly at her disposal, and quickly launched into an animated description of her summer, pausing only long enough to call Beau a perv when he interjected with his "hilarious" innuendos. If my brain hadn't been so static-filled, I might have enjoyed it all. But I was too on edge from these past couple of days—and Mrs. B's note.

Marissa was right—it was just a note, not a tumor. The sooner I got the conversation out of the way, the better. I wouldn't be able to avoid her forever. The school wasn't that big. And maybe it wouldn't be so bad, especially if I caught her at the end of lunch, when she wouldn't have enough time to quiz me about quitting the team. I stood abruptly and my chair tipped backward, clanging against the tiled floor. Marissa froze mid-sentence. Heads snapped in my direction.

"You okay?" Isaac asked.

"Fine," I squeaked. "I just need to check on something." I righted the chair. What was wrong with me? It was just Mrs. B. We'd had thousands of conversations. Why was I suddenly so nervous?

I picked up the note and my half-eaten lunch. Marissa nodded in understanding.

"See ya later, Supergirl," Beau offered through a mouthful of fries. Pieces of potato spewed from his mouth when Marissa elbowed him.

11

THE LOCKER ROOM WAS MOSTLY EMPTY EXCEPT FOR a few girls quietly pecking at their brown-bag lunches. A circle of black-and-gold star-covered curtains separated the dance team's section of the locker room from the rest of the space, and to the left of that sat Mrs. B's office. Through the open door, I saw her arms swirling as she talked to someone over a stack of papers. When she caught sight of me, her face broke into a smile and she nearly toppled a mountain of folders. Then she hobbled out of the small room and my heart sank with the usual spike of guilt.

The thick black boot on her foot thumped against the floor, but still Mrs. B moved with surprising speed. She'd gotten better at walking with crutches, and now a single cane that had black and gold ribbon twisted around it. I wondered if she had put the ribbon there, or if one of the girls on the team did it in honor of Monday's decorations.

It was hard to look at Mrs. B and not remember the way she used to move, the way she would glide across the floor like she knew how each piece of her body fit inside the music. She danced the way Gams taught everyone she loved to dance— like they were a song.

And now Mrs. B would never dance again.

"Whitney! I'm so glad you stopped by. I was worried you wouldn't come." She looked as beautiful as ever—hair coiffed into smooth curls, large diamonds glittering from each ear, long mascaraed lashes framing dark eyes.

With her free arm, she reached out and hugged me. I took the opportunity to squeeze my eyes shut.

"Hi, Mrs. B." I wriggled out of her grasp as soon as I could and turned toward the dark-haired man who emerged from the office, a tight grin on his face.

"Hi, Mr. Bower." I shrank back when our eyes met. Of course he would be there. As if seeing Mrs. B wasn't already worth its weight in guilt, I had to see them both together. Although I shouldn't have been so surprised. Mr. Bower had been Mrs. B's shadow since they were kids. They were high school sweethearts, and before they got married Mr. Bower used to wait outside Gams's old studio like a loyal puppy so he could drive her home from practice. He even volunteered to run back-of-house tech for a few of Gams's spring shows.

Once Mrs. B took over the Hornettes, he'd been a fixture at almost every football game and dance competition. He usually sat off to the side, away from the parents and the team, but it was hard not to notice him. He looked like something pulled straight from the pages of a glossy magazine, with a strong, straight nose, high cheekbones, and a square jaw that sent the newest team members into blushing giggle fits every time he said hello.

Mr. Bower smiled at me, flashing a row of perfectly straight white teeth. "It's nice to see you, Whitney. How are you? How's your grandmother?" His voice was warm.

"Good. Great. Everyone is great." I smiled a plastic smile.

"Peter, would you mind giving me and Whitney a few minutes?"

"Of course. I should get back to the office anyway." He bent down and kissed his wife's cheek, then turned to me. "Nice to see you, Whit. Tell your grandma hi from me." He smiled at me once more. Then he turned back to Mrs. B to give her one final peck. "See you tonight."

Mrs. B's office smelled faintly of tuna fish, likely coming from the sandwich remnants spread across the only non-paper-covered section of the desk. Everything else was buried under file folders, paperwork, and pictures of the teams she'd coached over the years. Despite her perfect outward appearance, her office always seemed to be in a cyclone of disarray, as if she couldn't bother to place files in folders or store things in drawers.

"I'm so glad you stopped by. I was afraid you were avoiding me." Mrs. B's smile was as reassuring as ever, but it did little to ease my discomfort. "It's okay if you're avoiding me. I would probably avoid me, too."

An apology stuck in my throat, the words made of Velcro.

"Look, Whitney. I'm not mad at you. It's your choice to leave the team and I have to respect that. You're practically an adult. I'm not going to lecture you or anything like that again. Okay?"

I nodded, blinking long and hard as the guilt squirmed inside me, as my choices marched inside my head like a macabre parade.

Mrs. Bower's dark eyes searched mine. "Whitney, I do hope you're at least talking to someone. A lot of the girls who were there that night are, especially as we get closer to the first game of the year. The events can be triggering. So I'd understand if that's the reason—"

I shook my head. "I'm fine, really. It's not you or the team. Of course it's not you. I—it's just . . . my technique . . . and college—" I couldn't seem to make my tongue work properly.

She reached for a framed photo on her desk and tapped the image. In it, two dark-haired girls in matching blue sequined costumes grinned widely, tap shoes strapped to their feet. They looked like twins.

She looked up at me, her eyes clear. "Did I ever tell you I had a sister?"

I shook my head, not sure why she was asking.

"Well, I did. She died when I was younger—" She broke off for a moment. "I was devastated, as you can imagine. She was my best friend." She gave me a sad smile. "It was dance that saved me. And your grandmother. I don't think I ever would have made it through those first years without my sister if it hadn't been for dance and your grandmother's willingness to teach me. I spent just about every free moment inside her studio, learning how to channel my emotions into my work. It helped me heal. The dance team could do the same for you, if you'd let us. We all need to do some healing, Whitney."

I swallowed again and tried my best not to look away. Every time I tried to dance now, my feet felt like boulders. All I could think about was that night at the football game—the crowd, the sound of gunfire, the choices I made. The memories held me in place, like the darkness reached inside of me and suffocated my will to move. The idea of dancing with the team and having to look Mrs. B in the face every day . . . I couldn't do it. Maybe it made me a coward, but I couldn't even stomach the thought of it.

There must have been something in my expression because Mrs. B held up her hands in surrender. "It's okay. I get it. I'm sorry, I shouldn't have brought it up. In fact I swore to myself I wouldn't. So much for promises, huh?" She gave me an apologetic frown. "Anyway, how are you? How's your first week of senior year going?"

I thought about my locker and graffitied car and forced a smile. "Good." I stepped back slightly. "It's a little strange not staying after school for practice, but it's good to be back."

"Well, we miss you. How are your dance classes going? I hope they're helping with your technique."

There was a bite to her sentence and I winced. But in some ways it made it easier knowing she still held some resentment toward me—it was deserved.

"Classes are good. I'm going to Gams's old studio. I'm even competing with their competition team this year." The lies tumbled out like the more details I added the more truthful they would sound.

"That's wonderful! Maybe we'll see you at competition. Wouldn't that be fun?"

"Yeah. Fun." I swallowed.

"How is Constance? I miss her. Things have been so busy lately that I haven't had the chance to visit since she moved into her new—home."

She hesitated on the last word, likely because she couldn't bring herself to think of Lone Star as a home. Not the way that Gams's old house had been a home, anyway. It was hard to think of Gams anywhere she wasn't in command of the spotlight.

"You should stop by for a visit. It would mean a lot to her."

"You're right. I'll give her a call." Mrs. B smiled, the fondness evident in her brown eyes. "I'm embarrassed that it's taken me this long."

"I'm sure she understands."

She smiled, then dug through a stack of papers until she found a sheet of paper with tiny X's all over it. "I hope you don't mind, but I actually asked you here to talk about the dance you choreographed when you auditioned for officer. You know, the one with the red dress?"

She pushed the paper across the table, shoving aside other stacks so I could see.

Everyone trying out for officer had to choreograph three dances—a halftime routine, a competition routine, and a solo. The sheet in front of me detailed the formations and transitions for *Red*, the competition lyrical piece I'd created for my audition. I'd envisioned the entire team in head-to-toe white, with the exception of one girl in a long, flowing red dress.

"I would love to use the number for competition season, but I wanted to check with you first. Would it be all right with you if we used it?"

I put my hands in my lap so she couldn't see them ball into fists. I'd always envisioned myself as the one in red. Now the role would go to someone else. Probably Penny.

"Of course," I answered, working to keep my tone even. "I'd be flattered if the team used it."

Mrs. B clapped her hands together, not noticing that my voice sounded like cardboard. "I'm so glad. It's such a beautiful piece. And I think it sends such a powerful message about not being afraid to stand out in a crowd. It's just what we need to bring home the trophy."

She beamed, and I didn't have the heart to correct her. The dance wasn't about standing out in a crowd. It was about the things I saw. The girl in red was like the darkness, twirling and twisting as she finally broke free from her cage. She was a dancing warning—a beacon screaming to be saved. Screaming for *me* to save her.

But I supposed none of that mattered anymore.

"So then you won't mind taking Penny through the choreography and formations so she can teach it to the team?"

And there was the rub. That explained the relief on Mrs. Bower's face. My penance, it seemed, would be an afternoon trapped with Penny.

"We're hoping to start teaching some of the competition routines next month, after homecoming. Do you think you could go over it with her in the next few weeks so we can start planning?"

"Of course. I'd be happy to." An afternoon with Penny was a small price to pay. I glanced at the clock, grateful to see that the bell was about to ring. "I should get to class."

I picked up my bag and stood, feeling the weight of Mrs. B's eyes on me as I made my way to her office door.

"Whitney? There's something—no, it's stupid."

"What?" I asked, trying to gauge her expression. Her mouth was twisted into a frown.

"It's just—there's something that's been bothering me. I know it's silly, but I thought about it a few times over the summer and I was just wondering—I had to ask—" Her eyes darted around the room, avoiding my face. Dread tiptoed down my spine. "The night of that game, after y'all performed and you were marching off the field, you broke formation. In all the years I've known you, I've never once seen you make a mistake, let alone break formation. Did something happen? It's just—well, it was so unlike you. And considering what happened after . . . I know it's silly, but I had to ask."

I swallowed. The walls of her office crept closer. Why was she just now asking me this?

"Broke formation?" I scrunched my forehead, trying to look like I didn't know what she was talking about. But in my mind, I saw the moment with perfect clarity—the way the first tuft of darkness appeared in the stands, followed by another and another. How could I *not* break formation?

I shook my head. "You know, I don't remember. I think maybe I heard someone call my name or something?" Somehow I managed to keep my voice even. "I'm sorry. I wish I could remember more, but the night . . . it's kind of all a blur. I've been trying not to think about it."

"Right," she said. Mrs. B looked down and smiled. "Right, of course. I told you it was silly." She shook her head, like she was shaking away the memory. "Thanks for stopping by, Whitney. And for agreeing to let us use *Red*. It's really such a lovely routine. I promise we'll make you proud with it."

I smiled and nodded back. "I'm sure you will."

"I'll have Penny reach out about scheduling rehearsal time, but let me know if there's anything else you need."

"I will, thanks, Mrs. B."

I waved once, trying to look casual as I reached for the

office door. It made a soft click when it closed behind me. I walked calmly through the locker room until I was sure she couldn't see me, then I sprinted to the nearest bathroom and threw up.

12

MY CAR HAD MULTIPLIED. THERE WAS A SECOND SILVER Accord parked next to it, identical down to the black faux-leather interior and tree-shaped air freshener dangling from the rearview mirror. If it weren't for the jagged scratch running the length of the other car's passenger-side door, I might have climbed into the wrong car.

"Looks like your car has a twin."

I shielded my eyes so I could see the figure approaching from the football field, the yellow numbers on his warm-up jersey glowing in the sun. Not that a visual was needed to confirm his identity. I'd know Kevin's voice anywhere.

"Looks that way," I replied, opening my car door. Maybe if I made it clear I was leaving, he'd go away.

His hair was shorter. The close-cropped curls suited him, making the cleft in his jaw more pronounced. But his smile hadn't changed. There was a time when that boyish half grin would have turned me into a puddle. Now it just made me rueful, like he was a stranger in a crowd resembling someone I used to know.

"You never answered any of my texts, so I figured the only way to get you to talk to me was to hunt you down."

He smiled as he spoke, but I didn't miss the edge to his words. I swallowed, thinking of the many pleas he'd texted over the summer.

Swear you won't tell anyone, Whit.

Promise me.

"How are you?" he asked, clearing his throat.

"Good. Great. I'm really great." How many times had I said that since getting back? I was like one of those talking dolls with strings that only could say three sentences.

"Good," he echoed, eyes grazing over the students weaving their way through the emptying parking spaces. The silence stretched for what felt like an eternity, then he finally raked his fingers through his curls and let out a grunt of frustration.

"Are you pissed about Penny? Is that why you never answered me? You're the one who broke up with me. You can't be mad at me for moving on."

I slammed the door shut with more force than intended. First Mrs. B, now Kevin. Why was it that everyone wanted to confront me today? Frustration broiled inside me. Of course I broke up with him. How could I not, after what Dwight told me he'd done? It was like I'd never really known him, like his good-guy act was just an outer husk masking the darkness inside.

"I don't care about Penny," I said, unable to stop my hands from fisting.

My issues with Kevin were much deeper than him jumping into the arms of my nemesis mere days after we broke up. I'd spent all summer trying to reconcile the two versions of him—how could the Kevin who'd had the show choir serenade me at lunch when he asked me to junior prom, who'd driven me to dance competitions and sat through hours of performances just to watch me dance a two-minute solo, be the same Kevin who'd tormented Dwight? Either I was completely naive or Kevin deserved an Academy Award. I wasn't sure which was worse.

"If you don't care about Penny, why are you icing me out?" He glanced behind him like he was checking to make sure no one was listening. Then he lowered his voice and added, "You didn't tell anyone, did you?"

Ah, so that's what he wanted. He was paranoid I'd tell someone about Dwight because I was jealous of Penny. As if.

I couldn't hold back my eye roll. "It would serve you right if I did."

Suddenly he was right next to me, his body too close. He squeezed my wrist, hard.

"Who did you tell?" His mouth was next to my ear, breath hot and sour. There was something dark and dripping in the way the words hissed out of his mouth.

I let out a yelp and tried to pull my wrist free. He squeezed harder.

"No one! Jesus, Kevin, stop."

His pupils were blown wide and his scowl transformed him into someone I barely recognized. Then just as quickly his face relaxed and he dropped my wrist like I'd burned him.

"I'm sorry— I just— You can't tell anyone, okay? I don't want people associating me with what Dwight did last year."

I gritted my teeth and rubbed at my wrist. It throbbed like Kevin's fingers were still wrapped around it. Was *this* what Kevin had been like with Dwight?

"Come on, Whit. It's not like a few harmless locker room pranks are what pushed Dwight over the edge. He was always a creep. It's not my fault he went psycho."

"I don't care if you thought he was a creep or not, what you did to him was wrong."

"Jesus, it was a joke. You're blowing it way out of proportion. Will you at least tell me who told you? You owe me that much."

I thought of the picture on my car last night. Could Kevin have put two and two together? Did he figure out I was the girl in the photo, and wanted to use it as leverage so I wouldn't tell anyone what he did to Dwight?

"Did you follow me last night?" I searched his face.

"Follow you?" He looked genuinely perplexed, but it's not like I could trust myself to read Kevin. If last year taught me anything, it was that people are like spotlights—they only show you what they want you to see.

I opened my mouth to ask about the photo directly, but the lights on the second Accord flared to life and I noticed Isaac approaching from the back entrance of the school.

Kevin narrowed his eyes.

"Hey, Whitney!" Isaac called, waving. His hair looked like a halo in the afternoon light, flopping as he jogged toward his car.

I rubbed at my wrist, still sore from where Kevin grabbed me. The fury must have still been visible on my face.

Isaac flicked his eyes back and forth between Kevin and me. "Everything okay here?"

"Fine. Nothing for you to worry about." Kevin's voice was as tight as his spandex football pants. "You're Gunter's cousin, right?" He sized up Isaac with a frown, eyes taking in the wrinkled shirtfront, frayed jeans, and hair hanging loosely over Isaac's forehead. Kevin was a big believer in irons, pleats, and respectable haircuts. Seeing the two boys together was like seeing a photograph next to its negative.

"Yeah, I'm Isaac." He palmed his hair back from his forehead before extending a hand, which Kevin proceeded to squeeze with more force than necessary. To his credit, Isaac didn't flinch. "Am I interrupting something?" Isaac looked to me for confirmation.

"No. Kevin was just leaving."

"Whitney—" Kevin started, but he flattened his mouth into a line and shot an annoyed glance at Isaac. "I'll text you later. We aren't finished talking about this." Then he turned and marched back toward the football field.

Kevin could easily have been the one who vandalized my car. He knew where Gams lived. He knew what car I drove. And he was obviously scared I'd ruin his perfect reputation by spilling his secret. Not to mention the way he'd just grabbed my wrist.

"Let me guess. Your brother?" Isaac leaned against the second Accord and gave me a smirk. "Kidding. Sticks up the ass are usually genetic, and you don't seem to have one."

I laughed, then I jerked my head toward his car to change the subject.

"So I guess this proves you really weren't trying to steal my car Saturday?"

"I figured it can't hurt to show you the evidence, just in case you had any lingering doubts. Hope it's not weird that I parked next to you."

His eyes scanned the parking lot. It had cleared quickly, leaving only a smattering of cars left by students with after-school activities. The breeze picked up, lifting my hair from my shoulders. I reached up and brushed it back, then felt heat rise in my cheeks when I noticed Isaac watching with more interest than the action called for.

"So I was wondering what you're doing next Friday," Isaac started, his blue eyes searching mine.

"Next Friday?" I blinked, my mind going completely blank.

"Yeah. I thought maybe you might want to hang out?"

"Like on a—date?"

"Bad idea?" He ran a hand through his hair and looked back at me sheepishly.

"No!" I quickly tried to backpedal. My stomach suddenly had a marching band inside of it. "It's just—next Friday is the first football game. I promised Marissa I would be there to cheer her on. They have this big halftime tribute dance they're doing. You know, to honor the victims? They've been working on it for weeks."

Despite many contentious debates, they'd canceled the rest of the football season after last year's tragedy. At least for a little while it felt like our lives were paused. But here we were again, almost exactly a year later, trying to pretend like we could move past it. The game would be at a different stadium, playing against a different team, but still . . . how could anyone sit in the stands and *not* think about what happened? How does anyone ever climb out from under a shadow like that?

I shivered despite the heat. I'd promised Marissa. I had to go. There was no way around it.

Isaac's face pressed into a frown, making his dimple look like an upside-down *C*.

"Right—the game. I forgot about that."

I gaped at him. The hallways were littered with signs advertising the upcoming pep rally, the game, and the planned tribute to honor those we'd lost that night. There were collection bins set up at every entrance to the cafeteria asking for donations to help the families of those impacted, and petitions for gun control circled daily. Not to mention the protesters that gathered across the street at the start and end of the school day. The anniversary of the tragedy was an albatross hanging over the school—how could he not have noticed?

There must have been something in my expression because he quickly explained.

"I mean, I didn't *forget*. I guess I've just been trying to block it all out. It was all anyone talked about at my old school, not that I blamed them. It just made it so hard to be there—and pretty much impossible not to think about it every second of every day. I guess I hoped that when I transferred things wouldn't be quite so heavy all the time. Which is . . . super thoughtless. I'm sorry."

I looked out toward the field where the football team had lined up to start their afternoon drills. Inside the gym, the dance team would be prepping for their first halftime performance of the year—their first halftime show since that horrible night. Isaac was so lucky he hadn't been at the game. He may have to live in its shadow, but at least he didn't have to live with the memory.

"It's not selfish. I think everyone who was there that night wishes we could forget, too."

Isaac ran a hand through his hair. "I'm sorry, I should have realized." His eyes searched my face, expression teetering between pity and something else I couldn't quite read. "Would you maybe want some company? At the game?"

His face was hopeful. My stomach did a pirouette. I'd never sat in the stands as a regular fan before—I'd always sat with the team. And I'd been dreading the idea of having to sit in the student section without Marissa by my side, especially on the anniversary. Maybe having Isaac there with me would make for a good distraction. Maybe the company would help.

"Yeah," I finally said. "That would be nice."

Isaac's smile was full wattage. He pulled the keys from his pocket. "Great."

"Great," I echoed.

"We'll make it fun, I promise. Or as fun as we can, all things considered." He opened his car door, then turned back to me. "Oh, I almost forgot to ask you the most important question of all." He smirked. "Would you rather spend the rest of your life with antlers or lobster claws?"

I furrowed my brows, pretending to think hard about my answer. "Lobster claws. People would probably try to use my antlers as a coat rack, and who wants to walk around with clothes hanging off their head all the time?"

"Touché."

We stood there smiling at each other, and I felt the marching band in my stomach start up again. What exactly was happening here?

Isaac's gaze lingered, jumping between my eyes and my mouth before he finally climbed into the front seat.

"See you tomorrow, Whitney."

The sound of my name on his lips sent a shiver up my spine.

I waved, unable to keep my smile from widening.

I had a date. A date with a boy who wasn't Kevin. Maybe I didn't deserve it, but there was something about Isaac that made me forget, just for a moment, about Dwight and the darkness and all the other thoughts that swirled inside my head at any given moment. And maybe having someone at the game with me wouldn't make the night feel so awful.

I opened the car door, then paused when I saw a piece of paper on the front seat. I might have mistaken it for something that fell out of my bag if it wasn't for how neatly it was folded—like someone took care to make the edges crisp before they slid it through my cracked window. But it was the black pen seeping through the page that made my hands start to tremble—there was something familiar about the dark tangle of ink.

I unfolded it slowly, like time could keep the message at bay, like I knew what I'd find before I opened it.

Just like in my locker yesterday, there was a black-and-white photograph with a thick cloud-shaped blob scribbled over a person's head. But this time it wasn't a picture of Dwight. It was a picture of Gams.

Over the top of her face, someone had drawn a thick black X.

I flipped the note over to see if there was anything else written on the back, but there was only black pen bleeding through from the other side.

Something in my stomach squirmed.

I turned it back to Gams's picture, staring at the raggedly drawn X darkening her face and the black cloud squiggled overhead.

Then I crumpled it into my palm, my hands shaking as the realization slammed into me.

Either someone was playing a very cruel trick or something bad was going to happen to Gams.

13

"EXCUSE ME! YOU HAVE TO CHECK IN. I CAN'T LET YOU IN if you're not a registered guest."

It must have been monochromatic Mindy's day off, because an angry-looking nurse I'd never seen before stood at the Lone Star Assisted Living front desk. I barely glanced at her as I barreled through the lobby and past the slow-moving elevators.

"Miss, you have to sign in! Wait!"

Blood roared in my ears, threatening to swallow me. The woman's voice was a dull echo at my back. I ignored her, throwing the door to the stairs open and rocketing up them two at a time. She didn't follow, which probably meant she'd gone back to her desk to call security. I didn't care who she called. I didn't care about anything other than Gams.

The drive to Lone Star was a blur—my muscles must have remembered the way because I couldn't recall driving. All I saw was the scribbled blob of black ink and the dark X covering Gams's face.

It had to be some sort of sick joke. Someone was trying to scare me.

I sprinted down the hall toward Gams's room.

The fluorescent lights were dimmed and the hallway curtains drawn, making it seem later in the day than it actually was. Gams hated it when they made everything dark and dreary. It made her feel like she was under the cover of rain clouds when she belonged in the sun.

The door to Gams's room was closed. I pounded my fist against it, calling out to her. An orderly emerged at the other end of the hallway, probably coming to see where the racket was coming from. But no one answered.

"Gams!" I shouted again, this time twisting the knob and pushing my way inside. I marched past the couch, past the tiny kitchen nook housing her electric teakettle and toaster oven, past the pictures and playbills of Gams and straight into her bedroom.

"Gams!" I called, nearly out of breath. I stopped cold when I saw her.

She was on the bed, on top of the covers. Her arms were splayed out across the floral duvet, one arm reaching above her like she was posed in fourth position. Her eyes were closed. Her hair was up in its usual bun, only a few stray hairs escaping. I might have thought she was sleeping, midway through a *pas de deux* dream, if it wasn't for the unearthly stillness in the room. It felt like all the air had been sucked out of the small space.

I ran to her side, still calling her name. Only I wasn't shouting it anymore—I was screaming it, my throat raw with the sound.

"Gams, please!" I grabbed her shoulders and her head lolled to the side. She felt impossibly fragile, like she might crumble into pieces if I shook her too hard.

Her chest wasn't moving. Her skin was too pale. There was vomit stuck to the edges of her dried lips, some of it still foaming and wet, like if I'd arrived just a few minutes earlier I could have stopped it.

Above her head, there was no death cloud. No choice to make.

I heard voices, then someone grabbed me from behind and moved me out of the way. I watched numbly as hands worked over her, checking for the vitals that I knew deep down in my gut were no longer there. The room tunneled in and out of focus. More people came in, this time with a stretcher. Then hands were at my back again, pushing me out of the bedroom and onto the couch.

Around me, Gams's pictures hung untouched on the walls. *Pas de deux. Port de bras. Grand jeté.* She was everywhere and yet she was nowhere at the same time. I felt the missingness of her, as if Gams's last breath took part of the world with it.

I knew death—the shape of it, the color of it, and the look on people's faces in that moment when I had the chance to save them. I knew that death was our only truth. The great equalizer. The one certainty. And yet nothing prepared me for this. It was like someone had reached into my chest and ripped out one of my organs, leaving a gaping, unfillable hole.

I closed my eyes. The scribbled black cloud that was drawn over Gams's head flashed against my eyelids.

This had to be the work of the person who'd been following me. The same person who'd left Dwight's photo in my locker and on my windshield. They'd followed me to school and left a picture of my grandma in my car and now Gams was . . . she was . . .

I couldn't bring myself to finish the thought.

The couch shifted as someone—my mom—sat down next to me. When did she arrive? How long had I been there?

Her arms slid around me. "Oh, Whit. I'm sorry," she said. "I'm so, so sorry you found her like that."

She kept talking, words garbling out of her mouth as if underwater. They didn't make sense. Nothing she said made any sense.

Overdose. Hoarding medication. Intentional.

"Your brother's on his way," she said, stroking my hair. As if having Will here could make things better. As if anything could ever be better again.

My locker. My windshield. The notes. The pictures of Dwight. This was more than just a prank meant to scare me. This was something much, much worse.

"It wasn't an accident," I said, finally looking at my mother's tearstained face.

"I know, sweetheart. The doctor thinks she was hoarding her medication—"

"No," I said, my voice firm even as a tear slid down my cheek. "That's not what I mean. She didn't do this."

"Honey—"

I pulled myself free of Mom's grasp and stood, turning to face the room. Someone who looked like a nurse or doctor hovered just outside of Gams's room, looking at me with worried eyes.

"She didn't do this," I said to them, my voice raising. Then I looked back at Mom. "You have to listen to me. I think someone may have—" I cleared my throat, but the accusation wouldn't come loose.

Because the expression on Mom's face—stricken, scared—was exactly the way she looked at me when I was little and I told her about the darkness.

I swallowed, Gams's rules whiplashing inside of me as I thought of what she would want me to do. How could I explain my certainty that this wasn't an accident without telling Mom about the photos? And how could I explain the photos without telling her about Dwight? The truth was too tangled up. No one would believe me.

I blinked back tears and lowered my eyes to the rug.

"I just mean someone should have noticed something was wrong," I said. "They should have been taking better care of her."

Mom nodded and wiped at her cheeks.

"You're right," she said, arms sliding back around me in a hug. "I'll speak to someone about it. Okay?"

The knot in my stomach tightened around the accusation I'd swallowed back—the one I was positive was true.

This wasn't an accident—someone murdered Gams.

And I couldn't tell anyone without confessing the truth.

14

COLD WIND WHIPPED AT MY FACE, STINGING MY CHEEKS. Gravel crunched against my shoes. I blinked against the bright light of the afternoon, trying to figure out where I was and how I got there. The Dallas skyline loomed in the background, skyscrapers jutting toward the clouds like crooked teeth.

It clicked into place—I was on a downtown rooftop. *The* downtown rooftop.

"Hello, Whitney," a gritty voice said at my back.

My heartbeat moved to my throat. I didn't want to turn around, but I couldn't stop myself. My body spun slowly, as if my feet were mounted to a stand like a ballerina in a music box.

Dwight Hacken stood before me, so close I could feel the cold when he exhaled. His skin was pale and gaunt. His clothes hung loosely against his thin frame. The pink line of his mouth reminded me of melted candle wax.

"You can't be real," I said to him, trying to squeeze my eyes shut. They snapped back open as if on springs. "You're dead."

"No, I'm not. You saved me, remember?"

Dwight stepped toward the ledge of the building, knees bending like he was ready to pounce. Above him a dark cloud thrummed, swirling and spinning as fingers of smoke reached down past his cheeks. It was a tornado of darkness—an endless, twisting tangle of night.

"Not everyone should be saved, Whitney," he said, then he sprang into the air and tumbled up and over the side of the rooftop.

I shot up in bed, body drenched in sweat and sheets bunched tightly around me. My heartbeat thudded in my ears.

I was in my bedroom, at my house, far from the roof and Dwight and the horrible darkness. It was just a nightmare.

The clock on my nightstand showed it was after two in the morning, which meant I hadn't been asleep long. I'd tossed and turned for hours. Now I wasn't sure I'd ever fall back to sleep.

My chest felt heavy and hollow at the same time as the reality of Gams being dead crashed into me. Would it always feel like this when I woke up and realized she wasn't here anymore? It was hard to imagine a moment when it wouldn't feel like drowning.

I squeezed my eyes shut, but the afternoon still came crashing back—Gams lying motionless on her bed, the empty feeling of her room, Mom's arms squeezing me as I cried.

After I'd swallowed back my accusation, Mom explained to me again what the doctors thought happened. They'd found an empty pillbox nearby with traces of Gams's medicine. Evidence, they said, that she'd been hoarding her medication. She'd eaten dinner just before, and they suspected she'd crushed the pills up and put them into her food. They'd seen this kind of thing before, they said. Depression was common in elderly patients as their mental health deteriorated, they said. They said, they said, they said.

Only I knew the truth. The horrible, unbelievable truth.

Gams wasn't hoarding medication. Gams wasn't depressed. I knew Gams like I knew myself. She would never do something like this without saying something to me first. Not without a warning, or a real goodbye. Or at least a note. And even if she hadn't told me what she was planning, I would have known she was thinking about it. I would have seen the danger hovering over her head when I'd last visited her, thick as a storm cloud, giving me the warning that I had to stop her.

Unless her mind was already made up and there was no saving her.

I shook my head. No, this was not a choice Gams made for herself. Someone else did this. The note said as much.

But what was I supposed to do? Gams was firm: No one could know that I helped Dwight that day. No one could know I was the girl in the picture, and no one could ever know that I had anything to do with what happened at the game last year. The truth was too unbelievable. People might come to their own conclusions about what happened. Dangerous conclusions. Ones that could end up with me handcuffed in the back of a police car and everyone I cared about hating me.

People are afraid of the things they don't understand.

I wiped at my eyes with the backs of my hands, holding in a sob.

Someone killed Gams. *Someone killed Gams.*

But why—to get revenge for what happened last year? Because of what I can see?

I thought of the way Kevin grabbed my wrist and the dark look in his eyes when he told me not to tell anyone about what he'd done to Dwight. I'd thought he could be the one behind the notes, but that was when I thought the person leaving them was just trying to scare me. Kevin was many things, but a murderer? It didn't seem likely.

But if not him, then who did this? A family member of one of the victims? Someone who'd been injured at the game that night? My brain kept spinning, but I couldn't come up with an answer. I had no idea who was behind this.

At this rate I was never going to fall back to sleep.

I started to toss the covers back, ready to pull out my laptop to start outlining a plan, when I heard a sharp squeak on the other side of the room. It sounded like someone stepped on the loose floorboard by the window. The same loose floorboard I always had to watch for when Marissa and I snuck out of the house during one of our regular sleepovers.

I froze. My pulse sped back up.

A floorboard can't squeak by itself.

"Mom?" I croaked, straining my eyes to see in the murky dark. Then I remembered Mom saying that Will was on his way. Maybe he'd just gotten home? "Will, is that you?"

Silence. I held my breath, trying to hear past the nighttime sounds of the house settling. My room was an endless pit of black.

"Hello?" I called again, the word barely making it out of my throat. "Will?"

This was stupid. The nightmare had made me jumpy.

Except I had every reason to feel jumpy, didn't I? Someone killed Gams. Someone knew what I'd done.

I squinted. There, by the window. Did a shadow move? It almost looked like a slice of darkness shifted to the right—

There was a loud click. I jerked upright, clutching the covers to my chest like a shield.

"Who's there?"

What if whoever left the notes was now standing in my room, watching? What if Gams was just a warning and I was next?

I nearly screamed when a puff of cold air blasted my cheeks. Then I clapped a hand over my mouth, stifling a laugh.

It was the air conditioner. The damn thing clicked and ticked so loudly it was amazing anyone could sleep through it. No wonder I jolted awake.

I shook my head and lay back down, feeling ridiculous. *It was just the AC*, I thought, trying to quiet the thundering in my chest.

I squeezed my eyes shut and pressed myself against the mattress. I needed to get some sleep if I had any hope of being able to think straight. I needed to be strong for Gams.

Someone killed my grandmother, that much I was sure of. And if no one was going to believe me, that meant there was only one option.

I had to figure out who it was on my own.

15

I SAT ON THE FRONT PORCH, STARING OUT AT THE too-bright sun in the too-blue sky. My itchy dress was completely wrong for the weather, but it was the only funeral-appropriate thing I owned.

Despite the brilliance of the late afternoon glare, everything about the day felt black—the exact opposite of what Gams would have wanted. She deserved a carnival-colored celebration, not a sea of macabre mourners draped in muted neutrals. But I didn't have the energy to argue with Mom about the arrangements, the wrongness of it all, or much of anything for that matter. The only bright spot was Will, who'd driven up from Austin. I hadn't realized how much I missed him until he walked through the front door.

Inside the house, guests milled over finger sandwiches, casserole dishes, and macaroni salads. A few even braved the makeshift bar, using Gams's love of martinis as the reason for the afternoon cocktail. That part, at least, Gams would have approved of—she always said the staff at Lone Star would benefit from a few stiff drinks. But everything else felt too forced, from the feigned conversations about our remodeled kitchen, to the musing about Gams and how beautiful she had been. Everything about her now was a *had been*, *was*, or *used to be*. Gams lived in the past tense, and I was stuck in this nightmare of a present.

"There you are," Will said, poking his head out while shielding his eyes from the sun. "Mom's looking for you."

He sat next to me on the front steps and gently thumped my shoulder with his. "I should've known you'd do the smart thing and escape. It smells like a department store in there. What is it with old women and perfume?" His nose wrinkled, a childhood habit I was glad he'd never outgrown.

"You didn't seem like you were having *that* bad of a time in there." I arched an eyebrow. When I'd left him, he'd been the centerpiece in a ring of martini-guzzling nurses, former dance students, and ex–dance moms.

He made a gagging noise and shoved my shoulder again. "I just got eye-fucked by one of Gams's nurses, and I'm pretty sure Mindy from the front desk pinched my ass while pretending to remove a piece of lint from my pants."

I tried to mirror his smile while looking out across the quiet street we'd grown up on. Anyone watching would immediately know we were siblings, but unlike me Will looked like someone who belonged at the center of a raucous party, with hair that didn't lie flat, hands that couldn't stay still, and an impish smirk that somehow managed to look equal parts sweet and deadly.

"You okay?" he asked, wearing the same frown my mother had worn for the last few days. The look didn't suit him. "Mom's worried about you."

"I'm fine." I feigned a smile. "I'm glad you're here."

"Me too. I mean, I wish I was here under different circumstances, but it's been good to see you."

He leaned back on his hands, shoulders straining against

the fabric of his suit jacket. He'd grown since I'd last seen him. In the two years since he'd left for college he'd practically doubled in size. What were they feeding him down there?

"I'm really sorry, Whit. It's hard on all of us, but it must be especially hard on you. Y'all were so close."

I nodded, scanning the tree-lined street. Our neighbors must have been out of town—patches of jagged weeds poked out of their normally pristine lawn. Above that, oak trees swayed and shushed in the breeze. In the coming months, they'd start dropping leaves and acorns, covering lawns in a blanket of fall. Gams loved the sound of acorns popping underfoot, like tap shoes clacking against a stage.

"I miss her," I finally said, the truth of it cutting deep. I looked away so Will wouldn't see me blinking back tears.

Will slid an arm around my shoulders and I rested my head against him.

"I miss her, too," he said, letting the words take shape around us, as if they could fill the emptiness. As if they could erase the last few days.

I glanced at Will, wondering what he would say if he knew the truth, imagining his face if he learned his sister was the catalyst for everything—last year's tragedy, Gams, and who knows how many other dominoes that had fallen because I saved people I had no business saving.

"For what it's worth," Will started, "I'm glad you made Mom call the Lone Star staff out for what happened to Gams. Someone should have been paying better attention—she shouldn't have stopped taking her meds without someone noticing. You did the right thing."

I bit the inside of my cheek, nodding numbly. As if *doing the right thing* was at the heart of what was bothering me. I studied Will's face, debating my next words.

"What if it wasn't Gams?" I blurted out, desperate for someone else to know that Gam didn't kill herself but afraid of what he might say if I told him the truth.

"What do you mean?" He furrowed his brows.

"What if someone else put the medication in her food? What if it wasn't her?"

"Whit—" he started, then stopped, like he was choosing his words carefully. I didn't need him to finish to know what he was going to say. Whoever did this not only knew about the darkness and Dwight, but they must have known Gams was the only person I talked to about it. They must have known no one would believe me. That without her, I'd be all alone.

"Never mind," I said. "Forget I said anything."

"Whit, the evidence was clear. I know it's hard to believe, but—"

"I said never mind." My words were clipped. I was stupid to even try to bring it up.

A tear slid down my cheek. I wiped at it with my thumb. Will squeezed my shoulder a little harder, then pulled me into a hug. We sat like that for a long time, the silence stretching. It should have been comforting, but somehow it made me feel even more alone.

"It's going to be okay," Will said. And even though it wasn't, I kept my mouth closed, holding on to the words crawling around inside me.

I had to think of something. I had to find a way to figure out who did this.

Will scanned the row of cars lining the opposite side of the street.

"Mom said your AC's on the fritz again. Want me to take a look? Maybe later, once I've had a chance to change out of this suit?"

"Yeah, that'd be great. Thanks. I was going to take it in, but—"

"Don't lie. You were saving it for me." He cracked his knuckles, a dangerous glint in his eye mixed with the relief of having something else to talk about. Will loved poking under the hoods of cars, or anything mechanical, to see how they worked. To him, a broken car was an art project in the making. It was no surprise to anyone when he got a scholarship to study mechanical engineering at UT Austin.

"You can only fix the air conditioner," I said, pointing a finger at him. "I need that thing to get me to school."

Will held up his hands, feigning innocence, as if he hadn't dismantled it for over a week the last time he told me he was "just going to fix the AC."

The front door to the house opened and Mom poked her head out.

"There you two are." Her eyes lingered a beat too long. "I was beginning to worry. The Bowers are heading out. So is Marissa. They've been looking for you."

Mom glanced back into the house. "She's out here," she called.

A few seconds later the Bowers emerged, Marissa trailing behind them. Mrs. B's eyes were swollen and bloodshot from crying. There was a smudge of black on Mr. Bower's shirtfront that looked like mascara.

Mrs. B leaned her cane against the wall and folded me in her arms. For a moment, I forgot about my guilt. I forgot about the boot encasing Mrs. B's foot and the fact that she would never dance again because of what I'd done. For a moment, we were just two people who loved my grandma fiercely.

"She was a really special woman," she said, pulling away from me. "I feel so blessed that she let me be part of her life."

"She was an amazing person," Mr. Bower added, his hand perched on the small of his wife's back. "If there's anything we can do . . ."

He trailed off the same way everyone did, unsure of what it was people were supposed to offer in times like this.

"Thank you," I managed to stutter, afraid that if I said anything else I wouldn't be able to hold back the tears.

"Thank you both so much for coming," my mom added, reaching out to hug them. Will followed suit.

Marissa grabbed my arm and pulled me into a tight embrace. "Are you sure you don't want me to stay? Just say the word and I'll move in."

"You're just saying that because Will's here." I said it quietly enough that Will wouldn't hear, but Marissa's cheeks flared pink at the reference to her old crush on my brother. "Kidding. I'll be fine. Go to practice and call me when you're done."

"I will. I promise."

I watched them walk down the sidewalk, my heart heavy. After they'd driven away, Mom and Will went inside to talk to the rest of the guests. I lingered, glad to finally be alone. I leaned back on my hands and shut my eyes. I heard Gams in the *shush* of rustling leaves and the bending chirps of mockingbirds.

I felt her in the breeze, whipping the grass in a tornado of chaîné turns as she danced, the whole sky her stage. Wherever she was, I knew she was dancing.

"I didn't expect to find you smiling. It's a nice change."

My eyes snapped open. Kevin's shadow blocked my view of the front yard. Leave it to him to ruin the first nice moment I'd had in days.

He slid his hands into the pockets of his slacks and sat down where Will had been a few minutes before. "Is the reception over?"

"What are you doing here?" I was tempted to walk back inside and leave him sitting there, but I wasn't sure which was worse—making small talk with the houseful of mourners or making small talk with Kevin.

"I thought you could use a friend," he said with a shrug, as if *friend* was a word we'd use to describe each other. I must have rolled my eyes, because he gave me one of his classic injured puppy stares. "Look, I know things are weird between us, but I still care about you. And I know how important your grandma was to you."

My chest squeezed, and I relaxed a little. Kevin was many things, but he had always been kind to my grandmother.

"I see your brother drove the 'stang up from Austin. Think he'd let me take it for a spin around the block?" Kevin nodded at Will's prized 1969 Mustang parked in front of the house.

I let out a snort of laughter. "Please. He barely lets anyone breathe near that thing, let alone drive it."

"He let me drive it once."

"He did *not*," I said, incredulous.

"He *did*. I swear! You were running late from dance practice, so I helped him work on it and he let me take it around the block."

The smile on his face was smug, and something tugged at my heart. Once, it wouldn't have been so hard to believe that my brother would let Kevin help with his car.

"Do you remember the first time you took me to the nursing home to see Gams?" he asked, a grin creeping into his voice. "She asked everyone who walked by if they thought I was good-looking enough to date you."

I laughed at the memory. "She was a character."

"She really was."

Before I could process, he closed the space between us and wrapped his arms around me. He was solid and warm—a buoy counterbalancing the weight in my chest. It felt good to be hugged by someone I wasn't related to. Comforting. I let myself sink into the feeling.

"I'm sorry," Kevin whispered, the words a hot puff of air on my cheek. "For the other day. For everything. If I could take it back, I would."

His familiar scent took me back to a time before things became so complicated. And when I closed my eyes, I could almost pretend it was last summer, before everything changed. When I was just a girl in love with a boy. I wanted so bad to go back in time and be that girl again.

I was so distracted that I didn't realize what he was doing until his mouth found mine.

I sat back with a jolt, pushing him off me.

"What are you doing?"

He shrugged like it was no big deal.

Ahead of us, someone cleared their throat. I snapped my

head in the direction of the sound and saw Isaac standing on the walkway in front of us, clutching a bouquet of calla lilies in his hand. His grandfather clung to his other arm, wearing the same gray three-piece suit he'd worn at Lone Star Assisted Living.

Heat fired in my cheeks. How much had he seen?

"Isaac," I said, wanting the earth to open its mouth and swallow Kevin whole.

"I brought this for you." His expression was unreadable.

I expected him to hand me the flowers, but instead he tucked the bouquet under his arm and pulled a paperback from his back pocket.

"*Breakfast at Tiffany's?*" I stared at the picture of Audrey Hepburn that graced the cover. The spine was worn and bent, and a corner of the back cover was ripped off.

"It's the book Constance and I were reading. She said it was one of her favorites. We were a little over halfway through when . . ." He trailed off, looking past me toward the house. "Anyway, I thought you might like to have it."

"Thank you." I clutched the book to my chest, fighting back tears. I had a sudden flash of me as a little girl, curled up on Gams's couch with a bowl of popcorn between us as *Breakfast at Tiffany's* played on the TV.

Isaac stepped around me, his grandfather glowering as they passed.

"I THOUGHT YOU SAID SHE WAS A NICE GIRL?" He leaned toward Isaac like he'd meant to say it quietly, but the words boomed as if they'd come out of a megaphone.

I waited until the door closed behind them, then turned to

Kevin. He was *smiling*, like the whole situation was funny to him.

"Did you—" I started, teeth clenched. "Did you know Isaac was there when you tried to kiss me?"

Kevin shrugged. "Does it matter?"

I took two deep breaths to slow my thudding pulse. It didn't work. "You are such an ass."

Kevin smirked, like he could give a shit. Like this was all part of his plan.

"You need to leave. Before your *girlfriend* finds out you were here."

His dark eyes disappeared beneath a furrowed brow. "So what, you're just going to act like a fucking bitch to me all the time now?"

"Like a—what?"

He made a scoffing sound, his face contorting into something I didn't recognize, and I was reminded of the way he'd looked when he'd grabbed my wrist in the parking lot.

It occurred to me that he'd been right next to my car when I found the picture of Gams. And he easily could have guessed that I would be visiting her after the first day of school. Football practice would have ended long before I left Lone Star Assisted Living—there was plenty of time for him to get there and vandalize my car.

Could his fear that I would tell someone what he did to Dwight be big enough that he'd do something to Gams?

"Did you leave that note in my car? And that . . . thing in my locker?" I blurted out, standing.

"What?" He let out another scoffing sound and stood as well.

"You know what? I don't care. I'm done with your bullshit."

Before I could say anything else, he cut across the lawn toward his car.

I blinked, speechless.

If he didn't have anything to hide, why had he just taken off like that?

16

THE DAYS FOLLOWING THE FUNERAL WERE A BLUR OF tear-filled family dinners, sleepless nights, and combing the internet. I practically barricaded myself in my room, determined to figure out who had been stalking me and who was behind Gams's death. That, and hiding felt safer than braving the outside world. If someone murdered Gams, what else were they capable of?

I pulled my blanket tighter around me, shivering despite the heat outside. A few sticky notes fell off my bed. My room was a disaster zone. I'd scoured social media and newspaper sites, making lists of everyone who might have a connection to the shooting—family and friends of the victims, people I remembered being at the game, the dance team. Then there were the more personal connections like Kevin, Penny, and Jenny Chan. I'd even included Mrs. B and Marissa. They'd both been at the game that night, and they'd both had their lives irrevocably turned upside down because of what happened. Until I had solid proof, I couldn't eliminate anyone just yet. No matter how much it pained me.

Outside, Will examined something under the hood of my car. His nose was pink from the sun and a smudge of grease marked his cheek. He'd finished fixing the air conditioner over an hour ago. I was afraid to ask what else he'd found that kept him working in the heat, although it wouldn't be the first time he turned fixing one small thing into a multi-hour mechanical engineering project.

I wished he didn't have to go back to school tonight. Having him home made me feel just a smidgen safer. If safe was something I could ever feel again.

What I couldn't figure out was why someone would hurt Gams. If I was the catalyst for everything that happened, why not target me directly?

Unless last year wasn't the real motivation. What if it was about what Gams and I could do? Gams had said it so many times it had become a mantra—*people are afraid of the things they don't understand*. Was fear enough motive for murder? And if they were scared enough of Gams to kill her, what would they do to me?

It was a terrifying thought.

I shivered again and pulled a sticky note from the wall, crumpling it in my palm. My trash can was littered with dead ends. The Dunburts and Copperstons, two of the victims' families, had moved out of state. Most of the others had social media posts or classroom conflicts that proved they were somewhere else when one or more of the notes were left. But more than that, I couldn't shake the feeling that my stalker wasn't a stranger.

Whoever hurt Gams either worked at Lone Star or was a regular enough visitor that no one thought twice about seeing them in the hallways. There weren't any signs of a struggle, which meant Gams either knew her killer or the person had easy access to her dinner and was able to slip her medication in unnoticed.

And I couldn't deny the other obvious connections: They knew which locker was mine. They knew my schedule. They knew where Gams lived and when I would be there visiting her.

They also knew about the darkness—the one thing Gams made me swear to never tell another living soul. Maybe she wrote about it in her journal and it got into the wrong hands. Maybe she told someone without realizing it. Or what if someone figured out what we could do because they saw the darkness, too? Could they have pieced together my history of *right place, right time* heroics because they knew what to look for firsthand?

But if that was the case, why wait until now?

My head pounded with the onslaught of questions, each one taking root like a weed. But regardless of all the possibilities, one thing was glaringly clear: while there were probably hundreds of people who would want to get back at me for what happened last year if they knew the truth, whoever was doing this knew me and Gams personally. There was no other explanation.

I willed myself not to cry, not to let the panic that was vibrating just beneath my skin take over. I had to focus. I had to figure this out.

I thought back to the afternoon I found the note with Gams's picture. It must have been placed on my front seat before I got to my car. And I would have been well on my way to Lone Star if Kevin hadn't interrupted me. That ten-minute argument may have been the difference between life and death.

I thought of Kevin's fingers squeezing my wrist and the

threat in his voice when he told me not to tell anyone about Dwight. Maybe he *was* trying to keep me from telling his secrets.

He certainly had the ability to drop the note in my car—I was so distracted by our conversation that I wouldn't have noticed. Except he wouldn't have had time to leave class, do something to Gams, and get back to the parking lot to deliver the note. Unless he was somehow able to leave school early, which wasn't impossible. A lot of seniors' last classes were study periods, and everyone knew that study periods weren't monitored.

But if it was him and this was all about keeping what I knew about Dwight quiet, why would he need to hurt Gams? Why the vague notes when he could threaten me outright? It didn't make sense. Something was missing.

Then there was Penny. Marissa was convinced that she was the one who vandalized my locker. And she definitely hated me enough to want to mess with me. But killing someone? That felt too extreme.

Still, I couldn't rule her out. At the very least, she might have information that could help me figure out if Kevin was involved. And Mrs. B had given me the perfect opportunity to interrogate her.

I pulled out my phone and shot her a quick text: choreography session at the rec center still on tomorrow?

She shot back a thumbs-up a few minutes later. Spending my evening with Penny was the last thing I wanted to do, but at least it gave me a way to do some sleuthing.

I jumped at a knock on my bedroom door. Mom poked her head in, eyes scanning the mess.

"You alive in here?" she asked with a smile, brushing back the fine wisps of blond hair that escaped her ponytail. "Must be one hell of a project you're working on."

"It's a beast."

She'd been doing this on an hourly basis—using one excuse or another to check on me, like I was at risk of melting into my mattress if she didn't maintain round-the-clock surveillance.

"I'm going to run some errands for a bit. Do you need anything? Or maybe you want to come with? We could go to Nordstrom Rack, maybe do some shopping—"

I shook my head and tried to ignore the concern in her eyes. "Thanks, but I've got to finish researching this paper."

"Right, of course." She lingered in the doorway a moment longer, making her smile wider, like forced optimism could somehow pull me out of my funk.

"I won't be long," she said, smile still tight. "Call if you need anything?"

"Sure." I gave her a small smile in return. At least she was trying, but scrutinizing me like I was a crystal vase teetering on the edge of a mantel wasn't exactly helping.

Music drifted in from outside, where Will had cranked up my stereo to full blast. The song was too full of hope. I squeezed my eyes shut and swallowed the lump in my throat.

All this research was getting me nowhere. I needed to get out of here. I needed to *do* something. And I knew just where to go.

I pulled on shorts and a T-shirt, grabbed my phone, and went outside to join Will. He was examining a tire. He adjusted his sunglasses and stood when he heard me approach.

"I need my car," I said, shielding my eyes from the glare of the sun.

He wiped his hands on his jeans, leaving a smudge of black. "I still need to change the oil. And you're almost out of wiper fluid. I can't let you drive without wiper fluid."

I swallowed. I'd probably used it all trying to get the fake blood off my windshield.

"I think it's a safe bet that I'm not going to need wiper fluid today." I pointed to the cloudless sky.

"What if something hits your windshield? It won't take me long. I'm almost done."

"You said that over an hour ago."

He shrugged. "Maybe if you took it in more often it wouldn't take me so long to fix it."

"Can I borrow yours?"

He snorted a laugh and glanced toward the front of the house, where his refurbished treasure was parked.

"Please," I said. "I won't be long. I just . . . I need to—" I cleared my throat, trying to think of a good lie. If I told him I was going to Lone Star he'd probably say no.

"There's a class," I finally said, hoping my words didn't sound as plastic to Will as they did to my own ears. "A dance class. I thought that maybe I'd . . . I don't know, try going."

Will blinked and glanced back at my Accord. The hood was propped open and both doors stood wide to the afternoon heat.

"If you can give me another half hour or so I'll be done—"

"The class will have started by then. Please? I won't be long—I'll just drive there and back." I saw him waning. After I'd been moping around the house, the idea of me wanting to voluntarily leave for something like a dance class must have been a relief. "Come on, Will. It's not like you need it right now. You're not driving back to school until tonight. It would mean a lot to me." I took a deep breath. "The last time I saw Gams she told me how badly she wanted me to get back to dancing. And I thought that maybe—if I went—" I didn't have to fake it when my lower lip wobbled and tears filled my eyes.

Will gave an audible sigh, then reached into his pocket for his keys.

"Fine, but just there and back."

"Thank you!" I shouted, practically jumping up and down with relief.

"Promise to be careful, Whit?" He handed the keys to me. They felt warm in my palm. "Hands at nine and three at all times and make sure to check the blind spot on the right when you back up." I must have rolled my eyes because he shot me a glare. "I mean it, Whit. She's temperamental."

"I'll be careful, I promise. You don't have to worry."

Unless he counted trying to track down a murderer as a reason to worry.

17

I LISTENED TO THE STEADY GROWL OF WILL'S MUSTANG, my hands perched dutifully at nine and three. He'd spent over a year restoring it to its classic muscle car glory. People kept giving it appreciative glances as it roared down the street.

A few minutes later I pulled into my usual parking space at Lone Star, like it was just another afternoon when I'd come to visit Gams. My stomach folded in on itself. It didn't seem right that I could do something so familiar in a world that was forever changed without Gams.

I killed the engine and took a few deep breaths. I could do this. I *had* to do this.

When I pushed through the entryway doors, I was relieved to see monochromatic Mindy working the front desk. Today she was dressed in a bright yellow blouse with large plastic lemons dangling from each ear. Her long nails were tipped white in a French manicure, with a yellow lemon painted on each thumb. She really knew how to run with a theme.

"Whitney, hi," she said in her usual sticky-sweet drawl, but there was something forced about it, like she was putting on a performance. "How are you, hon?"

I plastered on a wide grin and gripped the edge of the counter.

"I'm doing okay, all things considered. How are you?"

The guest registry was spread out on the counter, open to a half-filled page of the day's visitors. Every guest had to sign in and note the resident they were coming to see. Which meant the name of every person who'd visited Gams was somewhere in that log. I just needed to get my hands on it.

"I'm so sorry about your grandma, sweetie. I've just been sick about it. I've been praying every night for your family. I even have a prayer circle going on Facebook. How's your mom doing?"

I slid the ledger toward me. Maybe a few of the nurses would be willing to talk to me, too.

"She's hanging in there. She's been focusing on work to try to distract herself. But I guess it's good she's keeping busy."

I flipped it back a page, scanning the names to see how many guests came in on any given day. Outside of weekends, it couldn't be that many. It shouldn't take me too long to find who'd visited Gams recently.

Mindy's eyes flicked to the page I was scanning. "Is there something I can help you with, hon?"

"Um—yes." I swallowed and forced confidence into my voice. "Someone sent us this beautiful bouquet of flowers, but the card got wet and now I can't read the signature. The note said something about recently visiting Gams, so I thought maybe I could take a quick peek at the registry to see who it might have been so I can send a thank-you card. It should only take a few minutes—"

Mindy's hand snapped over the registry and she pulled it away from me. Her smile pinched down.

"I'm sorry, Whitney, but I can't share the names of visitors without permission. It's against policy. I'm sure you understand." The lemon earrings jingled.

"Please—the flowers were so pretty and I'd hate to be rude—"

Mindy's smile looked more like a grimace as she slid the registry off the counter and tucked it underneath, out of sight and out of reach.

"I'm sure whoever sent them will just be glad to know the flowers reached you."

"Mindy, please, I just need to see who came to visit Gams—"

"I'm sorry, but I can't do that." She placed both hands on the counter and matched my gaze, as if we were having some kind of guest registry standoff. What was her issue? In all the time I'd known Mindy, I'd never heard her say anything about policy or rules.

"I wouldn't want to get you in any kind of trouble," I said, looking around to see if anyone was watching. The lobby was empty. "Maybe you could look for me? Tell me who came to see her the last few weeks? Or maybe you noticed someone coming to visit her that seemed out of the ordinary?"

Mindy frowned and placed her hands on her hips. "I told you, I can't share the names of guests." Then she looked around and leaned across the counter, her voice dropping to a whisper. "You know they fired the orderly on duty when your grandma passed, and they put two of the nurses on leave until they complete an investigation. I am truly sorry for your loss, Whitney, but I need this job. I am not putting myself at risk because of what happened to your grandma."

I swallowed. This was not going the way I'd imagined.

"I'm sorry, Mindy. I didn't realize." I paused and looked up at the ceiling, trying to think of what to do next. She had to let me sign the registry if I was visiting someone, didn't she? I thought of the last time I'd come to visit Gams.

"Anyway, I'm not just here about the flowers. I'm here to visit Isaac's grandpa. I thought I might read to him for a bit," I improvised, leaning forward like I was sharing a secret. "Isaac was so kind to read to Gams all summer. I thought I might return the favor."

Mindy narrowed her eyes, looking down to the hidden guest log.

"I don't see your name on his list of approved visitors."

"You mean every visitor has to be approved before they can be let in?"

"Of course. We don't just let people walk in off the street." There was a defensive bite to her words—I wondered just how much trouble we'd gotten the staff into after we'd lodged our complaint.

If everyone had to be preapproved to visit, that meant I was right. Gams knew her killer. She would have added them to the visitor list. Assuming, of course, that Mindy wasn't just being extra because we'd gotten the staff in trouble.

My stomach clenched. I tried to keep my face neutral even though I thought I might be sick.

"Maybe you could give me the list of my grandma's approved visitors—"

"I thought I made myself clear, Whitney. I cannot share visitors' names under any circumstances." Her lemon earrings shook in a firm no, making it clear she wasn't going to budge, no matter how hard I tried.

"Fine," I said, jaw clenching. "Thanks for your help."

More like thanks for nothing.

Then I turned on my heel, a new idea forming.

〜〜

My fingers gripped the steering wheel with enough force to break it. I pressed my foot against the gas, feeling some satisfaction when the engine growled and the car lurched forward. Maybe there was something to the whole muscle car thing after all.

I was only a few blocks away from Isaac's house. I needed to get my hands on that registry, and he was just the person to help. My new plan was to convince him to check the guest log the next time he visited his grandpa. Maybe the staff would be more receptive to him. Except he'd been a little off since the funeral—which was all Kevin's fault. What in the hell made him think I would want to *kiss* him, at my grandmother's memorial no less? Hopefully Isaac knew I wanted nothing to do with Kevin. And if he didn't, I had to convince him there was nothing between us.

Behind me, someone honked, and I realized I was just sitting at a green light. They swerved around me, shouting as they passed, and I finally realized where I was. I didn't want to look, but I couldn't help myself, like there was a gravitational pull yanking my eyes toward the strip mall across the street, and the dance studio occupying the last storefront in the square.

Gams's old studio.

The awning was the same green, but the name had changed from NORTH DALLAS DANCE ACADEMY to DANCE TEXAS! with an image of a girl doing a backbend next to the white block lettering. Gams hated acrobatics. She would have had a conniption if she'd seen the new sign.

I'd taken classes there after she'd sold the studio, mostly at Gams's insistence, but I eventually stopped. The woman who'd bought it was nice enough. She'd known Gams from the dance circuit, and I'd danced with her daughter on a competition team when we were younger. And initially Mrs. B was supposed to teach a few classes there, but she backed out because of her time commitment to the team. Gams was the soul of the place, and Mrs. B the heartbeat. Without them the studio felt hollow.

Still, in that moment I missed Gams and her studio so much my toes pointed in anticipation.

From my car, I could see several girls around my age hovering near the front door. I glanced at the dashboard. Ten to three. A class was probably starting soon. Gams's voice echoed in my head:

You have a gift, dear . . . You can't keep punishing yourself. You need to be brave.

Suddenly the car felt too cramped and stuffy despite the cold air pumping from the vents. My legs began to itch. My hands began to shake. My whole body had the sudden compulsion to *move.*

Before I could overanalyze, I jerked the steering wheel and turned into the parking lot.

I climbed out and headed toward the studio entrance, legs shaking beneath me. What exactly was I doing? I was wearing shorts and a T-shirt—hardly dance-appropriate clothing. Plus I didn't know what the three o'clock class would be, who was teaching, or whether they'd allow walk-ins.

Twelve pairs of eyes sized me up as I walked through the

studio door. While the previous class wrapped, the next group stretched on the floor outside the classroom. They must have been regulars, judging by the curious looks they gave me.

At first glance everything inside the studio looked unchanged, but I noticed the subtle differences. Like the smell. The entryway had a musty air to it instead of the warm cloud of rose water and coconut I remembered. Gams's photos had been replaced with playbills and pictures from past recitals. The pink lace curtains that once edged the windows were now tan mini blinds, and the leotards, tights, and dance skirts hanging from the display racks felt too drab—outside of the obligatory black and pink ballet uniforms, Gams had a flair for sequins, feathers, and fringe.

"May I help you?" asked the dark-haired woman working the front desk.

"Do you have room in your three o'clock class for a walk-in?"

The woman smiled. "Of course. It's an intermediate contemporary class. Is that okay?"

I nodded, returning her smile. Contemporary was Gams's favorite. I pointed to a pair of simple black dance shorts and a sports bra hanging from the rack behind her.

"Could I get those? I wasn't expecting to stop in, but then I saw that people were going inside and I thought it might be fun . . ." I trailed off, not sure how to explain what it was that pulled me into the studio.

"You can change over there," she said, pointing to a stretch of curtains on the opposite wall. As if I didn't know every inch of the studio by heart.

I ignored the curious looks from the other dancers as I made my way to the dressing room. Once changed, I took a space on the floor and started to stretch. My muscles were tight—I felt an unfamiliar pull in my hamstring when I put my nose to my leg. I'd stretched over the summer out of habit, but not with the same frequency. My muscles would pay for it later.

When it was time for class to begin, I stood at the far back of the room. In another lifetime, I would have marched straight to the front, knowing I worked the hardest when I had an audience. But that was the old Whitney. This Whitney wasn't here to garner respect or push her body to its limits. She was here for Gams.

It turned out the woman at the front desk was also the instructor, and her sweet demeanor completely disappeared once in front of the classroom. She reminded me of Mrs. B, all smiles and how-are-yous outside of practice, but a fierce instructor with a meticulous eye for sickled feet and sloppy arms as soon as she stepped into the studio.

After taking the class through a series of warm-ups and floor exercises, she broke down a piece of choreography with staccato rhythm, stopping only to scold when someone lagged. Learning the routine was like riding a bicycle—the steps were wobbly at first, but soon I found my body sinking into the movement, until finally I stopped thinking about the steps and let the music take over.

"From the top, with music." The instructor motioned for us to spread out. I squared my shoulders and waited for the cue.

I'd forgotten how easy it was to get lost inside a song. My arms and legs became extensions of the words, my hips and head punctuation marks to the beat, until I forgot where I began and the song ended. With each movement I felt Gams watching, eyes alert and studying my every move. She was everywhere—in the music, in my muscles, in my pointed toes and raised chin. For the first time in what seemed like an eternity, a rush of joy washed over me. Something unwound, as if all these months of not dancing had caused my insides to tangle.

The piece ended. We returned to our original places around the studio, waiting for the critiques. The instructor went one by one through the twelve girls with corrections:

Watch your lines!

You're a half beat behind!

Point your feet!

But when she got to me she only smiled and nodded her head. "Nice job."

Heat fired in my cheeks as the other dancers turned to look.

"Again, from the top. But this time switch the lines—back line come to the front, front line move to the back."

I moved to the front of the room and took my opening position. The music started, and once again I let myself meld with the music, not just executing the routine, but feeling the dance all the way through the tips of my fingers. The choreography called for a double pirouette, but the music left enough time for a triple, so I improvised. The song's crescendo seemed more powerful than the grand jeté allowed, so I executed a switch leap, knowing I would barely be able to walk the next day but unable to stop my legs from completing the movement.

When the song ended, I felt the room watching me. I grew lighter.

We broke into three smaller groups, each taking a turn while the rest of the class watched. The small audience was exhilarating. It reminded me of the high I got after a performance, the way the world fell away until it was just me, the stage, and the music. And through it all, Gams was with me; I felt her heartbeat in every step I took.

I thought back to when I was little, when Gams first confessed that she saw the darkness, too. When she'd explained how she knew that I had the family's dark gift because of the way I moved. The same way she'd moved. The same way her grandmother had moved, like we were floating.

We move like the rain clouds.

Maybe dance and our dark gift were one and the same. Maybe they lived inside us, always hungry to break free.

When class ended, I quietly gathered my things and made my way toward the exit, but the dance teacher stopped me before I could sneak out.

"Whitney, is it?" she asked, smoothing her flyaways against the crown of her head. "What studio do you usually attend?"

"I used to take classes here, actually. But I'm on my high school's dance team now." The words fell easily from my mouth, like they had been waiting for me. And once the words were out a plan started to form.

The dance team gave me a built-in excuse to keep a close eye on both Penny and Kevin given that the football team practiced at the same time as the dance team. And beyond that, it gave me a built-in chance to keep a close eye on the people impacted by what happened at last year's game—the football team, the dance team, the cheerleaders, the band—even Mrs. B. All of them would be within viewing range. If one of them was my stalker, maybe they'd slip up; maybe they'd do something that would prove they had something to do with Gams and the notes. Or if they had some grand master plan that extended beyond Gams, maybe I'd be able to stop them. If I had any hope of finding out who hurt Gams I needed to do something. I needed to get back on the dance team so I could stop Gams's killer before anyone else got hurt.

Or before they came after me.

18

THE HIGH OF MY PERFORMANCE BOUNCED ME OUT OF the studio and into Will's car. All these months I thought the solution was to keep my distance from the team, but that was the last thing I needed. Especially now. Especially when there was someone who knew what I'd done.

Something rattled underneath Will's car—a soft but steady *thump* vibrated from the back, barely audible over the hum of the radio. The bucket seats put me lower to the ground than my Accord, making every bump and ripple in the road more pronounced. Maybe the sound was part of the macho muscle car experience, like the snarl of the engine after turning the key in the ignition or the steady grumble that followed. I cranked up the music to drown out the noise, then flipped to another song that matched my mood. I felt like someone had jolted me out of a coma. I couldn't change the past, but I could change the future. I could *do* something. And it started today.

When I got home, Will came outside to greet me. I had a feeling he'd be listening for the car.

"I can't believe it! She's still in one piece." Will smirked, walking around the car to inspect it. He made a show of checking the paint for scratches and looking at the bumper. His grin told me he was kidding, but still.

"If you treated your girlfriends the way you treated this car, maybe you wouldn't be single." I handed him his keys, matching his smirk. "Did you reassemble my car?"

"It's as good as new." He took his keys from my outstretched hand. "How was class?"

"Great, actually." I grinned when I realized I didn't have to lie.

"I'm glad. It's good to see you smiling, Whit." He glanced back toward the house. "I'm going to get my things packed. I left your keys on your bed."

"You're not going to stay for dinner?"

"Nah, I'll grab something on the way."

I followed him inside, then made my way to my bedroom. My keys were lying on my pillow, just like he said. I moved them aside, then tumbled face-first onto the mattress. I was exhausted, but at the same time still pulsing with energy. Tomorrow I'd get to school early and talk to Mrs. B about rejoining the team. Maybe she'd let me sit in on rehearsals right away.

A warm breeze blew in through the open window. The mini blinds thumped against the glass, blowing outward as the afternoon exhaled, then slapped back into place.

Strange. I didn't remember opening the window. Maybe Mom or Will had done it.

I sat up. Even this late in the afternoon it was still too warm to have the windows open. The blinds gave another thump as air billowed into the room. Above me, the air conditioner whirred.

"I'm heading out." I jumped at Will's voice, on edge. "Come and give your favorite brother a hug."

I climbed off my bed, laughing at the cartoonish way he

opened his arms. We weren't usually the hugging kind of sib-lings, but there was something about losing Gams that broke that barrier, like we wanted to hold on to our shrinking family a little more tightly. I wished he didn't have to go.

"Text when you get to the dorm?" I let him wrap his arms around me, then squirmed away when he tried to muss my hair.

"Sure thing, Mom. Speaking of, you should shut your win-dow. You know how Mom is about opening windows when the AC is on."

He gave my hair a final ruffle before leaving.

I crossed my room, reaching up to slide the window back into place. But something was off. The window opened straight into the front yard—the screen was gone. I leaned out, scan-ning the row of boxwood shrubs lining the house. Peeking out from behind one of the plants was the metal frame of my window screen. It looked like someone had hidden it there on purpose.

I thought of the other night when I'd woken from my night-mare, sure that someone was in the room, watching. Then I spun back toward my bedroom, my heart thudding. The room looked the same as it had when I'd left earlier that day—open calculus book on the desk, my bag unzipped on the floor. The pile of folded clothes my mother brought in that morning still sat next to the dresser. The same hodgepodge of perfume bot-tles, makeup brushes, and hair ties cluttered my dresser. The full-length mirror rested against the wall as usual, except—my heart jerked—a white piece of notebook paper was tucked into the edge of the mirror's frame, glaringly out of place.

I was hit with a horrible sense of déjà vu.

Through the open window, I heard Will making his way down to the Mustang.

My fingers twitched when I plucked the note from its nesting place. The writing bled through to the other side of the page, darkening the folds. Maybe I should have been surprised when I opened it and found a picture of Will with a cloud drawn over his head, but somehow I wasn't, like my subconscious had already put the pieces together. Below his picture, the words SAVE HIM were written in all caps.

Save him?

I ran back to the window. Will was already in his car. The engine roared to life.

"Drive safely," Mom called from the front porch before closing the door behind her.

My throat went dry, but somehow I managed to find my voice.

"Will!" I shouted. "Stop!"

Because pulsing over Will's head was a thick cloud of darkness.

19

I HEARD THE ROAR OF THE MUSTANG PULLING AWAY from the curb as I ran through the garage to my car. I wedged my phone under my ear as I slid into the front seat. My call went straight to voicemail. *Shit.* My hands shook. I fumbled against the dash, unable to gain traction. When I finally got the Accord started I jammed my foot against the accelerator, cutting the air with the squeal of tires on pavement. Will's taillights flashed as he turned onto the main street leading to the toll road. I could still make out the swell of darkness churning above him, the danger imminent. Was there something wrong with his car? Was he going to get in an accident?

I reached the intersection just as the light turned red. I slammed on the brakes. Will roared away from me, oblivious.

I knew where he was going—I just needed to get him to pull over so I could figure out what the danger was and how to stop it.

Please, God, let me catch up to him.

Beads of sweat pooled at my hairline. My heart was a snare drum inside my chest. I couldn't let something happen to Will. I couldn't lose him, too.

Come on come on come on.

The light turned green. I pressed my foot against the accelerator and squealed left, nearly colliding with another car. They laid on their horn. I pressed the gas harder.

I zipped through another light as it turned yellow, swerving around cars. Ahead, Will's bright red Mustang glinted in the fading sun. He was only two streetlights ahead of me. I had to catch him.

I floored it and soared through the next intersection, closing the distance. As soon as I thought I was near enough for him to see me in his rearview mirror, I leaned on my horn, pounding it with my fist over and over again.

Come on, Will. Look behind you. Look behind you!

I changed lanes so I could come up beside him, but his car bolted forward.

Ahead, signs pointed to the freeway. Above Will's head, the cloud churned. It swelled the closer he got to the on-ramp. I had to stop him before he got there. There wasn't much time.

I laid on the horn again, long and loud, then tried tapping out the rhythm of a song he liked. I started swerving side to side, one hand on the horn, motioning for him to pull over between honks. I couldn't see his eyes in the rearview mirror because of the storm cloud surging above his head, but his blinker flared to life.

Except he didn't slow down.

The Mustang barreled past the gas station he should have pulled into, blinker still flashing.

Ahead, the next light turned yellow. I laid on my horn again and pressed the gas, coming up close behind him. Still, he didn't slow.

The light turned red but Will plowed through it. I had no choice but to follow. There was a blast of horns as we sailed through the intersection.

He must have seen me. Why else would he have turned on his blinker? And Will didn't run red lights. Will didn't do anything that would put his precious Mustang in danger.

Then it hit me—what if he *couldn't* stop?

Suddenly Will cut to the right, tires squealing as he took the turn at full speed. I jerked my wheel as well. The seat belt dug into my shoulder.

He turned right again, this time into a parking lot. The Mustang rolled forward, zigzagging around cars and weaving in between the empty parking spaces like it had a mind of its own.

Then the air exploded in a crunch of metal as he bumped over a curb and connected with a tree. The hood buckled inward, the car finally coming to a horrible stop.

I squealed to a stop and launched out of my car, shaking from adrenaline.

"Will!" I shouted, feet pounding the pavement. Smoke billowed from the hood of the Mustang.

I reached the driver's side door just as it sprang open. A sob escaped my lips when Will tumbled out.

"Jesus, Will, are you okay?" I scanned his body, looking for signs of injury. "Are you hurt?"

The space above his head was empty—no cloud warning of danger. I pressed my hand to my heart, relief coursing through me.

"I heard you honking and saw you weaving back and forth. Then I realized I couldn't stop," Will said, his voice shaking. He began pacing next to the Mustang. "I kept pressing the brake over and over, but the car wouldn't slow down." His hands were in his hair, eyes round and wild. "If you hadn't been there—if you didn't try to get me to pull over—I would have gotten on the freeway. I would have been going even faster. How did you know—" Will stopped his pacing and stared at me, mouth agape. In the distance, cars whizzed by on the highway.

The color leeched from Will's cheeks as he started putting the pieces together—the warnings and suggestions I'd made to neighbors and friends throughout the years. My nonsensical chatter about rain clouds and death when I was little. The way I always seemed to be in the right place at the right time. It was all written on his face, confusion and horror mixing into an expression I couldn't identify.

I thought of the way Mom looked at me the very first day I told her about the rain cloud and waited for Will to draw the same definitive line between us—to look at me with unequivocal fear.

Instead, he marched forward and wrapped his arms around me, crushing my face against his chest in a bear hug.

"Jesus Christ, Whitney. You just saved my life."

20

I POKED AT THE SLICE OF PIE IN FRONT OF ME, ROLLING a cherry around with my fork. Will wasn't eating his, either. He'd practically gutted it, smearing the apple filling across his plate as he'd processed what I'd told him.

The police and tow truck had left over an hour ago, Will's beloved Mustang dragging behind it, but we were both too keyed up to go back home right away. That, and Will had questions for me. Lots and lots of questions. But he was listening. And that was a solid start.

"When we were kids, I just thought it was some weird game you were playing," he said, examining the mess that was once his pie.

I gave a snort of laughter. "A game of spot the soon-to-be-dead person? That's a pretty twisted game for a kid to play."

He shrugged and shook his head. "I don't know, I thought maybe you saw a show about it on TV or something. To be honest, it was pretty scary. I may be older, but I was still just a kid when you first started talking about the clouds. I guess I didn't want it to be real, so it was easier to think that it wasn't."

I nodded. I never really thought about it from Will's perspective, but it made sense that he would be scared. Hearing your little sister talk about dark clouds and death would be scary for any kid.

Will reached across the table and gave my hand a squeeze.

"I'm sorry. I should have been there for you. You were my little sister and I just . . . I don't know. I should have been a better big brother. I promise I will be from now on, okay?"

I swallowed back tears and squeezed his hand back. It was now or never.

"There's more," I said, the confession burning at the back of my throat. I'd been holding on to my secret for so long I didn't know if I could actually say it out loud, but Will's face was so open. And suddenly I needed to get it out—all of it, every last thing I'd been holding on to. So I told him. About Dwight. About the night of the game. About my locker and the notes. It poured out like bile; like I'd ingested poison and my body needed to squeeze out every single drop.

When I finished, I felt lighter. As if by sharing it the weight I carried contracted into a shape that was just a little bit easier to hold.

Will was quiet for a long time, his face unreadable. Then he got out of his seat and came to sit by me, sliding an arm over my shoulder. I'm not sure how long we sat like that, but when he pulled back his eyes were clear, his expression calm.

"I'm so sorry that happened to you, Whit. And that you felt like you had to hold on to it all by yourself."

My lip wobbled.

"You tried to tell me about Gams at the funeral, didn't you? When you asked if someone else could have put the medication in her food?"

I nodded and he frowned.

"I can be such a dick sometimes. I'm sorry I didn't listen."

"You're listening now," I said, unable to put into words just how much it meant to have someone other than Gams believe me.

Will looked down at the table.

"Maybe we should call the police," he finally said.

I sighed and looked out the window, shaking my head.

"And tell them what? All I have is a picture of you with a squiggle over it. That hardly proves that someone intentionally messed with your brakes. No one will believe me. Hell, the only reason you're listening to me right now is because I ran you off the road."

Will's jaw worked back and forth as he thought. "What about the window in your room? Someone broke in—that's evidence, don't you think?"

I chewed my lip, thinking of the way the screen neatly rested against the house. There wasn't broken glass or anything else to suggest forced entry. It looked like it did when Marissa and I snuck out, almost as if it was opened from the inside.

A light went off in my head. I couldn't believe I hadn't thought of it before.

"Will," I said, "there were dozens of people at the house for Gams's memorial. Someone could have opened the window from the inside. Couldn't they?" I screwed my eyes shut. Could Gams's killer have been at her memorial?

My stomach clenched at the notion that they could have been right there in front of our faces, in our home, pretending to mourn her.

Will shook his head. "Who would want to do all this?"

My phone buzzed inside my pocket.

"Just a sec," I said, sliding it free. "It might be Mom."

My blood ran cold when I saw the text waiting for me.

> CONFESS BY THE ANNIVERSARY. OR NEXT TIME YOU WON'T GET A WARNING.

"What the—" I started.

My phone slipped from my trembling fingers and clattered to the table.

"What?" Will asked, his voice thick with concern. "What happened?"

He picked up the phone and scanned the message.

"What the fuck is this?"

I shook my head. "I don't know—" I swallowed, ears ringing as I looked out the window toward the parking lot. "It just arrived a few seconds ago."

Was someone watching us? Were they here right now?

Will followed my gaze, then his eyes bounced around the restaurant, scanning the other patrons. "This is seriously fucked up, Whitney."

His thumbs flew across the keyboard, then he glanced back around the restaurant to see if anyone reacted.

"What did you text?"

He showed me the screen. His response was written in all caps:

> WHO IS THIS? WTF DO YOU WANT?

In the corner booth, a man sipped his coffee, quietly reading the paper. Two women talked animatedly over their own steaming cups of coffee. A waitress leaned against the wall, examining her nails. The cars in the parking lot all looked empty. If someone was watching us, they were doing a good job of hiding.

The minutes ticked by as we stared at the phone, but no response came through.

"It could be from a burner phone or something, which would make it untraceable. I'll look into it." Will fired off another WHO IS THIS? to the unknown number. "What do they mean, *confess by the anniversary?*"

"They must mean the anniversary of the shooting," I whispered. "The first football game. It has to be that."

Is this what they wanted the whole time? To get me to confess to what happened?

"Isn't that in four days?"

I nodded numbly. "It's on Friday."

"So what, you're supposed to go to the police and tell them you're the girl in the picture, otherwise they'll run me off the road again? Fuck that."

"They killed Gams, Will. And they almost killed you." I swallowed. "I don't think I have much of a choice. If I didn't find that note I never would have known to follow you."

"No way," Will said, his voice hard. "You can't. People will jump to conclusions. Bad conclusions."

"I'll tell them I was scared—that I was afraid people would think I had something to do with the shooting."

Will shook his head again, jaw set. "And what happens if they arrest you? People are always looking for someone to pin the blame on for things like what happened at the game last year. I don't think you understand how bad it could get if people find out you were the girl in that picture and you kept it a secret all these months." He sighed. "Think about it, Whit. How did you know to follow him up onto that roof? Why didn't you stick around to talk to the police? Why didn't you tell them what he said to you? There are too many holes. You're my sister and I love you, but if it wasn't for what happened tonight I have to admit that even I would wonder what you were hiding . . . if you had something to do with it all."

"I don't have another option. They're hurting the people I love—"

Will shook his head again. "There has to be something else."

Gooseflesh rose on my arms as I looked back out the window, following Will's gaze. Whoever it was, whoever was after me—they must have been watching the house. Otherwise how would they have known when Will was leaving? They'd been inside my house, touching my things. Inside my locker. Inside Gams's room. How long had they been watching me?

"What if the next time they don't leave a note, and something worse happens to you? Or what if they try to hurt Mom? Or Marissa?" I looked down at my pie as a shiver passed through me. "I couldn't live with myself if something happened to you or anyone else."

I thought of Marissa driving to and from practice alone. The way she cranked her music so loud she wouldn't hear if something was wrong with her car. And then I thought of Mom spending her evenings in the dark house, buried in work. Most nights she didn't notice I was home until I came into her office. Someone could bust in the front door and she probably wouldn't hear them. I couldn't let anything else happen to the people I cared about.

"You can stay close to Marissa, can't you?" Will said. "And I'll talk to Mom about setting the alarm and connecting the Nest Cam so we can see who comes and goes. Plus . . . I can stay here and help you figure out who's doing this."

"No." My voice was firm. "You can't drop out of school to babysit me. You'll lose your scholarship. Plus the farther away from me you are, the safer you'll be."

"Well, I can't just leave you here on your own. And I can't let you go to the police and risk ruining the rest of your life."

I bit at a hangnail. Outside, taillights flashed red as cars made their way toward the highway.

"There has to be a reason they're leaving you threatening notes instead of just going to the police," Will said. "Think about it—why go to all this trouble to scare you? Why leave the pictures of me and Gams behind? If their goal was to kill us they would be better off not leaving a trail of clues. It doesn't make sense."

"So what, you think it's all just to scare me into confessing?"

"Exactly," he said. "They must not have enough evidence that you're the girl in the photo. They need *you* to confess. They've been leaving the notes to make you think someone will come after your family if you don't do what they want."

"Someone *did* come after my family. They killed Gams."

Will was thoughtful for a moment.

"What if that was an accident?" he said. "What if they thought you'd see the note in time to save her?"

I chewed on my bottom lip. "Maybe," I conceded. If it hadn't been for Kevin stopping me in the parking lot—and I guess my conversation with Isaac, too—

I would have found the picture of Gams as soon as I got in

my car. I might have made it in time to save her.

Suddenly the idea of someone like Penny or Kevin being behind everything didn't seem so impossible. Maybe they hadn't planned to kill anyone. Maybe they really believed the darkness would allow me to save Gams. It had certainly allowed me to save Will, hadn't it? And if that was the case, maybe all they really wanted was to scare me into confessing, because they didn't have enough evidence to prove that I was the girl in the photo. Maybe running to the police was playing right into their sick game.

Which meant I couldn't confess. I couldn't give them what they wanted.

I pulled out the list of suspects I'd made and slid it across the table to Will. Many of the names had been crossed out, but there were still a fair number I hadn't yet eliminated.

"Maybe you could help me by doing some research," I said, explaining how I'd been checking social media and looking into people's class schedules to verify their whereabouts when I found the notes.

Will scanned the list. "Isn't Jenny Chan Luke Chan's sister? Luke is a good guy."

I blinked hard at the statement, and Will seemed to realize his mistake—Luke *was* a good guy.

"Sorry, I just meant that I knew him. I'm connected to a few of the people on here, so I think I can help." He continued to examine the list, his eyebrows shooting up. "Why are Mrs. Bower and Marissa on here?"

"It includes everyone from our school who was at the game or connected to the victims. Just to be thorough. I'm trying to be unbiased."

"I don't think someone who used to doodle my name in hearts could be a murderer," he said, referencing Marissa's crush that had mostly (I was pretty sure) waned as we got older. His finger traced the list again, thoughtful. "Wasn't Mrs. B hurt pretty badly at the game? When I saw her at the funeral she was still using a cane."

"Yes," I croaked, picturing her booted foot. The same foot that would never again don a pointe shoe or rise in relevé. "But she loves—" I cleared my throat, realizing my mistake. "She *loved* Gams. Plus I'm almost positive she was with the team at practice. Same for Marissa. I'm just trying to be thorough before ruling anyone out."

Will's finger traced a scratch in the dull metal surface of the table. "What about the kids at the game from the other school—Collin Creek? They have just as much motive as anyone attending the game that night. Shouldn't they be on the list, too?"

"Yeah, I guess. Except anyone still attending Collin Creek has a solid alibi—it's like over an hour from here with traffic. They couldn't be in two places at once."

"Maybe. I'll do some digging and see what I can find." Will took a picture of the list and handed it back to me.

"I really don't like the idea of leaving you alone to deal with this," Will said again.

"I know, but I'll feel much better knowing that you're four hours from here, where it's safe."

I could tell by his twitching jaw that he wanted to protest, but he was running out of arguments.

"Fine," he finally said. "But you have to promise not to do anything rash like go to the police before I get here next weekend." He studied my face. "I mean it, Whit. I'm not leaving here until you promise."

I pulled my car keys from my pocket and slid them across the table to him. We'd agreed it made the most sense for him to take my car back. I could always get a ride with Marissa.

"I promise. I won't do anything until we know who's behind this." I pushed my uneaten pie slice away from me. "But I need to figure out a way to keep Mom home when I'm not around. It's safer if she's home."

"She's on a work deadline, right?"

I nodded. "Yeah, but I think it's for a presentation that's happening early this week."

Will chewed on his lip, a dangerous glint in his eye. "Maybe that presentation will have to mysteriously vanish from her computer tonight. Let me see what I can do." He smiled. "It's going to be okay, Whit."

I nodded again, trying to believe him.

"For what it's worth, it helps knowing that you believe me and I can talk to you," I said. I wasn't sure he'd ever understand how much it meant to not be alone in this anymore.

Will reached out and squeezed my hand again, and I tried to smile like that was all I needed. Like there wasn't a ticking clock now planted firmly over my head.

Four days. That wasn't much time. And if we couldn't figure who was behind the threats, what would happen Friday night if I didn't do what they wanted?

"I still can't believe how lucky he was," Mom said. Blond wisps of hair blew around her face when she sighed. "I mean if you hadn't caught up with him and he'd gotten on the highway . . ." She let out another exasperated sigh and took a sip from her wineglass.

"I know, Mom. Let's try not to think about it. He's fine, that's all that matters."

I looked out the window into the backyard, where shadows pooled beyond the glare of the porch light. A fingernail moon hung in the sky, looking too much like a grin for the heaviness of the evening. Thankfully, Mom had accepted our version of the night's events without protest: Will left his phone behind, I caught up with him to give it back, and that's when he realized there was an issue with his car.

At least Will believed me now. There was comfort in knowing that someone else knew about the darkness and believed it wasn't just a figment of my imagination. Gams had filled that space for me in the past. Maybe now it could be Will.

"I almost forgot." Mom stood and walked toward the back of the house. She emerged a few moments later with a cardboard box, which she dropped onto the counter with a *thud*. "I picked up the rest of Gams's things this afternoon. Her clothes, bedding, photos, and such are in the garage—I thought we could go through them together, maybe over the weekend if you're feeling up to it? But these were the things you asked about—the stuff from her nightstand, bed, and end table. There wasn't much."

I pulled the box closer and reached inside. There was a marble jewelry box with inlays of flower petals and curling vines, a keepsake from a trip she'd made to India. A stack of novels with dog-eared corners. A few old magazines. A lavender sachet. A packet of tissues.

"Where's her journal?" I asked once the contents of the box

were spread out in front of me. "The one with the flowers on the cover that she kept under her mattress?"

Mom walked her wineglass over to the fridge, shrugging as she went. "I don't know, sweetheart. There was a lot of stuff to go through. It could be with her other things in the garage."

"But you checked under her mattress? You made sure you got everything?"

"Yes, sweetheart. There was nothing under her mattress or the bed. I checked everywhere. If it was in her room, it's here."

I frowned. I definitely put it back under her mattress the last time I was there. Maybe she forgot to put it back again. Maybe it was with her other things.

"You sure you didn't see something like it while you were packing up her things? Or accidentally throw it away?"

"I didn't throw anything away unless it was mail or trash. It's probably in the garage. I'm sure we'll find it."

"Where in the garage?" I stood, my hands gripping the counter.

"The back wall. Why?"

I turned and made my way toward the back of the house.

"Honey, it's late. You have school tomorrow. You should really get some sleep—"

I ignored her, wrenching the garage door open and flicking on the light. Mom's car glinted in the fluorescent glow, and behind that boxes were piled against the far wall.

It had to be here. *Please, God, let it be here.*

I ripped open the first box. Glasses, plates, and teacups were wrapped in newspaper, along with Gams's teakettle. I ignored the pinch in my heart seeing her things orphaned in cardboard, as if they were nothing more than fodder for a yard sale.

The next box held old files and books, but no journal. Same for the next and the next until the contents of Gams's life were littered around me, the journal nowhere in sight.

Mom called my name from the doorway. I moved back to the first box, ready to start over. I must have missed it. It had to be here somewhere.

"Whitney," Mom said, louder this time. She grabbed my shoulders. "Whitney, sweetheart. Stop."

She pulled me back against her, and I realized I was crying. I let her arms slide around me as I let out a gasping, heaving sob.

"It's not here," I choked out. "It's not here. Someone must have taken it. Someone—"

"Shh. It's okay, sweetheart. We'll find it. I'm sure it's here somewhere."

I shook my head. "You don't understand—"

It was unlikely that Gams had written anything that would explicitly give us away—she was always so careful. But at the same time, she hadn't been herself lately. What if she'd written about me and Dwight? What if she'd written something that could prove I'd been there that day on the roof? Was this how my stalker knew about the darkness—had they stolen Gams's journal?

But the journal had been there the day I'd gone to visit Gams. If someone took it, they did it *after* I found Dwight's picture in my locker and after my car had been vandalized. Which means that whoever was following me knew about the darkness before the notebook was lost.

Still, the lost journal had to mean something. It couldn't be a coincidence.

I thought about Will's theory—that my stalker didn't have enough proof to go to the police and needed me to confess. What if the proof they needed was inside the journal?

Don't panic. If they had something on you, they'd have already used it by now.

"It's okay, sweetheart. It's going to be okay." Mom ran her fingers through my hair, like when I was little. "I miss her, too. So much."

I hugged her back, realizing I'd been so distracted these last few days, I hadn't bothered to ask how she was doing. She was grieving, too.

I wiped my nose and pulled back from her grip. Purple half-moons ringed her eyes.

She gently squeezed my arm. "I'll call Lone Star tomorrow morning and see if they found a journal lying around. I'm sure we'll find it. Don't worry, okay?"

I swallowed. They wouldn't find the journal. I knew it in my gut—it was gone.

"You should get some sleep." She motioned toward the open boxes, remnants of Gams's life now littered across the garage floor. "We can deal with this mess tomorrow."

I nodded and let her lead me inside the house, suddenly exhausted. The weight of everything that happened today crashed into me, and in that moment the only thing I wanted was to sleep.

When I got to my bedroom, my eyes lingered on the window. The curtains were drawn tight, and the screen was now back where it belonged. Still, something twisted in my stomach. Something didn't feel right.

I scanned my room again, looking for anything else out of place. The note tucked into my mirror was gone now, too—I'd taken it with me when I chased after Will. Otherwise, I saw nothing out of the ordinary. Everything looked as I remembered. Had they just opened the window to put the note in my room? Or had they lingered, digging through my things? Searching for proof that I was a monster.

I paused, eyes landing on my bed. My heartbeat sped up.

No. They couldn't have. They wouldn't have thought to look under the mattress. Right?

My ears rang as I stepped toward my bed. With shaking fingers, I slid my hand between the bed and box spring, reaching for my pink ballerina-covered notebook—the one that contained the names and accounts of every person I'd saved since I first saw the darkness ten years ago.

I only touched fabric.

Panic rose as I swiped. I pulled the covers back, stuck my hand as far back as I could. Nothing.

I grabbed the mattress and yanked, pulling it onto the floor. The space where my notebook should have been was empty.

I checked under my bed. Nothing. Nothing tangled in my sheets. Nothing in my dresser drawers. Nothing inside my pillowcases. Around the bed. In my closet. In my schoolbag.

I searched until my room looked like the aftermath of a hurricane, but the book was nowhere.

Someone had taken it.

21

MONDAY ARRIVED WITH A JOLT. I BARELY SLEPT THE night before, every sound causing my eyes to snap back open. Now I sat across from Marissa, chugging a caramel macchiato and breathing in the mix of coffee, fried dough, and lemon-scented disinfectant that was the Holy Donut.

"Mffst fftnut ifs soo fffg goorf," Marissa said. A few donut crumbs flew onto her shirtsleeve.

"Huh?" I leaned back to avoid the spray.

Marissa motioned to her still-chewing mouth, then took a swig from her jumbo-size iced coffee. "I said, these donut holes are so effing good. Are you sure you don't want one? I only got a dozen so we could share."

She nudged the box in my direction. I took one, only to placate her. My stomach was twisted in knots.

Someone has my journal. Someone has Gams's journal.

The door pinged. I spun around, hoping to see Isaac. Instead, a cluster of guys joined the line, laughing. I bit down my disappointment.

"He'll be here," Marissa said, licking glaze from her fingers. "Staring at the door is not going to bring him any faster. You know, a watched pot never boils and all that. Besides, you'll look like a total creeper."

"Right," I said sarcastically, as if showing up unannounced to his favorite breakfast spot didn't automatically make me a creeper. Isaac messaged me to say he'd been busy with some school project all weekend and that was why his texts had dried up, but I still hadn't gotten a solid read on him since Gams's memorial. It's not exactly like I'd kissed Kevin back, but still. Was I being ghosted?

Marissa pulled the box of donut holes closer, inspecting the options. "Ooh, looky. A twin!" She held up two connected balls of dough with the blue-ribbon pride of someone who'd won a contest. Her face fell at my lackluster reaction. "Well, you could at least act impressed. This is, after all, my last box of donut holes ever. As in, no more donut holes for *the rest of my life*. You should be consoling me instead of sitting there with your judgy face on."

"I don't have a judgy face on."

"Yes, you do. You're one powdered wig and gavel away from Supreme Court justice."

I pinched the bridge of my nose. This was only about the bazillionth time I'd heard Marissa swear off her favorite morning meal.

"If you were a real friend you'd help me finish them." Marissa stuffed the twin into her mouth, garbling her words. "Especially since I'm only here so you can explain to your hot soon-to-be boyfriend why you kissed your hot ex-boyfriend."

"*Kevin* kissed *me*. I literally pushed him away."

"Riiight," she said, winking so I'd know she was just messing with me.

The door pinged again. Two girls from my English class entered, waving when they caught sight of us. I half-heartedly waved back.

"Will you stop already? He'll be here." Marissa glanced out the windows. They were covered in hand-painted pumpkins and autumn leaves tumbling in an imagined breeze, even though we wouldn't see anything resembling autumn for at least another month. "Did Will make it back to Austin okay?"

I nodded, unable to hide a wince at the mention of Will and the memory of everything that happened yesterday.

I flashed to Will's crunched-in bumper and the message on my phone. My stalker was still out there. They could even be watching me now.

My eyes darted around the coffee shop. Will had to be right—whoever was behind the notes needed me to confess because they didn't have enough evidence to pin me to Dwight. But what if the journals changed all that? What if everything they needed was written in those pages?

Marissa's face screwed up with annoyance and I realized she'd been talking.

"Sorry, what did you say?"

"I said, I'm meeting Mrs. B to finalize formations, so I won't be able to meet you at lunch."

"Wait, does that mean Mrs. B said yes? Are you officially a choreographer now? That's great, Riss!" I beamed. Marissa had always wanted to choreograph one of the halftime routines, but Mrs. B was *very* particular. Getting a piece approved was a huge deal. "Which routine are you choreographing?"

"The tribute for the anniversary. To honor the victims." She raised her eyebrows expectantly.

I did my best to smile through the panic that fluttered in my stomach at the mention of Friday's game.

"Wow, that's a huge deal. Congrats. Why didn't you tell me?"

Marissa's mouth flattened into a thin line. "I did. Last week. And then again in the car this morning. What is going on with you lately?"

I squeezed my eyes shut as a pang of guilt hit me.

"I'm sorry, I must have zoned out."

Because I was busy thinking about how I have less than four days to figure out who is after me or else something horrible could happen Friday.

She shook her head, frowning. "No, something's up."

I clutched my coffee cup and forced a smile. "I'm just tired, that's all. It's been a long week. I haven't been sleeping."

That part, at least, wasn't a lie.

Marissa shook her head, not buying it. "You've been saying you're *just tired* for weeks now. Even before everything happened with Gams. I know you better than anyone, Whit." She looked down at the table, then back up at me, her face somber. "You know it's okay to not be okay, right? You don't have to pretend like everything's fine all the time."

"I'm not—"

Marissa cut me off. "Look, Whitney, you're not alone, okay? We were all pretty messed up after everything that happened last year. A lot of girls still are. A lot of girls thought about not coming back to the team, me included. In fact," she said, clearing her throat, "I'm still talking to a therapist about it. It's helped a lot, actually. I could give you her name if you wanted—"

I shook my head harder than I meant to, the word *therapist* spinning my brain back to the parade of doctors my mom sent me to when I was younger. Then I looked at Marissa's serious face, her words landing with a thud.

"I didn't know you were still talking to a therapist."

She shrugged and looked out the window, the unspoken words hanging in the air: *You never asked.* But she didn't need to say anything—her disappointment was written all over her face.

I looked down at the chipped wooden table. Someone had carved initials into the corner in jagged, jerky grooves.

Marissa was right to be disappointed. Because since getting back from California I hadn't asked her how she was doing. Not once. Of course she would still be upset. Of course she would want to talk to someone. But I'd barely said three words to her about the game and what happened last year because I was too focused on my own guilt. I was afraid that if we talked about it I might accidentally let the truth spill. And I couldn't let anyone ever know the truth about the horrible choice I was forced to make that night, least of all Marissa.

"I'm sorry," I whispered, the words sounding inadequate. "I should have asked you how you were doing. I guess I just didn't want—" I shrugged and watched the ribbons of steam rise from my coffee cup. "I guess I thought that not talking about it would be easier."

She nodded and gave me a half-hearted smile. "We all deal with things in our own way. I guess I just wanted you to know that I'm here for you if you want to talk."

Hot tears sprang to my eyes. I wanted to tell her. I wanted to be a better friend. But how could I tell her that I was to blame for everything? It was as if the truth had become part of me, rooted in place along with my teeth.

"I'm sorry," I said again, swallowing thickly. "I haven't been a very good friend to you lately. I'll do better, okay? I promise.

In fact—" I cleared my throat. I'd planned to surprise Marissa once it was official, but now seemed like a better time to tell her. "I asked to be let back on the team."

Marissa's mouth popped open. "Seriously?"

"Seriously. I talked to Mrs. B. She needs some time to think about it since they backfilled my spot and only have budget for thirty girls, but she didn't say no. I miss the team. I miss *you*."

It wasn't a lie, just a partial truth. Because I *did* miss Marissa and the team. I just also needed a reason to keep an eye on the people whose names hadn't yet been crossed off my list, and most of them would be practicing after school in the same vicinity as the Hornettes. And I could keep an eye on Marissa, to make sure nothing bad happened to her. Even if Mrs. B didn't let me back on right away, no one would question me hanging out in the stands after school to watch practice now.

Marissa squealed and practically launched herself across the table, stopping just short of spilling my drink.

"Whit! This is amazing! I can't believe it. Maybe they'll let you sit with us at the first game?"

"Well, she still has to say yes. And there's Penny to deal with—"

"Screw Penny. Mrs. B just has to appease her long enough to make sure her head doesn't spontaneously combust when you two are in the same room again."

Spontaneous combustion felt like the least of my concerns.

"Well, we'll see what Penny has to say this afternoon—we're meeting after school at the rec center so I can take her through the choreography for *Red*."

Marissa rolled her eyes. "I know. She's letting Veena Patel run practice in her absence even though I'm technically second-in-command." Marissa clapped her hands. "This is going to be epic. We finally get to spend our senior year dancing together!"

I smiled. Despite everything, seeing Marissa this happy made me feel happy, too.

"Wait until you see the new uniforms. You are going to *die*—" The door pinged, and Marissa's eyes widened. "Whit, he's here."

My throat went dry.

I turned around. There was Isaac, hands in his pockets, sandy hair hanging loosely over his forehead, blue eyes bright under the fluorescent lights. He leaned down to get a better look at the glass-encased pastries. My stomach danced. Why did it always feel like I had a kickline in my gut when I saw him?

I stood, bumping the table. Marissa gave me two thumbs-up and popped another donut hole into her mouth.

"Isaac?" I asked, attempting my best what-a-coincidence-bumping-into-you-here voice as I stepped behind him at the register.

He turned, a coffee in one hand and a bear claw in the other. His dimple appeared.

"Oh, hey," he said. "I didn't know you hung out here."

I pointed to the table where Marissa was watching with rapt attention. She suddenly became very interested in the pumpkin painting on the window.

"I came with Marissa. But I'm glad I bumped into you. Can you talk?"

"Sure," he said and shrugged, motioning to an empty table. I followed, wishing I'd thought to bring my drink with me so

I'd have something to do with my hands. Our knees bumped as we sat, one of the benefits of us both being tall. Warmth shot up my leg.

"How are you?" he asked, voice taking on a serious tone. "I'm sorry we didn't get to talk at your grandma's service. You seemed . . . busy."

He averted his eyes, and I knew he must be referencing Kevin.

"Actually that's one of the things I wanted to talk to you about." I cleared my throat. "I'm not sure what you saw, but I just wanted you to know that—in case you think that there's something going on between me and Kevin—I don't like him like that."

"Okay," he said, his expression unreadable. "It's just"—he avoided my eyes—"I've been someone's rebound before and I got burned pretty bad. It's not something I want to repeat."

"You're not—" I stopped myself from saying that he's not a rebound, because it sounded too presumptuous. We hadn't even been on a date yet. "There's nothing going on between me and Kevin, okay?"

"Okay," he said, but I couldn't tell from his tone if he completely believed me.

"How did the school project go this weekend?" I asked, changing the subject.

"Good." Isaac took a bite of his bear claw. He had a small constellation of freckles on his nose, barely visible against his tan skin. "Although it's not really a school project. I'm doing some volunteer work at the hospital for college applications."

"That's cool. What kind of volunteering?"

"Mostly reading to patients and stuff. Kind of like what I've been doing at Lone Star but more official. I'm hoping to get into UT Austin's nursing program, but it's pretty competitive."

He tried to sound flippant, but I could tell by the way his blue eyes danced how badly he wanted to get in.

"I'm applying to UT, too. I've always wanted to be on their dance team. It's a long shot, but . . ." I trailed off, feeling myself blush.

"From what your grandma said about your dancing, you'd be a shoo-in. But that's really cool. Maybe we'll both end up there."

"Yeah, maybe." Cue the stomach kickline. "You'd make a great nurse," I added, thinking of the way he'd handled his grandpa that day at Lone Star and his calm demeanor when Gams had her attack.

"Tell that to my dad. He thinks anything other than becoming a doctor is a waste of time."

He shrugged like it was no big deal, but I could tell by the edge in his voice that his dad's approval mattered.

"Well, for what it's worth, I think the world needs more nurses," I offered. "Doctors may physically put people back together, but nurses are the ones who keep them from falling apart again."

Isaac gave me a dimple-exposing grin so warm it nearly melted me. I looked down at my hands, suddenly embarrassed.

"Totally," he said. "What about you? Are you planning to dance professionally?"

"I'm not sure," I said honestly. "I used to think I wanted

to, but now—I think I may try something else." I shrugged, thinking of Gams's pictures and playbills that covered her room. Gams was the star, not me. I wasn't sure I'd like being the center of attention all the time.

"What was the other thing you wanted to talk to me about?" Isaac asked after a lengthy silence. When he saw my confused expression he added, "You said your grandma's service was *one* of the things you wanted to talk to me about?"

"Oh, right." I shook my head. I'd almost forgotten the most important reason for ambushing him here. Every time I was around Isaac the world fell away.

"I have a random favor to ask. You know the guest log at Lone Star?"

I tried to act casual as I asked him for his help.

What I didn't say was that everything was riding on it.

22

I ARRIVED AT THE REC CENTER FIFTEEN MINUTES EARLY, but Penny had already beaten me there. Which figured—she treated on-time arrivals with the same competitive spirit she did just about everything else in life.

She was in the far corner of the mirror-covered room, her nose pressed to her knee in a stretch. My stomach twisted. It was hard to imagine that this girl I'd grown up with—no matter how much we hated each other now—might have something to do with what happened to Gams. Still, I couldn't be sure. And I wasn't leaving here until I had answers.

"Good, you're here." She sat up. Her voice had an exasperated edge to it, like I'd kept her waiting.

She shoved a stack of papers marking formations in my direction and motioned for me to join her on the floor. These days, most people asked how I was doing, or at least offered half-hearted condolences about Gams. But not Penny.

"I thought we'd start by running through formations," she said, barely looking at me. "Then I can record you doing the routine from a few different angles so I have it for reference."

"Okay." I took a seat beside her on the floor and spread out my notes.

We walked through the formations while I studied her face, looking for clues that she was hiding something.

She shoved a page covered in tiny X's at me and jabbed at the transition notes. "Don't you think the front line should stay in the front? I really don't like the idea of moving the weaker dancers too far forward. It lets the judges key in on our flaws."

"Or it shows them that you don't have any flaws. All the other teams will keep the same dancers in the front row. If you move the lines around, you show them that the entire team is strong."

Penny made a *hmm* sound, then jotted down a few notes. The determined look on her face reminded me of when we used to perform together as kids. Before we'd go onstage, she would squeeze my hand and say, "You've got this, Whitney," with such unabashed confidence that it melted my nerves. When did things between us sour so much that I'd be able to suspect her of stalking me?

"What?" she asked, brows furrowing together.

"Nothing." I shook my head and tried to shake off whatever hesitations I was having. Until proven otherwise, Penny was still a suspect. Which meant Penny could still be dangerous.

I plastered on a smile and launched into my questions.

"So what other classes are you taking? Did you manage to get a study period like Marissa? I feel like I'm the only senior without last period free." I made a face, like this was the worst possible thing I could imagine. Like I wasn't probing into her schedule to find out if she had any flexibility to leave school.

"I'm an office aide last period." She smirked, unable to miss an opportunity to brag. "Which is basically as good as getting an off-period."

"Wow, you're so lucky," I said. "Can you leave early if you want?"

She shrugged. "Sure. Mrs. Clims doesn't exactly keep track of the aides once we check in with her."

Blood rushed in my ears. That meant it was possible she could have left the picture of Gams in my car. Or even driven to the nursing home.

"What about Kevin? Does he have last period free, too?"

She bristled. "Why do you care about Kevin's schedule?"

I glanced in the mirror, pretending to adjust my ponytail. "I don't. I was just making conversation. You said yourself you didn't want things to be weird between us. This is me, trying not to make it weird."

Penny made a noise at the back of her throat that sounded a bit like choking.

"He's an aide with me last period," she finally said.

Bingo.

I went cold all over. That meant Kevin could have gone to Lone Star before he intercepted me in the parking lot, too. The timing would have been tight, but it was doable.

My hands shook. The evidence kept stacking up—was it really Kevin? Gams knew him. He had motive. He'd admitted to helping fix Will's Mustang once, which meant he could have enough car intel to know how to mess with the brakes. And he'd proven he had a temper. But still, it was hard to believe. He was an asshole, that much was clear, but a murderer? Even if Will was right and Gams's death wasn't intentional, I still wasn't sure Kevin was capable of it.

Penny stood abruptly and walked over to the tripod that she'd stationed at the front of the room.

"We should move on to choreo," she said. "We only have the room for another hour."

I watched as Penny placed her phone on the tripod, and for a second I thought about telling her. If there was even a fraction of a chance that Kevin was behind Gams and the notes, it meant he was dangerous. Didn't she deserve to know what kind of person she was dating?

"I don't have all day," she snapped, motioning for me to stand.

I stood and shook out my arms and legs, trying to act like I wasn't about to be sick.

"I'm not going to do it full-out. I'm not warmed up." It wasn't a lie, but mostly I didn't trust my legs to hold me upright if I danced. I was trembling all over.

"Fine," she said. "Just call out the movements you don't complete so I know what they are."

I swallowed and took the opening position. Music spilled from the sound system. I walked through the movements robotically, marking turns and calling out the steps. Every time I closed my eyes, I saw Kevin's face.

When I finished, Penny was frowning.

"What the hell was that?" she snapped.

"I told you, I'm not warmed up."

"Yeah, but that was pathetic. It was like you haven't danced all year or something."

My cheeks flushed. "I've been a bit distracted this past week. You might have heard my grandma died?"

Her tight-lipped smirk relaxed. Had it been anyone else, I might have taken the look for sympathy. But there was something forced about the gesture—like she was pretending.

"I heard about that." Penny avoided my eyes. "I'm sorry."

Why wouldn't she look at me? And why hadn't she said

anything about Gams's passing until now? She knew how close Gams and I were. And she *knew* Gams—she'd taken classes at her studio for years.

Suddenly Penny's avoidance of the topic seemed like a glaring spotlight.

It wouldn't have been that strange for Penny to visit Gams, since she was a former student. Maybe she went there and found Gams's book lying out. Maybe she read something she wasn't supposed to, and that's what triggered this whole thing.

I thought about what Marissa said—how some of the girls on the team were still having a hard time after last year. Penny was at the game that night. She was one of the last girls on the field before the team fled to the locker room. Grief does strange things to people. I should know. Would that, plus her general hate for me, be a strong enough motive?

I couldn't ignore the possibility.

I waited for her to say something else, but she didn't. Instead, she stepped behind the tripod again. Like she wanted to put distance between us. She tugged at her ponytail, tapped her hand against her thigh, pressed a button on the camera. All the while refusing to look at me. Was I making her nervous? Or was that guilt written across her face?

"Do you think"—Penny cleared her throat and glanced up at the clock on the far wall—"do you think you could run through the choreography a few more times? Before we lose the room?"

I almost laughed at the absurdity of the abrupt subject change. She sure seemed eager to stop talking about Gams, didn't she?

"Kevin stopped by my grandma's memorial. Did he tell you that?" I asked, refusing to budge.

Penny opened her mouth, shock registering on her face. If she was pretending not to know what I was talking about, she was a better actress than I thought.

"Why are you telling me this?" she said, her voice quiet.

I shrugged, keeping my eyes on her face. She looked a little pale. "I just figured he would have told you. I'm surprised you didn't come with him, actually. You took classes from Gams for years."

"What is this, Whitney? What are you trying to do?"

"I'm just making conversation."

Penny shook her head. "No, you're not. Are you trying to make me jealous or something?"

"Jealous about a *memorial*?"

"You keep bringing Kevin up, like you want to talk about him. You're up to something."

"I'm just—"

Penny held up a finger. "Do *not* say you're just trying to make conversation. I'm not stupid."

Penny looked at me for another beat and shook her head. Then she pulled her phone off the tripod.

"You know what? I think I have what I need. I told Mrs. B this was a bad idea." She slid her bag onto her shoulder.

I gritted my teeth. "You know I have other things I could be doing than teaching you choreography. You could act a little more grateful."

"Grateful? *I'm* the one who's trying to be nice. *I'm* the one trying to keep things focused on dance even though we both know what you did."

"What I did?"

"Stop acting all innocent. I know you were the one who took the flowers—"

I fisted my hands, fury bubbling up inside me. I just told her my grandmother died. How could she be talking about something as trivial as flowers on a locker? What was *wrong* with her?

"I did not take your stupid flowers!" My throat suddenly felt thick, and I swallowed back a lump. I would not let Penny Ansel make me cry. "You know what I think? I think it was *you*."

Penny reached for the door handle, scoffing. "You have some serious issues to work through, Whitney."

"Me? What about *you*?" My pulse quickened. "Are you the one leaving me messages?"

"What?" She shook her head, finally looking me in the eye.

I opened my mouth, but the accusation shriveled on my tongue. This was a girl who used to be my friend. A girl who'd taken dance lessons from Gams. It couldn't be her, could it?

"I don't have time for this," she finally said.

Then the door slammed behind her with a definitive *thud*. She didn't even bother taking her notes with her.

23

As the week dragged on, the tension at school became a living thing. The looming anniversary was impossible to escape. The hallways were littered with flyers about the upcoming tribute and how to make donations to the impacted families. Morning announcements included information about counseling sessions and grief circles. Teachers reminded us to talk to someone if we felt triggered and reinforced the security measures that would be in place for Friday's game. It didn't help that news crews had parked across the street for two straight days, recounting last year's events and ticking down the minutes until Friday. As if we all needed a reminder of what happened nearly one year ago. As if anyone could ever forget.

Especially me. There was only one day left until the anniversary, and I was no closer to figuring out who Gams's killer was.

No more notes had arrived since the one I'd found in my room with Will's picture on it. Will thought they may have given up once they realized I wasn't going to confess like they wanted. I wasn't so convinced. To me, every day that passed was another day closer to the guillotine blade dropping. I couldn't take any chances. And time was running out.

I pushed open the door leading to the courtyard and surveyed the hodgepodge of people peppering the grass. Marissa sat cross-legged in one of the few shaded spots, her lunch spread in front of her as she talked animatedly to Veena Patel. Near the far wall sat the line of student club tables, where they usually sold tickets to various events or campaigned for new members. Jenny Chan was perched dutifully at the student council table, asking everyone who passed to sign a petition for gun control. Her girlfriend, Olivia Touplee, sat at the adjacent table, a hand-painted sign requesting donations to support victims of gun violence taped to the front.

Above Jenny's head the same anemic cloud I'd seen the other day wafted like smoke. Which meant she hadn't listened to me.

Her eyes met mine, then quickly darted away. Her smile evaporated.

I wanted to believe Jenny's skittishness was because I'd creeped her out with my warning. But I couldn't ignore the other possibility given that one of the four *In Loving Memory* lockers was there to honor her brother. That, and I discovered she was absent the day Gams died, making her one of the few remaining names on my list that didn't have an alibi. She had a motive and the opportunity; I just didn't want to believe she was capable.

Olivia leaned down to give her a peck on the cheek before bouncing away, leaving Jenny alone at the table. I took a deep breath and made my move.

Jenny's mouth pressed into a line when I approached. I slid a five-dollar bill into the donation jar and offered a wan smile.

"You know they take Venmo," she said, voice steely. "You don't have to come over here every day to give them cash."

My face went hot at the notion that she'd seen me slipping money into the jar each day. It was silly—it's not like it would make a huge difference or anything—but the donations helped assuage my guilt just the tiniest bit, like I was doing something to help the people whose lives I'd ruined.

And Jenny had noticed, which meant she'd been watching me. Interesting.

"Are you feeling any better?" I asked, trying not to look at the sliver of darkness dancing just above her hairline. "I heard you missed school last week."

"Why are you so obsessed with my health? It's weird." She surveyed me coolly. "And how did you know I missed school?"

I shrugged. "I just want to make sure you're okay, that's all."

Jenny stared at me, her jaw working. "What you said to me the other day about going to see a doctor—that was really messed up." She lowered her voice. "You know I was sick a lot when I was a kid. Saying something like that to me . . . it's not funny."

"It wasn't supposed to be," I said, thinking about her when she was younger. I remembered her missing school. I remembered how gaunt she looked in the hallways. But still, she always had a smile on her face and a joke to tell. Jenny seemed like one of those people who saw the world for what it could be rather than for what it was. At least she did until last year, when her brother died. She didn't smile nearly as much these days.

I glanced at the wedge of darkness above her head. "Is that where you were last week, when you missed school? At the doctor?"

The question was a test. Because if she'd gone, the cloud

wouldn't still be there. Which meant she'd been somewhere else.

"No," she said after a pause, and I was relieved that she didn't lie. As badly as I wanted to get to the bottom of the notes, I didn't want Jenny to be behind them.

"So where were you then?" I asked.

She made a sound that was somewhere between a laugh and a cough. "Why is that any of your business? You've been acting really weird lately."

"Hey, Whitney!" Olivia returned, taking her seat in front of the donation jar. She was wearing her Hornettes jacket even though it was nearly eighty degrees outside. "Did I see you slip more money into the jar? That's so generous of you. Isn't that generous, babe?"

She turned to Jenny, who eyed me wearily.

"Yeah, generous."

I shifted awkwardly, trying to think of what else I could say that wouldn't add Olivia to the Whitney-is-a-weirdo club.

"I think your friend is trying to get your attention," Olivia said, pointing to the opposite side of the courtyard. I turned, expecting to see Marissa flagging me down. Instead, Isaac waved as he picked his way through the lunch crowd toward me.

"Right," I said reluctantly, realizing my conversation with Jenny was over. At least for now. I glanced once more at the ghost of a cloud hovering over her head. "Take care of yourself," I added.

Judging by the way her expression darkened, she picked up on my meaning.

Jenny didn't lie to me, which had to mean something. If she was guilty, wouldn't she want me to think she'd been at the doctor? I'd basically handed her an alibi. But I still didn't know where she was the day Gams died, which meant I couldn't cross her off my list.

"Hey, Whit." Isaac palmed the hair back from his forehead and gave me a lopsided grin. "How's it going? I haven't seen you at lunch the last few days. Is this where you've been?"

He shoved his hands into his pockets. My stomach gave a little kick at the idea that he noticed—that maybe he'd been looking for me. I'd convinced Marissa to relocate out here in an attempt to do recon. All of my free time the last few days had been devoted to what so far had mostly proven to be fruitless detective work.

"Yeah, we're trying to get our vitamin D before the weather turns," I answered.

"I can see why. It's nice out today." He waved at someone behind me. "I have to run, but I wanted to let you know that I'm going to see my grandpa this evening. I'll try to get a picture of the guest log like you asked."

"That would be amazing, thank you," I said, unable to mask my relief. I kept running into dead ends—maybe this would be exactly the break I needed.

"You must really want to send that thank-you note," Isaac said, referencing the excuse I gave him. "Anyway, I should get going. We still on for tomorrow?"

"Yeah," I said, hoping I sounded nonchalant even though the stomach kickline was back. Spending the evening with Isaac was the one bright spot in this whole nightmare of a week.

"Cool. I hope you don't mind, but Beau asked if he could tag along." He shrugged, like it was no big deal. Like he hadn't just dropped a Beau-shaped third wheel in my lap.

"I-uh-sure," I stammered, because what else was I supposed to say?

"Great. I'll text you."

I watched as he turned to walk away, trying not to let the disappointment sink me. Isaac was a nice guy. Nice guys did things like say yes when their cousins asked if they could crash their dates. I wasn't getting friend-zoned, right?

Still, I couldn't shake the feeling there was something he wasn't telling me.

I swallowed my pride and made my way over to Marissa. Across the way, I spotted Kevin and Penny. They were crouched just outside the entrance, their heads bent close. It looked like they were arguing. Kevin's head snapped up. He was scowling. His eyes narrowed. Then he grabbed Penny's hand and tugged her through the doors.

I'd been clocking them all week but had yet to come up with anything useful. I'd even spent my evenings in the stands watching the dance and football teams practice, using the fact that Marissa was my ride as an excuse. All of it had been a waste of time. Tonight, though, I had a different plan. I just had to hope Marissa would go along without asking too many questions.

"Hey," I said to Marissa, speaking low so Veena wouldn't hear. "I have a favor to ask."

～～

Six hours later, I was slumped in Marissa's front seat. We were parked three doors down from Penny's house, hidden behind a large pickup truck, watching Penny and Kevin.

"This has to be the most boring stakeout in the history of stakeouts," Marissa said, reaching for the bag of Twizzlers resting on the dash.

"I think I'd have more fun ripping out my eyelashes," I added, glancing at the clock. They'd been sitting in Kevin's car for nearly an hour doing absolutely nothing. My grand plan was turning out to be a complete waste of time.

Thankfully, Marissa bought my story that I thought Penny and Kevin might be up to something.

"I don't know exactly what," I had explained, "but I heard them talking at lunch. They said something about my locker and I know it sounds weird, but I just have this hunch they may try something tonight."

Marissa immediately jumped to the conclusion that Penny must have learned about my request to rejoin the team and planned to do something like the locker stunt to get me in trouble. I didn't correct her. I felt bad lying, but I was running out of options.

Now I was second-guessing everything. What exactly was I hoping to catch them doing?

"I think there's trouble in paradise," Marissa said, taking a bite of a Twizzler. "You don't sit in a car with your boyfriend for this long and *not* make out unless you're fighting."

I chewed on my lip. She had a point.

"Look, see there?" Marissa pointed. Penny's arms were circling animatedly. "Totally fighting. I bet they're fighting about you."

I watched as Kevin's hands made a similar gesture, then punctuated the air with his pointer finger. Marissa was right.

It didn't look like a friendly conversation.

"I bet she found out he kissed you." Marissa waggled her eyebrows, clearly pleased to finally have some drama.

I shook my head. "You, me, and Kevin are the only ones who know, and I doubt Kevin would volunteer that information."

Marissa took another Twizzler and offered me the bag, contemplating. "What about Isaac? Maybe he got jealous and decided to stir the pot."

"No way, he wouldn't do that. Plus I'm not even sure what he saw exactly."

Marissa gave me a look, and I knew she was thinking about my date going from a twosome to a threesome. Thankfully, she knew better than to throw salt on the wound and kept her mouth shut.

I leaned forward. It was hard to see from where we were parked, but it looked like Penny might have been crying. It wasn't exactly evidence, but it was at least an interesting development. I'd seen enough true crime stories to know that murderers often start lashing out at the people close to them. Could that be Kevin?

"Did you ever in a million years think you and Penny Ansel would hook up with the same guy? I can't believe you used to be friends with her."

I took a bite of Twizzler. "Believe it or not, she used to be fun."

"I refuse to believe the words *fun* and *Penny* can coexist."

I snorted, thinking back. Marissa didn't meet Penny until junior high, when she transferred to public school. That was right around the time when Penny started turning everything between us into a competition. Before then, though, she'd been someone I trusted.

"She could be funny when she wanted to," I added.

"What, like cracking you up by cutting the heads off Barbie dolls?"

I snorted again. "I used to get really nervous before performances. She would give me these pep talks. And when that wouldn't work, she'd distract me by making up secrets for the girls on the opposing teams. It was always ridiculous stuff, like eating jars of mayonnaise after everyone went to sleep or keeping souvenir bags of hair after haircuts. But it worked." I shrugged. "Then one day I guess she decided that I was her biggest rival, and everything changed."

"Actually, I think it's my fault." Marissa looked at me, her face serious. "Freshman year, when we were auditioning for the team, she told me that I stole you from her."

"You *stole* me?"

"Yeah. She said y'all stopped hanging out when I switched schools. That we thought we were too cool for her or something." She shrugged. "I guess I never mentioned it because by that time you guys were like full-on rivals and it didn't seem important."

"I don't think it would have mattered." I thought back to all the things Penny had done to me—hiding my solo costume right before a performance, claiming I'd stolen her choreography. "It wasn't your fault we stopped being friends. She did that all on her own."

"Her loss," Marissa said.

She was silent for a while, left hand twirling the silver ballet shoe stud in her ear. I had the same pair—she'd bought them for me after we'd made the team together. They were supposed to be our good luck charms, yet mine had been sitting in my jewelry box untouched for nearly a year. One more symbol of what a bad friend I'd been as of late.

"Some of the girls on the team were talking about you at practice," she finally said.

"Oh yeah?" I asked, trying to act nonchalant even though my pulse had kicked up a notch. There was an expression on Marissa's face I didn't like. "What about?"

"The game last year. About how you held the doors to the locker room closed so no one could get inside." She turned to look at me. Her eyes were wet. "There's so much about that night I blocked out. I completely forgot about that until they brought it up. It was really brave, Whitney."

I swallowed and looked away, hoping my face didn't betray my emotions. It was true that I'd held the doors closed. But I hadn't held them closed to keep Dwight from getting *inside*. I'd held them closed so Marissa couldn't leave.

She pulled a small card from her back pocket and placed it on the dashboard.

"No pressure, but I thought you might like the info for the therapist I'm talking to. Just in case you want to talk to someone, too. It's really helped me. Or, you know, you could talk to me about it sometime. If you want to."

She looked at me the same way she had at the Holy Donut, when she'd first confessed that she'd been talking to a professional. I fought to keep my eyes from watering. Because I wanted to talk to her. More than ever, I wanted to tell my best friend everything. About the choice I'd made. About the darkness and everything else that had happened. But Gams's warnings were planted too firmly. And the memory of Mom's face the first day I'd told her about the rain cloud was rooted just as deep. Mom showed me that even the people we love can be afraid of the things they don't understand. And the last week had only proven how far people would go when they learned the truth about me.

I opened my mouth to at least thank Marissa for the referral, but just then, the passenger door to Kevin's car opened and Penny stumbled onto the sidewalk. She shouted something into the open window, then marched toward her house. The taillights on Kevin's Prius flared to life.

"Whit, he's leaving!" Marissa said, sitting up straighter.

I reached for my seat belt as his car pulled away. "We have to follow him."

Marissa fumbled to put the car in drive, Twizzlers flying as she gunned the engine and pulled onto the street. The card she'd placed on the dash slid onto the floorboard.

"Let a few cars get in front of us," I said, ducking lower as she came up behind him at a stop sign.

"Obviously. That's like stalking 101." Marissa gripped the wheel.

We followed Kevin into a Kroger parking lot. Marissa hung back, waiting until he was out of his car, then slid into a nearby parking spot.

"I'm going inside," I said. "You stay here."

"Nooo. I want to come," she whined. "Waiting in the car is boring."

"It will be harder to hide if we both go." I gave her an exasperated look.

"I can be stealthy." She slid down in her seat and popped the collar of her Hornettes jacket in what I could only assume was her attempt at being stealthy.

"Come on, I'll be right back. Just—stay hidden."

"Fiiine." She pouted. "But buy me something while you're in there. Sour Patch Kids and a Dr Pepper?"

Inside the store, I scanned the aisles for Kevin. The bright fluorescent glow of overhead lights felt like a spotlight. There weren't many shoppers crowding the store despite the peak pre-dinner hour, making it hard to stay hidden.

What exactly was I hoping to find? Once again, my whole plan seemed ridiculous. Was I going to confront Kevin in the produce aisle? Demand that he confess to my grandmother's murder over a BOGO sale?

My phone buzzed, and I slid it from my pocket. My heart moved to my throat when I saw Isaac's text.

> Got the pictures you wanted. I was only able to get a few pages when Mindy wasn't looking. Hope it helps.

A second later another text arrived, this time with photos.

I stepped into a secluded corner of the store, then clicked on the images. There were four in total, the entries dating back to a few days before I found Gams sprawled in her bed.

I saw my name and Mom's, but no Penny, Kevin, or anyone else I recognized. Would they have signed in under another name to cover their tracks? I scrolled the column for residents, looking for Gams's name. Whoever it was, they would have had to note who at Lone Star they were coming to visit.

I zoomed in. There—the day before I'd visited Gams the first time, someone named Ellie Harris had come to visit Constance Lancing. Then again the day I'd found Gams in her room—the day I'd received the note.

Ellie Harris? I didn't know an Ellie Harris. And as far as I knew, neither did Gams.

But there was something familiar about it. Something that poked at the back of my mind, trying to get out. What was it?

I jumped when a hand clamped around my wrist and yanked me backward.

Kevin jerked me against the wall, his face scrunched into a furious scowl.

"Kevin, what the hell—" I tried wrenching my wrist free from his grasp but he only squeezed harder.

"Why are you following me?" He was so close I could feel the hot puff of his breath on my cheeks.

"I don't know what you're talking about."

"Bullshit. You've been on my heels all week, hanging out in the stands, watching me practice. And tonight you follow me here? What the fuck, Whitney?"

"I'm just running errands—"

"Were you running errands in front of Penny's house, too?" Spit flew out of his mouth when he spoke. "You think I don't know what Marissa's car looks like?"

My mouth popped open before I could think to mask my surprise. Then he leaned down so that his lips were almost against my ear.

"What the fuck is wrong with you, telling Penny that I

came to your house? Are you trying to break us up?"

"No— I don't—" The broken words shook on their way out of my mouth. There was something about the way Kevin was looking at me—something about the dark sheen in his eyes and the sharp edge to his voice.

A muscle in Kevin's jaw twitched. He started to raise one of his fisted hands, then dropped it as a shopping cart rounded the corner in our direction.

Like a switch had been flipped, his face broke into a beatific smile and all signs of his anger vanished. *Snap*—like a light.

The effect was chilling.

He waited until the person pushing the cart strolled past, then his smile dropped and he leaned down again.

"Back the fuck off, Whitney."

My whole body shook as he released me, shoving me backward like I was a used tissue. Some animal instinct flared to life, telling me he was dangerous. Telling me that he'd always been dangerous and I'd just been too naive to see it.

He started toward the front of the store with his shopping basket clutched in his hand, his face placid. As if nothing had happened.

I couldn't just let him leave. Not like this. Not with the deadline hanging over my head like a guillotine. I had to do something before it was too late.

My fingers trembled as I pulled my phone out and thumbed over the record button on my camera. Then I slid it back into my pocket, speaker facing outward.

I marched over to Kevin on wobbly legs.

"I know it's you," I managed to croak. "Whatever it is you

have planned, you need to stop. Or I'll tell everyone what you did to Dwight. I'll tell everyone that you're the reason he snapped."

The words had their effect. Kevin spun around, eyes wild. He closed the distance between us in a few steps.

"I didn't make him *snap*. I told you, it was just a bunch of stupid pranks."

"So you admit that you bullied Dwight." I raised my voice so the speaker could catch what I'd said.

Kevin let out a panicked *shhh*, eyes darting around the store. He didn't deny it, which was basically as a good as a confession. I could work with that.

"What is this? What are you trying to do?" He lowered his voice. I pulled my phone free and covered the screen.

"I know you put the medication in Gams's food," I continued, the words seeping out of my mouth like venom. "I know you're the one leaving me threatening notes. You need to stop."

Kevin flexed and unflexed his fingers. "I don't know what you're talking about."

"Yes, you do. And if you don't call off whatever it is you have planned, I will play this recording for the whole school. I will tell *everyone* what you really are."

I removed my hand from the screen at the same time that I stepped out of his reach. His eyes went wide when he realized what I'd done. The color drained from his face, no doubt trying to remember exactly what he'd said and how much he'd revealed. Not that it mattered. I had enough to scare him.

I didn't wait for him to respond. Instead, I turned and ran

out of the store, phone clutched tight in my hand.

I'd just gone right up to the hornet's nest and poked it with a stick. And while he hadn't confessed, he hadn't exactly denied it outright either. Which was almost the same thing.

There was just one problem—if Kevin was behind everything, who the hell was Ellie Harris?

24

THE ANNIVERSARY ARRIVED LIKE A KNIFE TO THE GUT.
I spent every second of the day expecting my stalker to pounce
from the shadows and twist the blade in deeper. The deadline
was here and I hadn't confessed. What did that mean for me?

Multiple news vans were positioned outside the school parking lot and across the street from the football field. They must
not have been allowed inside, because the solemn-faced news
reporters stood just beyond a metal barricade.

A woman with a sheath of shiny black hair and large white
teeth spoke into a camera, recounting the events that unfolded
last year. It happened at a different stadium, against a different team, but still. It felt like history was trying to rise from
the grave and drag us back.

Marissa drove past them in silence, her fingers white against
the steering wheel as she pulled into our school's parking lot.
She was so tense she hadn't noticed my own unease, which had
to be on full display. My fingers were trembling.

"You okay?" I asked, trying to get my own nerves in check. I
had to keep it together. I couldn't fall apart. Not now.

She gave me a tight smile and slid into an empty parking
space. The night of the first game usually had an electric qual-
ity to it; this one felt leaden. Not just for me, but for everyone.

They won't try anything with so many people around, I thought,
trying unsuccessfully to make myself believe it. But maybe

Will was right—maybe my stalker had given up. Maybe, even with the journals, they didn't have enough to pin me to Dwight. And now that it was clear I wasn't going to confess, they were finally backing down. Or maybe I was right about Kevin and my threats last night had the desired effect.

Or maybe they have something else planned.

I swallowed back bile. I had to stay strong, for Marissa if not for myself.

Marissa flipped down the vanity mirror, inspecting her teeth for lipstick. The gold sequins on her uniform made tiny sparkles all over the car's interior. Her lips were painted the standard Hornette red, fake lashes making her already large eyes enormous. Her usually unruly hair was strategically pinned under a sequined cowboy hat. Next to each eye, a single rhinestone winked when she moved her head.

"You look great," I told her as she applied another layer of blush to her cheeks.

"I look"—she turned to face me so I got the full effect—"like a disco rodeo hooker. The eye rhinestones were Penny's brilliant idea. 'Cause covering your body in sequins isn't enough for people to see you from the stands."

"The new uniforms are . . . nice." I stifled a laugh, relieved to have something other than my fear to focus on.

Marissa snapped the visor shut. "Let's see how hard you're laughing when it's your ass squeezed into this monstrosity. You can thank Mrs. B in person once she finally tells you you're back on the team."

"Let's hope so," I said, unbuckling my seat belt.

Last night, Mrs. B had dropped a casserole off at the house

and apologized for not having an answer yet.

"We only have the budget for thirty girls," she'd explained. "So I have to get approval from Principal O'Connell. But don't worry, I'm sure he'll approve it. I can be very convincing when I need to be."

She'd winked, then went inside to talk to Mom. When she'd left an hour later, it looked like she'd been crying. I could only assume they'd been sharing memories about Gams. Or maybe they were talking about the game tonight, about what had happened last year. There was a lot to be sad about.

Marissa's hands were shaking. She looked like she might be sick, too.

"Are you sure you're okay?" I asked.

"I will be. They've upped security and all that. I know that Dwight"—she swallowed—"I know he can't hurt anyone anymore. That it's going to be okay. It's just—do you think we'll ever be able to go to a game and not think about what happened?"

Her eyes were wide, and the guilt-knife twisted in my chest. Of course she was scared. How could she not be? It wasn't just the first game of the year, it was the first game since it happened. I bet everyone was scared.

You're not alone, I wanted to tell her. *I'm afraid, too.*

"I'll be in the stands watching," I said, like that meant anything, like having me at last year's game did any good.

"You know, it's weird." Marissa kept her eyes forward, staring at some unseen point in the distance. "I play that night over and over in my head, but lately I keep having these flashbacks of when you yelled for me to get inside the locker room.

I could swear I heard the gunshots *after* you pulled me inside, not before. It's like you knew what was going to happen or something."

"That's weird." I quickly looked away.

"Did you?" she finally asked, her voice flat. "Pull me in before it happened?"

"Of course not." Somehow, I managed to keep my voice steady. "Where is this all coming from?"

She looked toward the stadium and let out a shaky breath. "Sometimes I wonder what would have happened if I hadn't made it into the locker room."

"You can't think like that." I reached for her hand. I hated lying to her, but I didn't have another choice. "It's going to be okay, Marissa."

I hoped it wasn't a lie.

I felt the heft of my phone in my bag, taking solace in the recording I'd made last night. It wasn't a confession—not exactly. But regardless, I'd seen Kevin's face. I'd scared him. If it was him, he wouldn't do anything and risk me leaking the video. And if it wasn't, I had to believe they wouldn't do something with a crowd watching. It was the only way I was keeping it together.

"Nothing bad is going to happen tonight," I told her. This time my voice was firm. "I promise."

"I know you're right. It's just . . ." Marissa shook her head, then seemed to swallow whatever it was she was about to say. "Never mind. It's stupid. Let's go inside."

She straightened her shoulders and raised her chin like we hadn't just been talking about her near-death experience. Like the night didn't have a cloud hanging over it.

I squeezed my eyes shut as visions of black rain clouds snapped behind my eyelids.

We climbed out of Marissa's car. Across the parking lot, Mr. Bower and Mrs. B were tangled in an embrace. The boot encasing Mrs. B's foot had gold ribbon around it, as did her walking cane. I watched as Mr. Bower placed both his hands on her shoulders and spoke to her, his face somber. I wondered if he was giving her the same kind of pep talk I'd just given to Marissa. Mrs. B was brave for coming to the game. Maybe the simple act of trying to move forward made everyone at the game brave.

"It's so sweet how obsessed they are with each other," Marissa said, following my gaze. "I hope when I'm married my husband stans me like that. They were high school sweethearts, did you know that?"

I nodded, watching as Mr. Bower kissed the top of Mrs. B's head. It felt like we were intruding on a private moment. "Come on." I grabbed Marissa's hand and tugged her toward the football field.

The other Hornettes had gathered in a circle to the right side of the stadium entrance, sparkling in all their disco rodeo hooker glory. Some of them were embracing. A few held hands. In a few minutes, Mrs. B would lead the team in their standard pregame prayer and chant, then get them into formation for their march onto the field. Although I had a feeling tonight's prayer may be different. That their march into the stadium would feel heavier. Maybe the whole ritual would forever be changed because of what happened.

"Sure you don't mind filming the halftime performance for me?" Marissa asked, adjusting the bag on her shoulder so it wouldn't tangle with the fringe hanging from her shoulders.

"Of course not. You'll do great."

"Thanks. I'll come find you after the game, by the exit. Although," she said as she wiggled her eyebrows, "hopefully you won't be riding home with me."

"Oh!" I shouted just as she turned to join the team. "I almost forgot. Good luck with the tribute. I can't wait to see your choreography. I'm sure it will be beautiful."

I couldn't believe I almost forgot. Again.

Marissa gave me a funny look and opened her mouth like she was about to correct me, but one of the Hornettes called her name and she turned away with a wave.

Inside the stadium, the *rat-a-tat-tat* of the drum line started up. Clusters of black-and-gold-clad spectators made their way toward the main gates and the newly erected metal detectors that the spirit squad tried to camouflage with streamers and hand-painted signs. Above the entrance hung a banner of an angry cartoon hornet yelling STING 'EM, HORNETS! We were playing the East Dallas Razorbacks, one of the worst teams in the division, so our victory was assumed. Still, there was a current of nervous energy running through the crowd.

I scanned the parking lot for Isaac. We said we'd meet at the front, which in hindsight was a terrible plan. What if I'd missed him and he was already inside the stadium?

I felt exposed standing there even though I was surrounded by so many people.

You're safe, I told myself. *They won't do anything here.*

Still, my stomach was a fist.

Confess by the anniversary.

After last night, Kevin was the most obvious suspect. But he wasn't the only name on my list. That, and I couldn't stop thinking about the mystery name from the guest ledger.

I'd googled every variation of Ellie Harris I could think of— Elle, Ellen, Eleanor, Elena, Elizabeth—but the only thing I found were listings for lawyers, real estate agents, LinkedIn pages, and Facebook profiles. I didn't see anyone I recognized or any information that connected the name to Gams. How many Ellie Harrises could there be in the world?

I shivered and walked toward the stadium entrance. I couldn't shake the feeling that I was being watched.

"Whitney!" A hand clamped down on my shoulder. I jumped. "I'm so glad you came to the game." Mr. Bower smiled. His dark eyes glittered under the bright stadium lights. He seemed smaller when he wasn't standing next to Mrs. B; I wasn't used to seeing him without her. "The team will be so happy to see you. How is your family doing? Did you enjoy the casserole?"

His hand was heavy against my shoulder, like he didn't know his own strength.

"We're good, and we did, thank you. It was so nice of Mrs. B to stop by last night and drop it off."

"I'm glad to hear it. We've been thinking about y'all." His teeth were almost too white inside his smile. "You should stop by and say hi to the team. It's going to be a pretty somber night. I'm sure it would cheer everyone up if they knew you came."

I nodded, unsure if I would be brave enough to face them all.

"I should get inside," Mr. Bower said. "Have fun."

"Thanks." I offered a wave. "See you."

He waved back before heading into the stadium, flashing his brilliant white smile.

Across the parking lot, I finally caught sight of Isaac weaving between cars. Beau walked ahead of him, his long arms swinging from his sides like two wet noodles. Isaac looked warm in the fading light, his cheeks flushed pink and his sandy hair shining under the parking lot lamps. My stomach did a wobbly pirouette.

Beau cupped his hands around his mouth and yelled, "Let's go, Hornets! Time to sting some bitches!"

A group of parents shook their heads as Isaac jabbed an elbow into his cousin's side, laughing. I shook off my nerves and went to join them.

~ ~

Despite the packed stadium and the beating optimism of the band, the crowd was silent, as if holding a collective breath. Hadley Jones sang the national anthem, her voice breaking in a sob when she hit the line *home of the brave*. When the show choir joined her in an a cappella rendition of "Amazing Grace" the silence was palpable, save for the rustle of clothing as people pulled cell phones from pockets and raised them into the air, shining lights in memory of the students we lost. There was a speech. A moment of silence. Along the sidelines, the Hornettes lined up, their hands stoically folded behind their backs.

I gripped my seat, afraid that if I so much as breathed I'd burst into tears. My guilt was as thick as the crowd's silence. Why did I come here? Why did I think I could do this?

Isaac excused himself, looking almost as pale as I must have.

I supposed it was hard for everyone, even those who weren't at the game last year. Even for the people who didn't have the weight of everything that happened sitting on their shoulders.

Your fault your fault your fault.

Confess by the anniversary.

I forced myself to watch. Forced myself to be there for my best friend. For my community. The game started. Isaac slid back into his seat, still looking on edge. The crowd shifted, eyes flicking to the doors and exits, like we expected Dwight's ghost to appear at any moment. We scored a touchdown. A field goal. An interception. The cheerleaders cheered. The dance team swayed in time to the band music. Somehow, we moved forward.

At halftime, the Hornettes took their place on the field, performing the kick routine they'd rehearsed all week. Marissa's smile was electric as she hit the ending pose. The crowd was on their feet. I screamed her name, waving proudly.

I expected them to transition into Marissa's tribute routine, but instead the team marched off the field to thunderous applause. Did it get cut? Is that why Marissa gave me a funny look when I asked her about it?

"I could watch those sparkly cowgirls kick all day," Beau said, plopping down between me and Isaac with a plate of nachos.

I'd had many ideas about what might happen that night with Isaac: sidelong glances, small talk that morphed into real talk, accidental hand touches, intentional hand touches. But in none of those imagined scenarios had I pictured Beau Gunter wedged between us, his long body and camo hat obstructing any and all access to Isaac. Not to mention that Isaac looked like this was the last place he wanted to be, not that I could blame him.

"Nacho?" Beau asked, passing the paper tray to me. He nearly dumped it into my lap when he jumped to his feet. "Go! Go! Go! Yesssss!"

The crowd roared as the announcer yelled, "Touchdooooown Hornets! By number twenty-two, Kevin Hampshire."

Only Isaac and I stayed seated, wearing matching scowls as the band played our fight song for the fifth time that night. Isaac's eyes kept darting around the stadium, like he was looking for someone. His usually ruddy cheeks looked pale in the stadium light.

On the field, Kevin fist-bumped one of the other players. The sight of him made my stomach clench.

"When did that guy get so good?" Beau asked, still clapping when he plunked back down in his seat.

I wondered the same thing. At practice he could barely hold on to the ball. Now he kept running them into the end zone like Emmitt Smith incarnate.

Kevin ran down the sidelines, smacking his teammates' hands. Then he looked up into the stands, fist pumping the air as he shouted the final lines of our fight song along with the crowd.

Sting 'em, Hornets! Rattle the nest!
Show 'em that North Dallas High is the best!

His eyes landed on me and he froze. I couldn't make out his expression through the helmet, but still. A shiver rippled down my spine.

At least I knew he couldn't try anything now. Not in the middle of the game. Not when he was playing. And I had to believe my words at the grocery store had an impact. If it was him and he had something planned, he'd have to reconsider now that he knew I was onto him.

I glanced back over at Isaac. A thin sheen of sweat coated his skin.

"You all right, man?" Beau offered him the nachos, then seemed to think better of it. "Look, if you need to leave—"

My stomach twisted at the idea of Isaac leaving, but thankfully he shook his head.

"I'm gonna get some air," he said, even though we were outside. Then he slithered out of his seat without a backward glance.

"Is he okay?" I asked Beau, watching Isaac's freight train trajectory out of the stands.

"He'll be fine. He's just had a rough go of things lately. Coming to a game was probably a bad idea."

"What do you mean?"

Beau shook his head and shoved a chip in his mouth, then laughed nervously. "Nothing. Sure you don't want one?"

He held the tray out to me again, then must have seen the disappointment on my face because he threw one of his gangly arms over my shoulder.

"Aww, cheer up, darlin'. It'll be okay. But maybe next time don't take him to a football game where the guy he saw try to kiss you is having a *Rudy* moment."

So he *had* seen us. I knew it. Is that why he let Beau crash our date?

Beau handed me his Coke. "Here, have a sip. You'll feel better."

"No, thanks." I passed it back to him. You could smell the booze wafting off of it from Oklahoma.

"You know what your problem is, Supergirl?" Beau took a

sip and leaned back in his seat. "You need to lighten up. You're so serious all the time. Look around. You're at a football game, your team is winning, and yet you look like someone just murdered a puppy. Don't you know how to have fun?"

"Of course I know how to have fun." I realized after I said it how unfun it made me sound. I reached for a nacho. Nachos were fun, right?

"You need to loosen up," Beau continued. "Like your spunky little friend. I just want to wind her up, point her at things, and watch her go."

"Word to the wise," I said, and looked toward the sidelines where the Hornettes were lined up, pom-poms circling in time to the band music. "Don't call her *little* unless you want to get punched in the face."

Beau laughed. "She'd have to be able to reach my face. And anyway, her size is part of the appeal. She's like a feisty little chicken nugget. I like chicken nuggets." He stood and cupped his hands around his mouth. "Hey, Marissa!" he shouted down to the field. "Shake it, you sexy little chicken nugget!"

Marissa dropped one of her pom-poms. I slapped Beau's arm.

"You are seriously damaged," I said, fighting a grin.

"Is that a laugh? Did I actually get the ice queen to smile?"

His shoulder bumped mine, nearly spilling his drink.

"Watch it with that thing," I told him, jutting my chin toward the figure a few rows in front of us. "I think Mr. O'Connell expelled the last person he caught drinking at a game."

Mr. O'Connell stood at the railing, arms crossed as his head bounced between the game and the exits. His face was arranged in an expression he probably thought passed for amusement, but I could see the nervousness behind it. Behind him, Jenny Chan sat with some of the other student council members. They were all dressed in black, and one of them had their arm around Jenny's shoulders in a comforting gesture. It made my stomach squeeze.

I was surprised to see her at the game. Maybe she came to support Olivia. Or maybe she was trying to be brave, the same way we all were.

Or maybe she's here for you.

The dark thought slithered into my brain before I could stop it.

If she was the one behind the notes, claiming to have a doctor's appointment the day Gams died would have been the perfect alibi. Yet she hadn't lied. I took another nacho and looked down at where Kevin was seated on the bench. It couldn't be Jenny. I was sure of it.

My phone buzzed. I fumbled it out of my purse and was relieved to see it was just Will checking to see if I'd made it to the game okay. I was supposed to text him the second I arrived. Oops.

"New boyfriend?" Beau asked, peeking over my shoulder just as Isaac sat back down. His jaw twitched.

"Just my brother." I flashed my screen, then texted back.

> Here. Mom's barricaded in the house.
> Can you check in on her?

I'd made sure that all the windows were locked and curtains were closed tight, then I'd set the alarm so that I'd get a notice if anyone tried to enter or exit my house while I was gone. I'd also set the Nest Cam so that we could track anyone coming or going. It wasn't as good as keeping an eye on Mom myself, but at least I'd know she was safe until I got home.

Will was the real hero, though. As promised, the presentation Mom had been working on mysteriously vanished from the cloud, ensuring that she'd spent the week barricaded inside. It was worth it to ensure she was safe, but still. I couldn't help but feel guilty.

When the game ended, we filed outside with everyone else bumping and shoving to leave the stadium. I felt lighter, the weight of fear and anticipation finally lifting. We'd made it. Nothing bad had happened. Maybe Will was right and they'd given up.

I hoped it was my imagination, but it seemed like Isaac intentionally stayed a few paces behind me. At least the color had returned to his cheeks—whatever was wrong with him earlier, he seemed to have shaken it off.

"So," Beau said once we were free from the surge of people. "I think this victory calls for a celebration. How 'bout a little gathering at the Beau's?"

I looked behind me, searching the crowd for Marissa. I wasn't going anywhere without her, but I wanted to talk to Isaac. He'd barely said three words to me all night.

"Do you think you can get the chicken nugget and her sparkly cowgirl friends to join?" I watched Beau's hopeful face, and it dawned on me that he wasn't kidding when he said he liked feisty chicken nuggets.

"You realize you're like twice her size, right? And she kind of has a thing against people who talk about themselves in the third person."

He placed his hands over his heart and closed his eyes dramatically. "The heart wants what the heart wants, Supergirl."

I laughed. This courtship would be highly amusing, especially since Marissa had no idea it was happening. Poor guy didn't stand a chance.

"The team usually goes out to dinner after the first game," I told him, doubting Marissa would want to miss out on the tradition. Especially given the heaviness of the evening.

Then I saw her face.

"Get me out of here before I kill your twin," Marissa said, looking like a teapot on the verge of exploding. "God help me, I'm going to murder that girl."

Veena joined Marissa. She pried off the rhinestones winking at the corners of her lashes and rolled her eyes.

"She wants us to stay and *practice*. Like, right now."

"Can she even do that?" I asked.

"We're not sticking around to find out." Marissa yanked off her hat and started pulling bobby pins from her hair. "She told me I was a half beat late on my jump split, which is total BS. And"—she jabbed a finger at Beau—"*someone* made me drop a pom-pom, and now she's threatening to yank me from next week's performance. I'm going to slap the sequins off her if she says one more word to me."

I wondered if part of the reason Marissa was so upset was because her tribute routine got cut. I'd have to ask her about it later, when we didn't have an audience. She'd worked so hard on it—I hoped they found another opportunity to perform it.

"Y'all are in luck." Beau handed Marissa his "Coke" and slung an arm around her and Veena's shoulders. "There's an after-party at my house. You're all invited, and whoever this horrible twin person is, is not. In fact, I'll drive with y'all to make sure you know how to get there, and you," he said, and nodded to me, a mischievous grin on his face, "can go with Isaac to keep him company. Lead the way, ladies!"

"But Marissa's my ride," I said, not wanting to leave her alone. We'd made it through the game unscathed, but what if my stalker had something else planned? I couldn't risk it.

"Veena's riding with me and Beau needs to tell us where he lives." Marissa looped her arm through Veena's, like they were suddenly besties. "*You* should go with *Isaac*."

I narrowed my eyes at her. "But you know where Beau lives."

Marissa and Beau gave me a look that said my antennas were up but there was no reception, and suddenly I realized what they were up to.

They were trying to get me and Isaac alone together.

"I don't mind riding with Isaac," Veena said, smiling at him. Was she blushing?

"Sorry," Marissa said firmly, dragging Veena away. "You're with me. Hurry up before Penny sees us."

Then she leaned over to me and whispered, "Go get him, Supergirl."

25

ISAAC HAD JUST PULLED OUT OF THE PARKING SPACE when Marissa's car pulled up alongside us. They'd managed to cram even more people into the car; the back seat was a mass of bodies and sequins. Beau dangled out the passenger-side window and motioned for us to stop.

"What?" Isaac asked, sounding irritated as he rolled down his window.

"I need you to swing by Eddie's and grab beverages. I already called and he said he'd hook y'all up."

"Don't you have stuff at your house?"

"Not enough. And I don't want to keep all these lovely folks waiting." Beau spread his arms out toward the back seat, where people were perched on laps and packed onto the floorboard. "Come on, bro. It'll take you like ten minutes. Eddie said he'd have a few cases waiting for you. You just need to swing by and grab them."

Marissa gave me a wink and a thumbs-up from behind the steering wheel, making me wonder if this was a ploy to give me more time alone with Isaac. Beau was starting to grow on me.

At least I knew Marissa wasn't alone. It's not like my stalker would try something with a carful of witnesses. And I was with Isaac. Plus, Mom was safe inside the house, and Will was four hours away. It would be fine, right?

"Who's Eddie?" I asked after Marissa's heaving car pulled away.

Isaac kept his eyes on the road and his voice flat. "Just this guy that hooks Beau up sometimes."

We turned down a darkened road, in the opposite direction of traffic. Isaac flipped on his brights, illuminating trees and a narrow two-lane road.

"And where is it we're going exactly?"

"To Eddie's," he said, as if I should know exactly where that was. I waited for him to elaborate, but he didn't.

The two-lane farm road was sparsely lit. I could make out the shadows of trees, fences, and the occasional porch light from one of the few houses set back from the road, but it was too dark to see much else. Beau had said it would only take ten minutes, but it felt like we were driving into the middle of nowhere.

Next to me, Isaac was a tightly wound spring. His white-knuckled hands squeezed the steering wheel and the corners of his mouth were tight and drawn. Had I said something to upset him?

"So what'd you think of the game?" I tried to make my voice cheerful even though my pulse felt like it had a microphone attached to it. The silence in the car was thick enough to eat.

Something in my stomach squirmed at the look on Isaac's face, and I realized how little I really knew about him. I'd only met him a couple of weeks ago. Sure, Gams liked him, but how much did she really know about him? He was basically a stranger.

A stranger with access to my school.

A stranger who was at Lone Star the day my car was vandalized.

A stranger who was with me in the parking lot when I found the picture of Gams.

A stranger who went to Collin Creek, the high school where last year's shooting took place. He said he hadn't been at the game, but I'd never checked. I hadn't even put him on my suspect list. What if I had it all wrong?

Suddenly the seat belt was too tight across my chest. I pulled at it, then reached over and cracked the window to let in some air. There was no one around. No one to stop him if he tried something. I reached for my phone.

"Maybe you should take me home—" I started, but Isaac cut me off.

"What do you even see in that guy?" he snapped, like the words had been thrumming inside of him and finally boiled over.

"What?" I asked, startled by the anger in his voice.

"Kevin. Your ex or whatever he is. What did you even see in him?"

I stared into the darkness, watching the shadows bounce with the headlights. Where was this coming from?

"You know he cornered me after school today? He had three other guys with him." Isaac rubbed at the back of his neck, scowling.

"Wait, what?"

"He told me I better stay away from you, or else. Even jabbed his finger into my chest, like some tough-guy asshole." He scoffed. "He didn't even have the guts to talk to me one-on-one. He had to bring backup. Maybe I should be flattered."

"Isaac, I'm so sorry. I had no idea." Suddenly Isaac's anger made sense. No wonder he bristled every time the announcer said Kevin's name. My cheeks heated at how quickly I'd jumped to conclusions about this boy who'd never been anything but nice to me. And to Gams.

It sounded just like what Dwight told me had happened to him—how Kevin and his friends cornered him. Only Kevin did more than poke Dwight in the chest.

I thought about the look on Kevin's face when he cornered me in the parking lot last week and the grocery store yesterday. The way he'd gripped my wrist like he could easily snap it. The way his hand fisted just before the other cart came around the corner. Why had it taken me so long to see him for what he was?

"Isaac, listen—"

Headlights rose behind us, filling the cabin with white, glaring light. Isaac squinted into the rearview mirror.

"What is it with everyone acting like an asshole today? Turn your brights off, buddy!" He held up a hand to block the glare reflecting off the rearview mirror.

I looked out the back window but couldn't see anything other than two squares of light riding way too close to Isaac's bumper. The driver leaned on the horn.

"All right, Jesus! Calm down."

Isaac turned on his blinker.

"Wait, you're pulling over?" Cold fingers walked down my spine. Outside of the headlights, the road was pitch-dark.

We'd be stopped on an empty, unlit farm road.

"I want this guy off my ass."

As if on cue, the car pulled even closer and laid on the horn again.

A small flicker of darkness appeared above Isaac's head.

Oh no. Not here. Not now.

"Don't stop!" I shouted, making Isaac jump and the car jolt. My hand jerked out and grabbed on to his arm. "Keep driving."

"Whoa, calm down. It's fine, we'll just pull over quickly and let them pass. This person's just being a dick, that's all."

Was this it? Was this the payment that had been promised if I didn't confess?

I turned around again. The car was inches from Isaac's bumper. The headlights made it impossible to see the driver or make out details on the car, but based on the size of the lights it had to be an SUV or truck—something much larger than Isaac's Accord. And it was painted a dark color, likely black. I quickly ran through a mental list of my suspects. Kevin drove a white Prius. I was pretty sure Penny drove something small and compact. Jenny had been driving her brother's truck the other day, but it wasn't black, and it was also a total clunker. I couldn't think of anyone else whose car matched the description.

But that didn't mean they couldn't have borrowed another car.

"How far is this Eddie guy from here?" My voice shook on the way out.

"Not far. Why?"

I wrapped my hands around the seat to keep them from shaking. The sliver of darkness hovered over Isaac's head like it was pondering its next move, pulsing in and out as I tried to figure out what to do. Which choice was right—pull over or keep driving?

Another blast of horn bellowed behind us, this time long, loud, and threatening.

"Look, let's just pull over. I don't like how close they're riding me."

Isaac started to slow again. The sliver grew into a thicker tuft of darkness, making the choice clear. We had to keep driving.

"Do you trust me?" I asked, unable to keep the quaver from my voice. Was there a cloud over my head too? Would I see my own darkness if I was in danger? "You need to keep driving. Don't stop until we get off this road and find someplace that's better lit. Please."

There must have been something in the way I said *please*, because Isaac nodded, gripping the steering wheel as he sped back up. The cloud above his head shrank to a small tendril.

Behind us, the car revved its engine and swerved side to side, taunting. Lights fanned back and forth across the dash.

"I don't like this, Whitney."

Another burst of horn and rev of engine, then Isaac's car jerked forward. My body snapped against the seat belt.

"Holy shit, they just hit my car!" The whites of Isaac's eyes shone in the darkness.

"I'm calling the police." I leaned down to grab my phone, but we were hit from behind again. My head smacked against the glove box and the phone fell from my hand.

"Shit! Are you okay? Whit?"

Bursts of color exploded behind my eyes, but I pushed myself upright and managed a nod. There was blood in my mouth. I must have bitten my tongue.

"Eddie's is just around the bend. Can you hold on until then?"

The headlights cut to the left, followed by a loud roar of the engine.

"They're coming up beside you!" I screamed. The dark sliver became a black smoky snarl over Isaac's head, thick and hungry. "Speed up! Move to the center of the road. Whatever you do, don't let them pass!"

I turned back around, trying to get a look at the license plate.

The road veered to the right. Isaac steadied the car, keeping tight to the center so the other car couldn't get past us. I held my breath.

"Hold on," he yelled, then cut the wheel to the right. The car fishtailed as we turned into a long gravel driveway.

There was a loud blast of horn as the other car flew past. We lurched to a stop, neither of us speaking while we waited to see if the other car would turn around and follow us in.

Twenty seconds passed.

Thirty.

An eternity.

The car didn't appear behind us, and the space above Isaac's head remained blissfully empty. I checked my own reflection, just in case. Not that I was sure I'd even be able to see my own darkness. Still, a gush of air released from my lungs when I saw the emptiness above my head.

"What the hell was that?" Isaac finally asked, breath heavy. The driveway floodlight came to life, illuminating a small squat house a short walk up a gravel walkway.

I closed my eyes, waiting for my thrashing pulse to slow. Every inch of my body quaked. *Too close. That was too close.*

Isaac reached out and took one of my trembling hands, then gently ran his thumb back and forth against my palm. It should have sent a thrill up my spine, but I was too numb to feel anything. I couldn't believe I'd suspected him of being the one to hurt Gams. What was wrong with me?

"Hey, are you okay?"

I closed my fingers around his hand to anchor myself. Then I squeezed my eyes shut and thought of dance. Anything to stay calm.

When executing multiple pirouettes, find something on the wall to anchor to and whip your head back to that spot as quickly as possible while keeping your neck long.

"Hey, it's okay. We're okay." He slid an arm around me. I felt his heart thumping underneath his T-shirt. I let myself fall against his chest. He smelled like the football game—popcorn and cotton candy wafting through warm fall air.

You could have died. I put you in danger. This is all my fault.

I had the urge to tell him everything. I wanted to let it spill out of my mouth until the words became waves that swept us both away. But when I closed my eyes I heard Gams's voice in my head: *People are afraid of the things they don't understand.*

The front door of the house banged open, spitting a short,

rotund twentysomething man onto the porch. He shielded his eyes against the glare of Isaac's headlights.

"That you, Isaac?"

Isaac let go of me and slid out of the car. I still felt the ghost of his arms around me as he walked toward the porch.

26

"YOU SURE YOU DON'T WANT ME TO TAKE YOU HOME?"
Isaac asked for the third time. I'd finally stopped shaking, but
I didn't know if my pulse would ever return to normal.

We eased back onto the darkened road and looked over our
shoulders, like a phantom SUV would be hiding in the shadows, waiting to pounce. We probably should have called the
cops, but the cases of beer weighing down the back of the car
were all the motivation we needed to keep our mouths shut.
That, and I wasn't sure what I would say to them.

*I think someone is stalking me. I think that same person killed my
grandma because I see death clouds and saved the school shooter last
year. Oh, and I'm the girl in the photo you were trying to find.*

"No, let's go to the party," I said, watching my reflection
in glass. A stricken ghostlike girl stared back at me. "I don't
want Marissa to worry."

And I need to make sure she's okay.

I couldn't stop my mind from spiraling with dark possibilities. What if there was another note somewhere and I'd missed
it? Or what if this was exactly what the text had threatened—
Confess by the anniversary. Or next time you won't get a warning.

Did that mean it was over? Or was there something else
planned?

I was beyond relieved when both Will and Mom texted me
back, letting me know they were okay. Now I just needed to
check on Marissa, who had yet to respond to my texts.

Unless I was the target all along.

I shivered and looked out the window, grateful to finally see lights and other cars as we left the dark farm road behind.

"That driver was out of control," Isaac said, eyes flicking toward the rearview mirror. "Talk about road rage. I've read stories about people like that flying off the handle. You were right to make me keep driving. How's your head?"

"Fine, just a little sore." I felt the tender place where I'd connected with the dashboard. A small lump had started to form.

Isaac reached across the seat and took my hand in his. His fingers were light and feathery. I waited for him to pull back or make some comment about us just being friends, but he didn't. The weight of his hand was warm and reassuring and helped slow my stuttering pulse.

What would have happened if we had pulled over? Was Kevin driving the car? If not him—who was it?

When we finally arrived at Beau's, the street was lined with cars. Clearly word about the after-party had spread. Marissa's car was parked directly in front of the house, and the sight helped me relax a smidgen. At least I knew she'd made it here okay.

"Question for you," Isaac said, climbing out of the car. I immediately missed the weight of his hand against mine. "Would you rather only age from the neck down or the neck up?"

I let out a surprised laugh, then paused to consider my answer.

"Neck down. I'd just avoid bathing suits. Or wear a wet suit."

"What about summer? You can't survive in Texas without shorts."

"Sure you can. That's what air-conditioning is for." I smirked and grabbed a box of the alcohol we'd picked up from Eddie's and followed Isaac into the house.

"Where are Beau's parents?" I asked, shouting to be heard over the music that greeted us when we opened the front door. Laughter floated in from the kitchen.

Isaac dropped his cases of beer onto the entryway tile and motioned for me to do the same. "Not sure. But my aunt goes to these monthly church retreats, and my uncle has a deer lease he runs off to every other weekend. So I'm guessing that's where they are."

We followed the sound of voices and found the kitchen filled with sequin-covered Hornettes. A few had changed out of their uniforms, but the majority must have come straight from the game, not even bothering to remove their hats. So much for Penny's after-game practice.

Jenny sat among a circle of sparkling girls around the kitchen table. She still wore the all-black outfit she had on at the game. Her arm was draped over the back of Olivia's chair.

When she saw me, her eyes narrowed. Something slithered down my spine.

You creeped her out, that's all.

I thought about the headlights rearing up behind us and the truck Jenny had been driving the first day of school. It wasn't a dark color, but it was so dark on the farm road maybe I had it wrong—maybe the shadows were enough to make any car look black.

Had I been too quick to dismiss Jenny? Isaac and I had stayed at Eddie's for a while—she would have had plenty of time to get here before us.

I swallowed and met her steely gaze. That's when it hit

me—there wasn't a cloud above her head. I'd been so distracted at the game, I hadn't noticed. She must have finally taken my advice.

"Hey," I said, looking between Jenny and Olivia so I wouldn't be too obvious that Jenny was my focus. "When did y'all get here?"

"About half an hour ago?" Olivia said, glancing to Jenny for confirmation. Jenny shrugged.

"Did you come together?" I asked, looking at Jenny this time. I couldn't imagine Olivia being game to run someone off the road. If it was Jenny, she would have had to do it alone. Jenny's scowl deepened.

"I'm going to get some fresh air," she announced, pushing back from the table before anyone could protest. "Wanna come?"

She aimed the last question at Olivia, who stood and followed without question. I'd have to try to catch Olivia on her own and ask her who she rode with then. Maybe she'd also know where Jenny was the day Gams died. Why hadn't I thought to ask her sooner? Jenny seemed hell-bent on avoiding me.

Veena Patel emerged from the kitchen with a deck of cards and a half-empty bottle of tequila. She took Jenny's open chair and motioned for me to sit in Olivia's.

"Has anyone seen Marissa?" I scanned the crowd as I slid into the seat.

Veena pointed toward the hallway. "She went upstairs to change. Said she'd be back in a few minutes."

Relief flooded me. Good, that meant she was okay.

Isaac appeared in the doorway, dragging an extra chair he

swiped from the nearby dining room. The girls scooted closer to make room.

"What are y'all playing?" he asked, reaching for the deck of cards.

"Nothing yet. Any ideas?" Veena leaned forward and traced her finger around the edge of the tequila bottle, eyeing Isaac with a look that could only be described as sultry. Was she flirting with him?

Isaac met Veena's dark gaze with a dimple-exposing smile, and I tried to ignore the spire of angst that jabbed into my gut.

"Do you know how to play assassin?"

When no one spoke up, Isaac launched into a detailed account of how to play the game. It was hard not to notice the way his eyes kept falling on Veena, or the way he grinned when she took off her hat and let her dark hair spill over her shoulders.

"Here," he said, dealing cards to everyone at the table. "Put your heads down and close your eyes." Then he lowered his voice, making it deep and ominous. "The city sleeps, unaware of the danger creeping in the dark. Because there's a killer in our midst, looking for their next victim." He paused dramatically so that we all jumped the next time he spoke. "The assassin strikes!"

Isaac's hand pressed against my shoulder, which meant the assassin had picked me as the first kill. The pressure of his hand was gone too quickly.

"I'm sorry to inform you that Whitney has been murdered by an unknown assailant."

The girls gasped in pretend shock. Veena giggled and flipped her hair over her shoulder, eyes never leaving Isaac.

I shivered, the irony of the game landing in my stomach with a thud.

Since I was dead I couldn't speak, so I had to watch silently while everyone discussed their theories, bantering back and forth until it was decided Jenny, who'd returned from her jaunt outside, was the assassin.

"I told you it wasn't me!" Jenny said, huffing when she flipped over her card.

"Shh. You can't talk anymore." Isaac plucked Jenny's card from her outstretched fingers and shuffled it back into the deck. "Everyone, heads down."

Before Veena put her head down again, she winked—actually *winked*—at Isaac, like they were much more acquainted than I'd originally thought.

I'd always liked Veena, but in that moment I wanted to reach across the table and wring her sequined neck. I leaned over to say something to Marissa, then realized she still wasn't here.

"Did Marissa come back downstairs?"

A spike of cold panic shot up my spine when they all shrugged. Her car was out front and some of the girls at the table rode with her, which meant she must have made it to the party okay. And Veena said she'd gone upstairs to change. But that would have only taken a few minutes. She should be back by now.

I pushed back from the table, checking my phone. The last text was from Will, asking if I was okay.

I ignored the gelatinous feeling in my legs as I slid the door to the backyard open. Outside of a cluster of guys near the back fence, the space was empty.

"Hey, have y'all seen Marissa? Curly hair, about this tall?" I held up my hand to just below my chin.

"No, sorry. Haven't seen her."

"Yeah, sorry."

I closed the door. Maybe she was in one of the upstairs rooms.

I followed the sound of voices down a hallway and pushed open the door to what I could only guess was Beau's room. A cloud of smoke plumed out of the mouth of a long-haired guy holding a vape pen.

"Have you seen Marissa?" I asked, fighting the quaver in my voice. He shook his head, then passed the plastic device to his friend, who also shook his head.

I let the door close with a heavy click.

She's fine, said the rational side of my brain. *She probably got distracted.*

But the other side—the side that jerked me awake when hot screams pierced through my sleep—began clawing at the puzzle pieces, forming a picture:

My brother speeding toward the highway, darkness churning above him.

Bright headlights on Isaac's bumper while a black cloud swirled overhead.

A ticking clock that said I had to confess before the anniversary—before tonight—or next time there wouldn't be a warning.

What if Marissa is payment for not confessing?

I shouldn't have left her alone. I shouldn't have let her out of my sight.

I ran from door to door, wrenching them open while my heart scratched at my chest.

A closet.

A bathroom.

An empty bedroom.

I circled back through the living room, pushing my way through the cluster of sequined girls dancing in a circle near the speaker. The couch was stuffed five people deep, all clutching drinks and laughing. A couple leaned against the far wall, heads close together. Four guys counted to three then tipped open cans of beer toward their mouths.

Marissa was nowhere to be found.

The primary bedroom was at the back of the house, down a long stretch of narrow, picture-lined hallway. I marched down the tan-carpeted corridor, tears blurring my path as I reached for the knob.

If she wasn't in there—

If something happened to her—

I jerked the door open. Moonlight spilled in through the edges of the curtained windows, barely illuminating the outlines of furniture as my eyes adjusted to the shadows. I felt along the wall for the light switch, stumbling over something left on the floor. The plastic knob was cool against my fingers when I finally found it. My pulse moved to my ears. The air didn't feel right. It was too dense. Too sticky.

Like someone was in there.

Maybe she's in here sleeping. Or maybe it's someone else and Marissa went home and I'm overreacting.

I clicked the switch, bathing the room in light.

27

I SAW MARISSA'S MATTED DARK CURLS FIRST, CLUMPED against the sides of her head. Then the smear of red across her face, bright under the overhead light.

Blood.

No, that wasn't right. It was a smear of the standard Hornette-performance-red lipstick.

I blinked, digesting the tangle of blankets and disheveled shapes sprawled across the king-size bed.

Beau sat up and brushed the hair back from his forehead. There was a matching red smear on his grinning mouth.

"Hey, Supergirl. Y'all back from Eddie's already?"

Marissa sat up too, eyes wide and cheeks flushed like she'd been caught red-handed. Or, in this case, red-mouthed.

"Hey, Whit. Beau and I were just . . . talking." She cleared her throat, eyes jumping around the room to avoid my stunned face. Music played softly on a stereo near the nightstand. I'd been so worried about finding Marissa that it hadn't even registered.

"Right." I shook my head at the ridiculousness of it all. At the ridiculousness of *me*. "Right, sorry. I'll just get out of here and let y'all . . . talk."

Marissa's blushing face matched her lipstick smear.

I covered my mouth to hide a laugh, then clicked the light off and closed the door. I couldn't *wait* for Marissa to explain how this happened. I might have felt stupid about my over-reaction if I wasn't in shock. Marissa and the Beau.

I thought of our conversation at the Holy Donut earlier that week. Maybe if I had been a more attentive friend, I would have noticed the sparks between them. I would have been there for her.

When I rounded the corner, I didn't notice the person standing by the front door until I'd run smack into them.

Penny Ansel whirled around, blues eyes narrowing. She'd changed into black-and-gold Hornettes warm-ups. Her blond hair was pulled into a slick ponytail and her car keys were clutched in her hand like she'd either just arrived or was about to leave. I wondered who told her about the party.

"What are you doing here?" I asked, unable to mask my surprise. Like the football and cheer coaches, Mrs. B had firm rules about postgame drinking. It didn't stop most people, except for the Pennies of the world, who viewed rules as things to be staunchly followed, even if it made them unpopular. She'd probably come to see the action for herself so she could narc to Mrs. B.

"Of *course* you're here," she said in a voice that sounded more like a snarl. She shook her head and glanced toward the living room, where the music was blasting by a few more decibels. A Hornette started down the hallway toward us, then retreated in the other direction when she saw Penny. "Was this whole thing your idea? Are you trying to make me look bad?"

"What, by throwing a party?" I said innocently, even though that was clearly what she meant. "It's not my party. This isn't even my house."

She rolled her eyes. "I know it's not your house. But I saw you with Beau at the game and y'all looked *quite* cozy. Seems pretty convenient that everyone ended up at his place after you spent all night hanging on him."

I pressed my lips together to suppress a laugh when I thought of who was currently hanging on Beau. But judging by the look on Penny's face, she thought I was laughing at her.

"You know it's a tradition for the team to go out to dinner after the first game of the year. You had to ruin that for us, didn't you? Just like you had to ruin the first-day decorations. You just can't stand the idea of us moving on without you." She shook her head.

"I had nothing to do with—"

Penny held up a hand. "Where's your little sidekick? I need to talk to her."

"I think she's changing?" I lied, knowing that if Penny was looking for her it couldn't be good. That, and if Marissa heard Penny refer to her as my *little sidekick*, Penny would lose one or more appendages. "I'll go look for her—"

"Actually I need to talk to you, too."

Penny's hand snaked out and grabbed my wrist. I thought of Kevin, grabbing me like he wanted me to break. Even Penny deserved better than him.

"Okay." I took a step back and yanked my wrist free of her grasp. "I have something I should tell you, too."

"I bet you do." She crossed her arms, face pinching in a look of disgust. "I know what you did. Don't even try to deny it."

"What *I* did?"

"What I did?" she parroted, voice taking on a nasally, mocking tone. When we were kids, I used to think that voice was funny. Now she just sounded like a bully. "I know you kissed Kevin. Don't even try lying."

"*I* kissed Kevin? Hardly. I had to shove him off me." I scoffed. "Kevin isn't a good guy, Penny. That's what I need to talk to you about."

Penny let out a snort of disgust. "Right, how convenient. Now that I know what you did, you suddenly want to talk to me." She stepped toward me, her normally blue eyes arctic. "I heard you *begged* him to come over to your house—that you used your dead grandma to make him feel guilty, and then you threw yourself at him. No wonder you were asking me all those questions at the rec center. You're obsessed."

"Is that what he told you? That's not even close to what happened. He's the one who showed up at my house. I didn't invite him. And he's the one who kissed *me*. Penny, you need to listen. He's been following me—"

"*He's* been following *you?*" She let out another snort. "You're the one who parked in front of my house like a stalker. And you followed him to the grocery store. There is something seriously wrong with you. I can't believe we used to be friends."

It was my turn to snort. "Right, like you were ever really my friend. You only ever saw me as a threat."

"No, you just made it impossible to stay friends with you—and you ditched me for Marissa. Stop trying to turn this around. Not everything's about you, Whitney. Some of us actually have to work for the things we want in life."

"What's that supposed to mean?"

"It means that not everyone got to grow up in a dance studio

and have everything handed to them on a silver fucking plat-
ter. It means that you can't just take things that aren't yours
just because you want them." She took another step toward
me, close enough that I smelled the sticky-sweet scent of her
shampoo. "Stay the hell away from Kevin, and stay the hell
away from my team, do you understand me?"

"Or what?" I gritted my teeth.

"Or I may have to do something we'll both regret."

She reached for the front door and yanked it open, then
marched down the walkway without giving me a chance to
respond. She didn't even bother closing the door behind her.

Blood roared in my ears. I clenched my jaw, grinding my
teeth in frustration. How dare she show up making ridiculous
accusations, acting like all the drama between us was *my* fault.
She was the one who turned everything into a competition,
not me.

And what did she mean, she'd do something we'd both
regret? It didn't sound like an idle threat. It sounded like she
knew *exactly* what she'd do.

Or what she'd already done.

I jogged down the sidewalk after her but stopped cold when
I saw her car. Lights flashed on a large black SUV, big enough
that she had to hoist herself up to get inside. Had Penny always
driven that car?

Square headlights sat high on either side of the grille—the
kind that would make it impossible to see if you happened to
get stuck in front of them on a dark two-lane road. But that
wasn't what made my breath hitch in my throat.

It was the long scratches running across the bumper.

Penny turned to glare at me.

"What happened to your car?" I asked before she had a chance to shut the door. I stepped closer, bending down to inspect the damage. Sure enough, deep scratches ran the length of the bumper, surrounded by other dings and scrapes. They were the same height they'd be if she'd rear-ended a small car. Like Isaac's.

"It's none of your business."

It was too much of a coincidence, wasn't it? The scratches on Penny's car were in exactly the right places, and her SUV fit the description to a tee.

I rubbed the spot on my forehead, still sore from when it connected with the dash.

"Did you follow me after the game? Are you the one who rear-ended us?"

"For the love of God, can't you just leave us alone?" Penny said, then slammed the door in my face. The SUV roared to life and her tires squealed, leaving me staring in stunned silence as she tore down the street.

28

I WALKED NUMBLY BACK INTO THE HOUSE, MY HEAD spinning and temples throbbing. It was all too much.

The music from the living room had gotten even louder—the walls rattled with bass. I headed toward the kitchen, expecting to find Isaac and the other girls still playing assassin. Instead, I found an empty tequila bottle and a vacant table. I followed the living room noise and saw a makeshift dance floor was in full force, bodies grinding to the music pulsing from the speakers.

I wanted to go home, but I couldn't leave until Marissa did. Instead, I hastily texted Will what happened and asked what time he'd be here tomorrow. He'd know what to do next. He'd be able to help. Maybe he'd go with me to talk to the police. Maybe the recording, texts, plus Will's account of what happened to the Mustang was enough to get them to look at Kevin or Penny as potential suspects.

I surveyed the crowd for Isaac but didn't see him. When I turned, I found Jenny watching me.

"Hey," I said awkwardly.

Her dark eyes studied my face, like she was looking for something. She looked lighter without the cloud hovering over her head, as if the shadow of potential death had been weighing her down.

"I'm glad you went to the doctor," I said before I could stop myself, then realized what I'd done. What was wrong with me?

"How did you know I went to the doctor?" Her eyes narrowed.

"I didn't— I just assumed—" I stammered, trying to backpedal.

She blinked at me, then let out a sound that was somewhere between laughter and disgust.

"I can't tell if you're messing with me or being serious." She tucked her dark hair behind her ears, shaking her head. "You know I canceled my appointment the day before you first told me to go to the doctor. I'm supposed to get checked out every year, but I've been in remission for so long I figured . . ." She shrugged. "I just wanted to put it all behind me. To be normal." She paused, like she expected me to say something. "Did you know that I canceled my appointment? Did someone put you up to this?"

"No." I swallowed, feeling trapped. I took a step backward, my back finding the wall.

"Then how did you know?"

I shrugged, trying to act like it was no big deal. Even though Gams's rules and warnings flashed inside my skull. "Does it matter?" I finally said.

She stared at me for a beat more without saying anything. Then Olivia marched over and grabbed Jenny's hand, tugging her toward the dance floor. The gold fringe on Olivia's uniform shimmied.

"Come on," she said. "Let's dance." Then she looked at me and smiled. "Hey, Whitney. I thought you left."

"No, I just . . . needed some air."

Jenny looked like she wanted to say something else, but I kept my eyes trained on Olivia, grateful for the distraction.

"Have you seen Isaac?" I said.

Olivia shook her head. "He wandered off somewhere with Veena." Her eyes lit with realization. "Wait, are y'all, like, a thing?"

"No. Maybe. I don't know. It's complicated." But was it? He'd seen Kevin kiss me. He'd invited Beau to the game. Maybe the moment in the car was nothing more than an attempt to comfort me after the road rage incident. Maybe Veena's flirting had worked. I thought of the empty bedroom I'd stumbled into while searching for Marissa.

Maybe it wasn't empty anymore.

"Do you have another one of those?" I asked, pointing at Olivia's White Claw. She motioned to the case on a nearby end table, then watched with a smirk as I cracked open a can.

"I didn't know you drank."

I shrugged and took a sip. It didn't taste as bad as I expected.

My brain flashed back to the way Isaac had watched Veena's hair tumble free from her hat, the way she kept touching her mouth, like she wanted to guide his eyes there.

Olivia tipped her head back and took a long swig. I did the same.

I closed my eyes and saw the two headlights roaring up behind Isaac's car as a gray cloud danced over his head. Then felt the swell of panic as I ran from room to room, so sure something horrible had happened to my best friend. I saw the dark clouds scrawled on slips of paper and smeared against my windshield. I saw Marissa's face earlier, when she'd asked me if I pulled her to safety *before* the gunshots started.

I took another, longer sip. Then another and another until my drink was empty and I had to get a new one.

Someone turned the music up. It vibrated through the room, rattling the walls and the floor. I wished it could rattle the thoughts out of my head.

"I love this song!" someone shouted, raising their hands over their head as they started to move. I followed, letting my feet find the rhythm.

"Me too!" I shouted, even though I'd never heard it before. It felt good to move. To dance. And I *did* like the song, whatever it was. It was loud and pulsing and numbing and perfect.

Pulsing. That was a funny word. I laughed, then jumped up to touch the low-hanging wooden beams that ran up and down the living room's ceiling. I missed and tried again.

Another song started, then another. My drink was suddenly empty again, and I realized that the second one tasted better than the first. I reached for another. Beau was right—I needed to have more fun. Why didn't I have more fun? This was way better than moping around.

Sequins sparkled all around me. The room felt heavier and I danced harder, feeling sweat pool along my hairline. People made a circle around me, moving back to give me space. I did the robot and laughed when everyone else laughed. Time slowed and sped up as the room bounced. The music ran through me.

Somewhere in the house Veena and Isaac were tangled together, his hands on her skin, her fingers in his hair. I should have kissed him when I'd had the chance. But then again maybe Isaac was better off without me. I didn't deserve him, did I? I was a selfish person who made bad things happen. I was the kind of person who saved the Dwights of the world and wreaked havoc.

My drink was empty again. How'd that happen? I should get another drink.

Kevin's face popped into my head, and I felt a hot spike of anger. How could I not have seen what a terrible person he was? How could Penny not see? I should call her and tell her about Dwight. I should tell her that her boyfriend might be a murderer.

Unless she was the murderer. Unless it's been her this whole time.

I thought of Penny and the gashes on her bumper that matched perfectly to the gashes on Isaac's bumper.

Why wait for my brother to get here? I could call the police now. Leave an anonymous tip telling them that Penny was in a hit-and-run. They would have to check it out, wouldn't they?

I stumbled out of the circle. Everything felt bouncy.

I flopped onto the couch, laughing at the looseness of my limbs. What was I looking for again? I couldn't remember. Oh, right. My phone. Where'd I put that thing?

"You're quite the dancer."

I turned my head. The room followed a second later. Isaac was perched on the arm of the couch, his hands in his pockets. When'd he get here?

"Thanks." I searched his mouth for Veena's lipstick, but my eyes couldn't focus.

"Let me know when you're ready to go home. I'll give you a

ride." His blue eyes looked dark in the dimly lit room.

"What about Veena?" I giggled when I said her name. It felt sticky inside my mouth.

He arched an eyebrow. "How about I get you a glass of water?"

I let my head fall back against the seat. It felt good to flop.

Isaac came back a few seconds later and pushed a sweating glass of water into my palm. He kept his hand under the base and guided it to my lips.

"You don't drink very often, do you?" he asked.

I shook my head. The room shook with it. "Beau says I'm not fun."

"Oh, I'd say you were having plenty of fun out there." He pressed the glass to my mouth again, forcing me to take another large swallow. "Do you think you can handle the car ride home, or should I get you another glass of water? How many beers did you have, anyway?"

I held up three fingers. Then four. Then three again. I couldn't remember. "I had White Claws. The raspberry ones. But they didn't really taste like raspberry."

The dimple appeared on his cheek. A perfect little *C*. I reached out to touch it, then laughed when I realized I'd just poked him in the face.

He took my hand and gently pulled it away, then grabbed my other hand to help me stand. "Come on, let's get you some fresh air."

The room tipped as I stood. Everything was in motion, like I'd done too many fouettés without spotting. I grabbed on to Isaac's arm to steady myself.

"Is this how drunk you were on the night I saved your

life?" I asked. My mouth had a mind of its own.

"When you saved my life?" Isaac smirked, then placed a hand on the small of my back to steer me out of the living room. "I think you might have me beat on level of drunkenness. You're kind of a lightweight. Here, let's get you outside."

He kept his hand on my back while he maneuvered the front door open. I let him guide me to one of the wrought iron benches flanking the porch, then plunked down. It wasn't as comfortable as the couch. Maybe I should go lie down on the couch?

The moon was hidden under a thick blanket of clouds. Where the light from the porch ended, shadows stretched out in dark, inky pools. It made me think of the dark farm road. Of the darkness I'd seen ghosting over Isaac's head.

"You okay?" Isaac asked, taking a seat next to me. "You look a little green."

Everything spun too fast.

"I think I might be sick." I leaned forward to steady myself. He reached a hand up toward my hair, gently pulling it back from my face.

"Just in case."

I wished everything would stop spinning so I could focus on the warmth of Isaac's hand on my back. Maybe if I scooted closer, he would kiss me. I bet he was a good kisser.

I meant to close the inch of space between us so that our legs would touch. Instead I lurched forward, barely missing Isaac's shoes when I puked.

29

I WOKE UP WITH AN ARMAGEDDON-SIZE HEADACHE, STILL in my clothes from the previous night. I'd managed to get my shoes off and my body under the covers, but I hadn't bothered to remove my shirt or jeans, both of which smelled like puke. Or was that my hair?

The night came back in jerking flashes. The way my vomit sounded when it splattered on the pavement, the feel of Isaac's hands as they held my hair back from the deluge, the stupid things I'd said to him on the blurry ride home.

"I wish you wanted to be my (hiccup) boyfriend. But I don't blame you. I'm not a good (hiccup) person. I want to (hiccup) save everyone (hiccup) but I can't because of what happened. So I don't (hic) blame (hic) you (hic) for (hic) not (hic) wanting (hic) to be with me."

When we finally got to my house I'd realized my purse was still at Beau's, so there was a bumbling search for the key Mom kept hidden. (*I think it's under this rock. No wait, that one. Or is it that big one?*) To cap the fabulous night off, I was pretty sure (although the blurry stop-motion memory made it hard to be certain) that I'd tried to kiss Isaac. *Tried* being the operative word.

I wanted to find a very large rock, or mountain, to disappear under.

The worst part was that I couldn't clearly remember everything I'd told him. The ball of dread in my stomach told me I might have confessed more than my memories could serve up. What if I'd told him about last year? Or worse, what if I'd told him about the darkness?

The only saving grace was that I'd somehow remembered to turn off the alarm so that my mother didn't wake up when I stumbled through the door and put myself to bed.

Now, fingers of muted afternoon light filtered through the slats of my blinds, jabbing into my skull like an accusation. The clock read 12:30, but it felt like I'd only just closed my eyes.

I pried myself up from my bed and managed to stumble into the bathroom.

Ouch, ouch, holy hell ouch.

When I walked back into my room I found my mom sitting on my bed, hands folded in her lap and mouth pressed into a thin line. Maybe she hadn't been asleep when I came home last night after all.

"Sorry to startle you," she said when she saw my face. She looked tired. "Mrs. B called. She's worried—she's been trying to call you all morning, but your phone keeps going to voice-mail. Is everything okay?"

"Mrs. B? Did she say what she wanted?" I wrapped my robe more tightly around my body, wishing I could disappear inside it.

Mom smoothed her hair back against her head, tucking a few loose strands behind her ears. "No, but didn't you say you talked to her about rejoining the team? Maybe she wants to talk about that."

Her face was hopeful, but I felt the color drain from mine. If Mrs. B just wanted to talk about the team she could have done it on Monday, at school. Calling on a Saturday must mean bad news.

"Is everything okay?" Mom studied my face. "Where's your phone?"

"I must have left it in Marissa's car when she dropped me off last night." *Shit*, I had no idea what happened to Marissa. I needed to check on her. I had to get my phone back. "Can I borrow your car to get it?"

"Sure." She stood, glancing around my room and wrinkling her nose. "You should open a window. Something smells funky in here."

Last night's clothes were in a pile on the floor. I moved to block them from her view.

"You okay?" I asked my mom, eyeing her sleep-filled eyes.

"Yes, just tired." She gave me a weary half smile. "I haven't been sleeping well. I've been swamped with work, which isn't helping." She pinched the bridge of her nose and closed her eyes.

We hadn't spoken much about Gams or anything else since the night of Will's accident. Maybe losing Gams affected her more than I realized.

"You should take some time off," I offered. "Give yourself a break." I felt a tiny twinge of guilt knowing that Will and I had added to her workload when he'd erased her presentation.

"It's fine," she said, forcing the corners of her mouth into a barely passable smile. "Just a busy time at the office."

I opened my mouth to say something else but stopped when

I realized I was the last person who should dole out grief advice. I'd run halfway across the country to escape my problems, and what good had that done? Maybe hiding behind a mountain of work was her version of running to San Francisco.

"Oh, I almost forgot." She turned to look at me just before leaving my room. "Will called. He's got a massive test on Monday and he should be studying, but for some reason he has it in his head that he's going to come up here this weekend. Can you please tell him to stay there so he can focus? He doesn't need us distracting him."

My stomach squeezed, but I nodded. She was right. It was better if he stayed put.

I had a vague, blurry memory of looking for my phone last night with plans to call the police about Kevin and Penny. Maybe drunk-me was onto something. I may not have any physical evidence, but Isaac could vouch that someone tried to run us off the road. And Penny's dinged-up bumper might be enough to at least make them consider talking to her. We should have dumped the alcohol and called the police last night. If I hadn't been in such a hurry to check on Marissa, maybe this would all be over.

Although maybe it was. The deadline had come and gone. Maybe last night's incident was a last-ditch effort to scare me into confessing. Maybe they were finally ready to give up. The idea made the ball of dread that had taken up residence in my stomach these past couple of weeks unwind just the tiniest bit.

"The keys are in the bowl by the front door," Mom said. "Call if you're going to be longer than an hour, okay? I still have a few errands to run."

I nodded, even though I had no intention of staying any longer than necessary.

～ ～

The sky was a thick ceiling of gray clouds, matching my mood. Rain fell in a steady drizzle, turning the world into a smudgy charcoal drawing.

I eased Mom's car through a puddle as I parked in front of Beau's house, my stomach clenching at the Accord already parked there.

Of *course* Isaac was at Beau's. They were practically welded at the hip. Why hadn't that occurred to me before I left my house? Another vision of me trying to kiss Isaac assaulted my brain, and I squeezed my eyes shut. I must look beyond pathetic to him.

I climbed out of the car and ran to the porch, wishing I had thought to bring an umbrella. That, and maybe a time machine.

Get in, grab your purse, and leave. He doesn't even have to know you're there.

I knocked instead of ringing the doorbell, praying that Isaac wouldn't answer. I might not be able to avoid him forever, but I could certainly try.

Thankfully Beau opened the door, looking rumpled in a pair of loose-fitting shorts and a dark T-shirt. His face exploded into a grin when he saw me standing on the stoop.

"Supergirl! To what do I owe the pleasure? If you came to clean up your puke don't worry about it. My cousin took care of it this morning."

I winced when he motioned toward the bench where the

contents of my stomach had erupted. *In and out. I could do this.*

"I think I left my purse here last night. Any chance you found it?"

"Haven't seen it, but you're welcome to come in and look." He opened the door so I could step through, then padded into the house behind me, his bare feet slapping the floor. They were comically large, like feet you'd find inside a clown's shoe.

The tables were cleared of cans and the rugs looked freshly vacuumed, but the sour, yeasty smell of beer lingered in the air. My still-delicate stomach squirmed.

Isaac, mercifully, was nowhere in sight.

Beau picked up a plate of what looked like a half-eaten bologna sandwich with mustard oozing out the sides. He threw himself onto the couch and pushed the sandwich in my direction. Cue the stomach gurgles.

"You want one?" he asked.

"No thanks." I kept my eyes off his lunch and began lifting couch cushions and pushing aside throw pillows. The last time I recalled seeing my bag I'd been in the living room. Not that I could rely on my alcohol-blurred memories.

"I'd offer you a drink," Beau mumbled through a mouthful of bologna, "but I'm pretty sure you drank everything last night. I have to say, I didn't think you had it in you. I'm so proud. It's like my little girl's all grown up." He fake-brushed a tear from his eye and held up a hand to high-five me. I ignored him and moved to the love seat on the other side of the room.

"You're sure you haven't seen it?" I asked again, ducking to look underneath the couch. There were dust bunnies and some loose pocket change, but no purse.

"What did it look like?"

"Like a purse. You know—small. Black. Purselike."

"Like this?" called a familiar voice from the kitchen.

Another vision from the night before assaulted me—Isaac jerking out of the way to dodge my puckered lips. Me, going in for a second try, only to have him duck out of the way again.

Now would be a great time for the earth to swallow me whole.

I turned to find Isaac leaning against the wall, a smirk on his face and my purse dangling from his outstretched fingers.

"Oh, that," Beau said, like he suddenly remembered he had purses lying around his house by the dozen and couldn't be bothered to keep track of them all. "I thought maybe the chicken nugget left it so she'd have an excuse to come back. Y'all do that kind of thing, right?" His voice was hopeful.

"More like you hid it so Marissa would have to come back and see you," Isaac said to Beau before pushing off the wall to hand me my bag. "Someone must have kicked it under the couch. I found it there when I was cleaning up. I figured you'd be back for it so I charged your phone. It's been buzzing non-stop."

He wore a baseball cap with the brim pulled low over his forehead, but it did little to camouflage his amusement.

"Thanks." I slid the strap over my shoulder, keeping my eyes firmly planted on the ground. The awkward pause that followed stretched on for the better part of an eternity, punctuated by smacking lips as Beau chewed on his disgusting sandwich.

"I should go," I finally said, staring at the brim of Isaac's hat so I didn't have to look him in the eye. "My mom needs the car."

I turned before I lost my nerve and marched toward the front door. Isaac's footsteps weren't far behind.

"Whitney, wait." He caught the door when I tried to shut it behind me and wedged his way onto the porch. I heard the smile in his voice. "How are you feeling? Did your mom wake up when you went inside last night?"

"I'm fine, all things considered. And no, thank God."

His dimple was out in full force. My blood did little piqué turns beneath my skin, but unless the earth planned to slurp me into its center afterward, I didn't want to stand around and rehash last night's mistakes.

"Look, I really have to get going. I told my mom I wouldn't be long."

I meant to spin around and walk back to the car, shoulders thrown back like I didn't care that I'd nearly puked on his shoes or attempted to mouth-molest him last night. But instead I stared limply at his black hole of a dimple, suddenly sympathetic to moths and flames.

"Whitney." He said my name softly, like it was a secret. "I was worried about you. You said some pretty strange things last night."

I closed my eyes. Rain splattered against the porch. The memories strobed inside my skull. What had I said? How much had I told him?

"Like what?" I asked, even though my skin felt too tight and my brain screamed at me to get the hell out of there.

"Something about saving people. About . . . knowing things. I don't know, you were slurring a lot. It didn't all make sense." I swallowed. Jesus, what was wrong with me?

"And," he continued, "you kept talking about Veena. I think you were jealous." He chuckled, shaking his head. "You know nothing happened with her last night, right? I mean, she's a nice girl, but . . ." He reached for his hat and turned it so the bill faced backward, exposing his eyes. "I like someone else."

He reached out and slid his fingers between mine, weaving our hands together. I sucked in a breath, sure that he would jerk his hand back, insert a *but*, or do something equally devastating, because how could he not after last night? But his hand stayed put, fingers points of fire against my skin. The only movement came from the trees shifting in the rain.

Shhh, they said. *Be still.*

I didn't move when his arm slid around me, afraid that if so much as a hair stirred the spell would break. I didn't move when his face leaned toward mine, or when his other hand danced across the edge of my jawline, soft as the satin of a ballet shoe. It was only when our lips pressed together that I finally let myself sink against him.

I melted, re-formed into a girl, then melted again.

When we broke apart, I couldn't stop the smile from twirling across my face. Isaac made time travel possible. I didn't feel like the girl who made horrible things happen. That girl was far away in San Francisco waiting for the fog to swallow her. This girl, with her burning lips and idiotic grin, was a girl without regrets. There wasn't room in my brain to obsess about all the stupid mistakes I'd made because there was only

Isaac, Isaac, Isaac filling every nook and crevice inside me.

"I've wanted to do that for a while now," Isaac said.

"Me too," I replied, breathless, head still spinning at the turn of events. "But what about last night? You didn't want to kiss me."

He let out a loud laugh. "Well, yeah. You'd just puked a river. Plus you weren't exactly *you*, if you know what I mean." He reached up and brushed a hair back from my cheek. "I thought it would be better to wait until you weren't drunk."

"Right," I said. "God, you must think I'm such an idiot."

"Nah. It was kind of cute. You're usually so much more . . ."

"Uptight?" I offered, quoting Beau.

"I was going to say reserved." His smile made me want to leap across a stage—grand jeté, tour jeté, cabriole. "You were the star of the show on the dance floor last night. Maybe you can teach me some moves sometime?" He pumped his fists and smacked the air with his hand, then jerked his arms and torso around in what could only be described as the world's most awkward robot.

"Stop!" I said, covering my eyes with my hands. "Please. You're going to make me throw up again!"

"Is that even physically possible?" He reached out and took my hand again, looking at me in a way that sent all the blood in my body shooting to my cheeks in a single gravity-defying *whoosh*.

I wanted to ask him what it meant. But the trees and the rain whispered again, telling me to *shhh*.

"You sure you can't stay and hang out for a little while?" His face was hopeful, eyes round and pleading. I thought my head might turn into a balloon and float up into the sky.

I needed to call Will. I needed to check on Marissa. I needed to figure out what my next move was going to be. But something inside me fluttered to life, telling me that waiting an hour or two wouldn't hurt. Plus the deadline had come and gone. My stalker's plan had failed. Everyone was okay.

"I may have overexaggerated the urgency of my mom needing her car back," I admitted.

"Yeah? So you can stay?"

I nodded calmly, but what I wanted to say was *Yes, yes, yes, a million times yes.*

"Well, in that case, would you rather watch a movie or watch Beau play a fourth consecutive hour of *Grand Theft Auto*?"

"It's a tough call, but I'm going to go with movie."

Maybe Gams was right. Maybe things really could go back to their natural order.

Yessh, yessh, yessh, chorused the trees, like everything was going to be okay.

30

WE WERE OVER HALFWAY THROUGH *TOP GUN: MAVERICK* when my phone buzzed and I remembered that I was supposed to call Mrs. B back. I'd checked in on Marissa and Will, but somehow the primary event that triggered me coming to Beau's in the first place had completely slipped my mind.

"Shoot," I said, pulling my phone from my bag. Mrs. B's name flashed across the screen. "I gotta take this. Can you pause for a sec?"

"Sure," Isaac said, his smile mirroring my own perma-grin. Who was this grinning fool that had taken over my face?

"You better hurry if you want to finish the movie." Beau emerged from the kitchen, a Dr Pepper in his hand. "The vigil starts in a little over an hour and I promised the chicken nugget I'd be there to watch her tribute routine thingy."

"The what?" I said, glancing down at my buzzing phone. "Hold on."

I pressed accept, my mind swirling as I stepped into the other room.

What was Beau talking about? The tribute was last night.

"Whitney!" Mrs. B's voice cheered from the other end of the phone. "There you are. I was worried. Is everything okay?"

"Yeah, sorry. I just— My phone died." I squeezed my eyes shut. Something was niggling at the back of my mind. Something I was supposed to remember.

"Well, I'm so glad I caught you." Her voice was warm. "Did you have fun at the game last night?"

"Yeah. I mean, it was hard being there. But I'm glad I went. The halftime routine looked great." I glanced out the window, watching as tributaries of rain slid down the glass and merged into bigger streams. It was really coming down now.

"I'm so glad you think so." I could hear the smile in her voice. "The team worked really hard on it. They wanted it to be special." There was a heaviness to the last statement, the unspoken motivation of why the routine needed to be special weighing it down. "Anyway, that's not why I called."

"Right." My mind whirred with potential scenarios for what she might say, all of them bad.

"I wanted to thank you for your patience. I'm sure it's been frustrating that I haven't been able to give you an answer about the team, but I hope you understand. We only have enough uniforms and funding for thirty girls, and since we backfilled your spot it's put us in a little bit of a bind. That, and we've been worried that it might be confusing for the girls to have you go from officer to regular line member. We've had a bit of a challenging start to the year, as I think you know."

The pit in my stomach widened. Just as I'd feared, she'd called to tell me it was too late.

Initially I'd wanted to get back on the team to stay close to Penny and Kevin, but now that the opportunity was slipping from my fingers, I realized how badly I wanted this for *me*. I'd been stupid to think I could actually fix things.

"But," Mrs. B continued, "I ran some numbers with Principal O'Connell and we think we can make it work. You'll have to learn the routines outside of regular practice time, and since we've already set formations for the next two weeks you'll have to sit out the next few games. Which is fine, I think, because it will take at least that long to get you fitted for the new uniform."

"Wait, so . . . I'm back on the team?" My heart leaped into my throat.

"Yes, Whitney. You're back on the team. I'm so happy you decided to give us another chance. We've really missed you." There was pride in Mrs. B's voice as she spoke. "And I'm glad I was able to catch you before this evening. If you're up for it, I thought you might like to sit with the team at tonight's vigil. We won't have a uniform for you to wear, obviously, but I still thought it would be nice to have you join as part of the team."

"The vigil?"

"For the anniversary. I assumed you were going? They moved it to the auditorium because of the rain, but it's still on. Marissa worked so hard on the choreography for the tribute. It's really a beautiful piece. You're going to be so proud of her."

My ears rang. I squeezed my eyes shut, thinking of Marissa's face last night when I'd wished her luck on the tribute routine—she'd looked confused. I thought of all the times she'd brought it up and I hadn't been paying attention, her words tangling with the other thoughts swirling in my head. I thought of the posters littering the hallways at school. Of morning announcements. They kept mentioning a vigil, but I'd assumed it was part of Friday night's game—that the game and the vigil were one and the same. Not that I'd been paying attention lately. My head had been so filled with static that details seemed to slip in and out with ease.

"But the anniversary was last night," I croaked, my throat suddenly dry. Because even as I said it, I knew I was wrong. How could I have not put two and two together? I'd been so focused on the football game that I'd completely failed to realize that the anniversary of last year's tragedy wouldn't fall on a Friday again. That's not how calendars worked.

It would have to fall on a *Saturday*.

Mrs. B was silent for a moment on the other end of the phone. When she spoke next, the world split in two.

"Last night was just a game, Whitney. The anniversary is today."

31

BLOOD ROARED IN MY EARS, THE SOUND MATCHING THE
rain beating against the windows.

The anniversary was *today*. The vigil was *tonight*. I'd had it
all wrong.

I walked back to the living room on wobbly legs. The fear
must have been evident on my face, because Isaac stood, his
brows pinching into a look of concern.

"Are you okay? Did something happen?"

"No, I just—" I swallowed, trying to think of what to say.
Trying to make sense of the thoughts swirling in my head.
Would my stalker try something tonight at the vigil? Or
would they try something again like they did last night, when
they nearly ran me and Isaac off the road?

Maybe it was time to finally go to the police.

"What time did you say the vigil is?" I asked Beau, trying to
keep the panic from my voice. How long did I have?

"It's in a little over an hour. But the chicken nugget said to
get there early because there won't be as many seats now that
they moved it inside."

I glanced at my phone and saw that I had over two dozen
missed texts. Several were from Mom asking me to bring the
car back, but most were from Marissa asking what time I'd be
at the school.

Shit. How could I have gotten it so wrong?

I could go to the police now, but what if they didn't listen to me? I wouldn't have time to make it to school before the vigil started.

Of course it was possible that nothing bad would happen. Just like at the game, there would be too many people to try anything without an audience, if they were planning anything at all. But at the same time, if they did have something planned, I'd be the only one who would see the danger before it happened. I was the only one who could stop it. I couldn't just leave Marissa alone to fend for herself. I had to make sure she was safe.

Outside, the rain beat fists against the pavement. We were twenty minutes from the school, but with the rain it would take longer. I could go there now. Warn Marissa that something bad might happen and not to go anywhere alone.

Then I thought about Mom, alone in the house. Had I set the alarm when I left? Turned on the camera?

Panic rose in my chest. I couldn't think straight.

Isaac's hand touched my shoulder and I realized he was talking to me. I couldn't hear him over the blood pounding at my temples.

"I need to go home," I said, my voice like an echo inside my skull. "Could you follow me to my house so I can drop off the car and then give me a ride to the vigil?"

There was no other option.

⌇ ⌇

Twenty minutes later, I pulled into my driveway. Isaac's car slid in behind me, water sloshing onto the sidewalk as he skated through a puddle.

"I'll be right back," I shouted, the rain giving me an excuse to run up the walkway. It was coming down in sheets, the sky a solid wall of greenish gray.

"Hurry!" Beau shouted from the passenger-side window. "I want to get a good seat!"

Inside, I found Mom in the kitchen, a cookbook open next to her. I was relieved to see the empty space above her head—she was safe, at least for now. I had to make sure it stayed that way.

"There you are. I was beginning to worry—"

"I can't stay," I said, marching toward her and wrapping her in a tight hug. My heart was a bird in my chest. When I pulled back, I saw the confusion on Mom's face.

"Is everything okay?" she asked.

Tears welled in my eyes when I shook my head. There wasn't time to explain, and even if there was, she would never believe me. Instead, she was just going to have to trust me. Just this once, I needed her to listen.

"I can't explain—there's no time. But I need you to listen to me. Can you keep the doors locked and stay inside tonight? Please?"

Her brows furrowed. She looked back to her cookbook. There was a handwritten list next to it—probably what she was planning to get at the grocery store. Mom loved scouring her cookbooks for elaborate meals to make on Saturday nights.

"I'm serious," I said, my voice high and desperate. "I promise I'll explain everything once I'm back, but for now I just need you to trust me."

"Did something happen?" She brushed the hair back from

her face with a trembling hand. "You're scaring me."

"I know, I'm sorry. Call Will. He'll explain. Just—stay put. And don't open the door for anyone, okay? No matter what. I'm leaving the car here in case of an emergency, but please. Stay inside."

I gave her one final hug, then left her standing in the kitchen wearing a look that was a mix of fear and confusion.

On my way out, I set the alarm. Now I just had to hope like hell she'd listen to me.

"All set?" Isaac said when I slid into the back seat. I nodded and looked nervously out the window, watching the rain slide down the glass.

Please let me be wrong. Please let everything be okay.

Traffic was worse than I'd feared. An accident blocked the main road leading to the school and the side roads were back-logged from the rain. I drummed my fingers on my leg, trying to will the car to go faster. In the front seat, Beau screamed song lyrics, his voice comically off-key and so loud it drowned out the music. At least it made for a distraction. If anyone noticed my anxiousness, they didn't say anything.

A line of cars leading to the school snaked around the block. I craned my neck, trying to see where it ended. I didn't have time for this.

"I'm going to get out here," I said, opening the car door. "I'm going to see if I can catch Marissa before the show."

I didn't wait for them to respond, instead launching myself into the rain and making a run for the back entrance of the school that led to the gym and locker rooms. For our spring shows, we always had to get ready in the locker room because the auditorium dressing rooms were too small to fit the entire dance team. Chances were the team would be waiting there while the audience took their seats. Maybe I was being paranoid, but I needed to see Marissa as soon as possible. I needed to see for myself that there was no darkness ghosting above her head. I needed to make sure she was okay.

"We'll save you a seat!" Beau yelled at my back.

I fumbled my umbrella open as I sprinted toward the cover of the gym. The rain fell around me, pinging off the sidewalk and soaking my ankles.

I kept my head down, trying to avoid the deluge, and almost missed the figure crouched underneath the awning. Their face was covered by their hands, but I'd know that blond hair anywhere. It was Penny. She was crying.

It's not my problem, I thought, shaking rain from my umbrella as I reached for the door handle. At the same moment Penny let out a hiccupping sob, her body trembling with the fury of her tears.

"Penny?" I took a step closer. Instead of a costume, she wore her Hornette warm-ups. Her hair was in a messy ponytail and she wasn't wearing any makeup.

My heartbeat sped up, a sharp stab of panic racing down my spine. "Did something happen? Is the team okay?"

She looked up, her face folding into a scowl when she saw that it was me. I took a deep, relieved breath. Whatever it was, it couldn't be *that* bad if she was able to manage an eye roll.

"Of course it's you," she said, standing and wiping at her blotchy cheeks. "Of course it's fucking *you*."

"Are you okay?"

Penny made a scoffing sound. "Do I look okay?" She motioned to her face with her hand. "Not like you give a shit."

Penny's lower lip wobbled. Something in my guts twisted. I'd known Penny a long time, and I didn't think I'd ever seen her cry.

"Did something happen?" I asked, looking through the window behind her. It was nearly time for the vigil to start. The team should be lining up by now. Unless they were already in the auditorium. Unless I had it wrong. "Why don't we go inside—I can take you to the locker room and we can get you cleaned up."

I reached a hand toward her, but she jerked away.

"Just leave me alone," she said, eyes watering again.

"Penny—"

"I said leave me alone!" She jerked back from me like I was trying to hurt her.

"Fine," I said, reaching for the door handle. I was running out of time. "I was just trying to help."

I stepped inside the hallway, letting the door click shut behind me. Guilt immediately twisted in my gut. Why did Penny have to make things so difficult? But when I turned to go back outside, she was running through the parking lot, away from the school. Her hair matted to her head and her white Hornette warm-up jacket was immediately soaked. Rain battered the sidewalk, pounding in fat drops that sounded like marching feet against the pavement. I didn't have time to go after her.

My heart sank when I found the locker room empty. I was

too late. The team must be waiting backstage to go on, or seated in the audience with Mrs. B. Which meant I might not be able to see Marissa before the performance.

Still, I had to try.

I ran through the hallways toward the front of the school, my wet feet squeaking against the linoleum floor. I shouldn't have stopped to talk to Penny. I should have gone straight to the locker room. Or I should have gone straight to the auditorium with Isaac and Beau. What the hell was I thinking?

A crowd was gathered outside of the main doors. The overhead lights flicked on and off once. Twice. The show was about to start. *Shit.*

I rounded the corner toward the backstage entrance and reached for the handle. A hand snaked out and stopped me.

"You can't go back there." A boy dressed in all black crossed his arms over his chest, glaring at me. A constellation of pimples speckled his cheeks.

"I'm with the team," I said, then clarified, just in case another team was performing that night. "The Hornettes."

He looked me up and down and shook his head. "Only performers are allowed backstage. Sorry."

"Please," I begged, my voice catching. "I need to see my friend. It's important."

Another shake of the head. "Can't. Mr. O'Connell's orders."

He widened his stance, like he was a bouncer at a posh club and not some gangly tech kid taking his job way too seriously.

The lights flicked again, signaling a final warning to take seats. The few remaining people in the hallway scrambled toward the theater doors. I glanced once more at the kid, weighing my options. The look on his face told me he wasn't going to budge.

Suddenly the hallway was empty except for me and the boy. A shiver ran down my spine. I had the eerie sensation of being watched, but when I looked behind me there was no one there.

"You need to take your seat," the boy said.

Inside the auditorium, I heard music. An announcer.

You're fine, I told myself. *There's no one watching you.*

Then I walked as fast as I could toward the amphitheater doors.

32

THE THEATER WAS DARK AND PACKED WITH PEOPLE. Onstage, Principal O'Connell spoke into a microphone. Behind him, the show choir stood in a half circle holding flashlights made to look like candles.

I pressed myself against the wall at the back of the amphitheater, hands still trembling from the eerie sensation of being watched. At least here, I was in a crowd. I was safe.

Except being in a crowd hadn't saved anyone from Dwight last year, had it?

I shook the grim thought away. A scan of the audience told me there weren't any clouds—no immediate danger. I needed to stop freaking out.

A woman dressed in a dark blue suit stepped up to the podium. My heart lurched when she introduced herself as the mother of Ken Burgstrom, one of last year's victims. I squeezed my eyes shut, not wanting to see the way her chin quivered as she spoke. Not wanting to see the devastation I'd caused.

Instead, I scanned the audience again, looking for Marissa and the rest of the team. There was nothing but a sea of silhouetted heads. Would I even be able to see the darkness hovering over someone's head if it appeared now? Or would it disappear into the blackness, unnoticed?

Several more parents took the stage, warbling out stories

that left me gutted. A few made pleas for more gun control and mental health support at school. Then finally, they left the stage. A screen was lowered. Music began to play.

Marissa was the first to appear onstage, costumed in a long white dress. Her hair was in a slick bun, face somber. In her hand, she held a plastic candle, its faux flame flickering in the darkened theater. Marissa raised the light over her head at the same time she developpéd, her leg raising in a perfectly controlled arch. Behind her, a picture of the outside of Collin Creek High flashed, along with pictures of the eight students who'd lost their lives last year. Another dancer appeared onstage, joining Marissa as she swept her leg in a fan kick, dress sweeping like a butterfly wing. The image on the screen changed, this time showing the front of Robb Elementary School in Uvalde. A sea of faces appeared below it—nearly two dozen. Another dancer appeared onstage, then another, until the stage was filled with dancers in long white dresses holding candles, their legs rising to the music spilling from the speakers and the lights in their hands shining like beacons in the dark. With each girl who stepped onstage, another image of a school appeared, followed by pictures of kids smiling into the camera as if their lives were a long road spooled out in front of them.

Except their lives weren't roads. Not anymore.

It hit me like a punch to the gut—this wasn't just a tribute to the students *we'd* lost. This was a tribute to shooting victims from schools all over the country. Oxford High School. Saugus High School. Santa Fe High School. Marjory Stoneman Douglas High School. Marshall County

High School. Marysville Pilchuck High School. Sandy Hook Elementary School. And so, so many others.

All this time I'd only thought about the impact of Dwight's actions to my immediate community. And really, if I was being honest, the impact it had on me and those closest to me. But it was so much bigger than that. There were so many people who knew the pain we felt because they'd experienced it, too. So many hearts broken. So much devastation. How had I not seen it before? This wasn't just a single tragedy. This was an epidemic.

An epidemic I'd contributed to when I chose not to tell anyone what Dwight said to me.

I could have stopped it from happening.

I could have saved more people.

Bile rose in my throat. Suddenly the room was too hot. My clothes were too tight. The music was too loud and the room too cramped.

I knelt down, gulping in air. I couldn't breathe. I couldn't *breathe.*

I stepped toward the exit, reaching desperately for the door handle. I felt the cold bite of the metal beneath my palm.

Then the air split with a sharp, electronic whine and everything went black.

The music had cut out. The slideshow and stage lights had gone dark. The only light came from the battery-powered candles held by the dancers on the stage, but it was clear from their helter-skelter movements this was not part of the performance.

Had the storm caused the power to go out?

Murmurs filled the room. A few people shouted. Phone

flashlights clicked on. Outside, the rain thrummed against the auditorium roof.

Then the screen flashed white. There was another sharp cut of static, a long beep, and then an image flashed onto the screen. But instead of the images of schools and pictures of students from the slideshow, a picture of the front page of a newspaper appeared, the headline ripping through the darkness. Below it was the black-and-white photo of the outside of Collin Creek High with crime scene tape strung in front of the football stadium entrance.

8 SLAIN IN HALFTIME HORROR SHOW

My stomach dropped to my feet. It was one of the many headlines from last year. *Halftime Horror* was one of the media outlets' preferred nicknames, as if they'd had a competition to find the most gruesome alliterative title for the terrible event.

Murmurs of confusion filled the theater. A few people stood, shouting at the screen. Onstage, the Hornettes marched off toward the wings, their candles bouncing in their hands.

The screen jumped from the headline to a series of spliced-together news reports from last winter, each showing grim-faced news anchors bleakly delivering their updates into the camera. I pressed my nails into my palms.

"Nine confirmed dead so far, including the gunman—"

"Countless others injured, some still in critical condition—"

"It was the first game of the year, so the stands were packed—"

"—reports of people cowering behind seats—"

"It was horrible. He just kept shooting—"

"Among those confirmed injured, a North Dallas High biology and dance teacher. No updates yet on her condition—"

"A tragedy for this North Dallas suburb, simply a tragedy, bringing the question of gun control to the forefront yet again—"

"Police are looking for any information about the woman shown in a photo taken a few days before the shooting. They believe she may have information about the suspect's motives—"

"—possible she may have been an accomplice—"

The room spun as though attached to a string. I had the sudden sensation that I was outside my body, watching my too-pale face as it took in the horrors flickering across the screen. *The deadline.* This was really happening—this was their plan. I wanted to give my shoulders a sharp shake and scream at my unmoving form to *do something*. But my mouth felt welded shut and guilt pinned me in place with angry fingers, forcing me to watch.

Watch what you did, Whitney. Watch the death and devastation you caused.

Inside the auditorium there were shouts of outrage. Onstage, images snapped across the screen: people fleeing the stands, their screams cutting through the unseasonably cold September air; a circle of sobbing kids holding one another; a woman sobbing into a microphone, her white blouse speckled with red spots; a sandy-haired boy with a single dimple piercing his cheek, his shoulders wrapped in a blanket as a police officer knelt in front of him. A smear of blood snaked across his forehead—

He looked exactly like Isaac.

But no, that couldn't be right. Isaac couldn't have been there. He wasn't at the game that night. Right?

Unless he lied. Unless he's been lying this whole time.

My vision blurred. The image jerked away, replaced by another.

It was a photograph of that day on the roof—the day I saved Dwight. The same photo I'd found on my windshield. The same photo the police had posted in the weeks following the shooting, looking for any information about the person with Dwight. In it, two people stood near the edge of the roof, talking. One of them was clearly Dwight, but the other was unrecognizable—their face covered by a hat and scarf so that only a small stretch of blurry face showed.

Only Gams and I knew that the other person in the picture was me, or so I thought. Gams had made me promise not to tell anyone—she made me swear to keep it a secret.

"No one can ever know," she'd said. "There are too many conclusions people would jump to. It's better that we keep it a secret."

In the photo, we looked cozy—almost intimate. You wouldn't know from the picture that I was trying to convince him not to jump. You wouldn't know that I had barely been able to see his face through the thick black cloud storming around him. Outside of the oddity of the rooftop location it probably looked like we were two friends having a nice conversation.

Or two people plotting.

The image zoomed in just as another picture appeared on the

screen next to it—a photo of me in my old Hornettes uniform.

The audience's murmurs grew louder as everyone tried to figure out what was going on. A few people gasped in recognition.

Because when you put the photos side by side, even with the winter gear covering all but a sliver of my face, you could see the resemblance. The girl was the same height as me. The same build.

Words appeared on the screen below the image of me and Dwight and the side-by-side picture of me smiling.

WHITNEY LANCASTER KNEW WHAT
DWIGHT HAD PLANNED.

There were gasps as people took in the words. I shrank against the exit, grateful that the darkness hid me. My head buzzed with static.

The words disappeared, and another sentence replaced them.

SHE COULD HAVE STOPPED HIM.

The screen went dark. For a moment, I wondered if someone finally thought to pull the plug to make it all stop, but then the photo of me and Dwight flashed on the screen again, along with two final words:

SHE DIDN'T.

First there was silence, then everyone seemed to move at once.

It was my fault, I thought as it all rammed into me. *It was all my fault.*

And now everyone knew my secret.

33

PENNY WAS THE FIRST ONE WHO HAD NOTICED DWIGHT
Hacken watching the Hornettes practice after school. His pale
face hovered in the windows at the back of our rehearsal room,
watching as we ran through floor exercises.

"He's a creep," she'd told Mrs. B. "Is he allowed to gawk at
us like that?"

Mrs. B asked him to leave, but a few days later we saw him
again when we were rehearsing outside, this time sitting in
the stands by the football field, his dark eyes intense as he
watched us mark formations. There were other students in the
stands—on nice days it wasn't uncommon for people to gather
there—but Dwight was the only one who studied us, tracking
our movements like he was committing them to memory.

Mostly Dwight kept to himself, head bowed low like he was
trying to make it through the between-class crowds without
being seen. It was odd to see him so blatantly watching, like he
didn't care that we knew he was there. Maybe he was a creep
like Penny said. Or maybe he didn't have anywhere else to go
after school; maybe sitting in the stands gave him someplace
to be other than his home. Regardless, there was something
about him that made me feel both sympathetic and uneasy at
the same time.

I was on my way to meet Marissa the Sunday I saw him sitting at the stoplight.

An early fall cold front had crunched over North Texas, putting an abrupt end to our usually warm September. Icy fingers reached around me as I walked toward my car. My entire winter ensemble belonged to Gams—from the wide-collared black coat to the bulky scarf and hat. My coat was buried somewhere in the garage with the rest of our winter gear. I didn't expect to need it this early in the year. Thankfully, Gams didn't believe in tossing out clothing that she could still fit into, even if she hadn't worn it in nearly a decade.

A blast of wind shot down the street, ripping the knit hat from my head. It tumbled down the sidewalk, rolling end over end toward the intersection.

I'd just managed to catch the knitted tassel with the toe of my boot when I saw Dwight. His head was down and he was kneading the skin between his eyes. Then he slammed his hand hard against his steering wheel, yelling something at the empty interior.

A small black cloud rippled above his head.

Another car pulled up behind him, the driver waiting a beat before leaning on the horn. The honk jolted Dwight into an upright position. He scowled at his rearview mirror, then pulled the car slowly forward.

I thought of Dwight's pale face watching us in the stands and the palpable loneliness that followed him down the hallways. I didn't hesitate when I tugged the hat back over my head and ran back to my car.

His car zipped in and out of traffic, making it hard to keep pace with him. He drove faster the closer we got to downtown, and when he jerked his car toward an exit I almost missed it.

I followed him into a parking garage. The cloud above his

head thrummed like it was making up its mind, swelling in size and then shrinking back down to a small tuft of darkness. When he climbed out of his car, his coat wasn't zipped, the ends flapping in the wind. His ungloved hands hung loose at his sides.

I kept my footsteps soft as I followed to avoid attracting his attention. The buildings marking the Dallas skyline loomed like sentinels, staring down at me and the few other pedestrians brave enough to leave their heated cars to face the cold.

He walked like someone with a purpose, each step a decisive *thud* against the pavement. Instead of his usual hunched posture, his back was straight. His dark hair blew around his face, ears and cheeks red from the cold, but if it bothered him, he didn't show it. The only sign he even noticed the cold were his hands, balled up into fists at his sides.

I pulled my hat low over my head, wrapped my scarf high on my chin, and ducked my head as I followed Dwight into the seven-story office building. The lobby was eerily empty, but it was Sunday, so it made sense that no one would be there.

I slid into the elevator after him, angling my body so that I faced away.

The button for the top floor glowed. I pressed it, acting like I was in a hurry and needed the doors to close. Dwight kept his gaze focused on the digital numbers slowly counting up the floors. In the reflection of the metal doors I saw that the cloud had tripled in size, curling fingers of smoke spreading wider and wider with each second.

I had to change his mind. I had to save him.

The elevator rumbled as we approached the top floor, then lurched to a creaking stop. I looked down at my nails, pretending to be engrossed in something else so that he'd walk out first. Then I quietly followed his marching form down the dimly lit hallway.

He paused for a second before opening the door marked ROOF ACCESS but the cloud above his head didn't waver. I caught the door the second before it banged shut behind him, listening to his footsteps echo up the stairwell. I reached in my pocket for my phone, then realized I'd left it in my car. Instead, using my hat to keep the door propped open, I went into a nearby office and dialed 911.

"There's a kid on the roof of a building downtown," I whispered when the voice on the other end picked up. "I think he's going to jump. I don't know the address, but it's across the street from McMurry's restaurant. Tan bricks. Green awning. Please hurry."

I hung up before they could ask questions. Then I retrieved my hat from the door, shoved it onto my head, and walked up the flight of stairs leading to the roof.

Cold air slapped my face when I stepped onto the roof. I squeezed my elbows against my body and pulled my scarf up to cover my nose.

Dwight stood on the opposite side, a few feet from the lip of the building. Through the cloud, I saw that his head was bowed. I might have mistaken his pause for hesitation if it weren't for the confident darkness still storming around him.

"Why are you following me?"

I jumped, startled by the sound of his voice. He kept his back to me, head angled toward the street below.

I thought of Gams and her rules and how she always told me to leave the darkness alone—but how could I ignore this?

You can do this. You can help him. No one has to know.

"You looked like you could use some help," I answered. My voice sounded stronger than I felt. I forced my legs to move, boots crunching against the graveled roof.

"I don't need any help."

He took a step forward, then another, until he stood inches from the seven-story drop. The cloud thrummed. It looked hungry.

"I don't believe you." I moved closer. From the ground, the building hadn't seemed that tall relative to the other giants that made up the skyline. Now the sky felt too close; the seven floors beneath us felt like miles.

He laughed, a cold, dry sound. "So what? You're feeling guilty and you want to suddenly help me, is that it? Clear your conscience?"

"Clear my conscience?" I swallowed and shoved my hands deep into my pockets. What was he talking about?

He turned to face me, dark eyes meeting mine through the swirling darkness surging around him. His dark hair flopped back and forth against his head, tangling behind his exposed ears and catching in the moisture on his lips. He didn't bother to wipe the strands of hair from his face.

I shivered, this time not from the wind.

"You don't have to do this," I told him.

"What do you know about me and what I don't have to do?"

"I don't— I mean, I'd like to know. If you'll tell me. Whatever it is can't be so bad that you need to do this."

He let out a sharp bark of laughter and shook his head, disgusted.

"You and your friends are really something else, you know

that? You think you can treat people like shit one minute, then act like we're friends the next. You think the whole goddamn world revolves around you. Fuck you. You don't know anything about anything."

I took another step toward him, heart hammering in my chest. "Dwight, I don't know what you're talking about—"

"You're going to tell me that you didn't sic your dipshit boyfriend and his asshole friends on me?"

I shook my head, confused. "What? No, of course not."

He huffed out a foggy breath and looked back toward the lip of the building. "You know they used to piss on my gym clothes? They thought it was so funny the first time I put them on, not knowing—" He shook his head, eyes closed like he was watching it all play back. "They made me their personal punchline. And then last week I get jumped for minding my own business. Like I give a shit about your stupid dance team. Like I was watching *you* or something."

The threads knit together as I thought of Penny telling Mrs. B he was a creep for sitting in the stands, watching us rehearse.

"Are you saying that Kevin did something to you? And that he . . . did that to your gym clothes?" My throat went dry. Had I said something to Kevin about Dwight watching us practice? And if I did, Kevin wouldn't do something to him for it—would he?

He let out a disgusted huff, shaking his head. "Right, like you didn't know your boyfriend was an asshole. Like you didn't know he's always been an asshole. He's the worst of all of them." He glanced toward the ledge. Another gust of wind slammed against us and I wrapped my arms more tightly around my coat. "Everyone thinks I'm a joke. Everyone always thinks I'm a fucking joke." Dwight's voice trembled as he spoke. The cloud above his head rippled, black tendrils reaching down past his cheeks. "Even my own father thinks I'm a joke."

"I'm sure that's not true." The words sounded inadequate. "Please, Dwight, let me help you."

"I should teach them all a lesson. I could make them all sorry, you know?" He wiped his lips with the back of his hand, eyes looking everywhere but at my face. "I think about that a lot. About getting back at people. I have this fantasy where I walk into a game filled with all the people who ever laughed at me—like my dad and your fucking asshole boyfriend—and I've got a gun in my hand and *I'm* the one laughing. I finally get to make them the joke, you know?" He made his hand into an L, like he was holding a gun, and pointed it at me. "I could do it, too. It would be easy."

The cloud above Dwight's head quivered, pulsing in and out, in and out, like a dark creature trying to catch its breath. I took a step back from him. Something in his eyes had shifted. His pupils had gone wide, opening like a window. They reminded me of a cave where shadows and dark things slithered.

"You don't mean that." I had the sudden urge to step farther away from him, but instead I stepped closer. Because I could save him. I knew I could save him. Saving people is what I did. "Look, Dwight, whatever it is, whatever is going on with you, with your dad, we can get you help."

In the distance, a siren whined. Dwight leaned down and looked over the ledge, this time so close that I thought for sure he was going to jump. Except the cloud above his head had started to shrink. I was changing his mind.

"You called the police." A statement, not a question.

"I told you, I want to help. Please, Dwight, step back from the ledge. Let me help you. Whatever you need. I can talk to Kevin—tell him to stop."

Dwight gave a half-hearted laugh, shaking his head. "People like him don't stop."

He squeezed his eyes shut and when he opened them again they'd changed back to their original dark brown. He didn't look scary—he looked like a broken boy who needed my help.

"How did you know to follow me?" he asked.

"Just a hunch." His pleading eyes and the shrinking cloud told me I was getting through to him, so I continued. "You're not alone. Please don't do this, Dwight. Please."

I reached out my hand toward him. His Adam's apple bobbed when he swallowed, and in that moment he looked so sad and so incredibly helpless.

Somewhere nearby, someone must have snapped a photo. Maybe from a nearby building—close enough to see the two of us standing together at the roof's edge but too far to capture details of my face hidden behind the tightly wrapped scarf and hat.

Dwight smiled a sad smile, and the darkness above his head pulled in on itself until it was barely a smudge—barely even a shadow.

"Thank you," he said. "Your nickname suits you."

I smiled, my chest swelling with pride. "I should go before the police arrive. It will be easier if they think it was a false alarm, don't you think?" I eyed the now empty space over his head. Gams's rules circled inside my head, warning me to steer clear of the authorities and their questions.

276 ~

"Right," he said, giving me a small smile. "I'll tell them someone made a mistake and I was just checking out the view."

"You're going to be okay, Dwight. I promise." I hoped he felt the sincerity of my smile.

He jutted his chin toward the opposite side of the roof, where there was another door labeled ROOF ACCESS.

"You can get out that way."

I hesitated, just for a second, thinking of what he'd said about making people pay. Of the L shape he'd made with his hand. He didn't mean it. He couldn't mean it. It was just an idle threat from a boy in pain. Plus the cloud above his head was gone; the danger had passed. There was no need to involve anyone else.

Below, I heard car doors slamming. Sirens screamed more urgently.

"Take care of yourself," I finally said. Then I shoved my hands into my pockets and walked toward the door on the opposite side of the roof.

That Friday we played the Collin Creek Wild Cats at their home turf. Most away games were sparsely attended by the visiting team, but the first game of the year always drew a big crowd. The stands were packed. There was an electric charge to the air—the excitement of football season kicking off and the Hornettes' first big performance.

The audience jumped to their feet when we hit our ending pose at halftime, the sound of applause thunderous. Mrs. B was in the front row, hands cupped around her mouth as she cheered, and I knew we'd nailed it. Missy Allen, the captain, counted us down. Then we started our synchronized march off the field and into the locker room, our grins wide and chests heaving with the adrenaline of a perfect performance.

I don't know why I looked behind me, but something pulled my head back to the crowd. Something made me break formation and look.

There, in the audience—a dark cloud. It appeared in a blink, and then just as quickly another appeared. Then another. And another. Each one unfurled above its victim like a sail, pulsing and undulating as if a breeze had blown through the stadium. I'd never seen more than one at a time.

"What are you doing?" Missy hissed. "You're holding up the line!" She grabbed my arm and pulled me toward the waiting locker room, motioning for the other girls to keep moving. Then she shoved me inside with both hands. "What is *wrong* with you?" she shouted, mad that I'd broken formation. Mad that I'd ruined our perfect exit. But my eyes were on the door—at the girls still making their way off the field. Marissa was one of the last girls in the line.

There was a smudge of darkness hovering over her head.

No.

I shoved past Missy and the other girls gathering around the benches, oblivious grins on their faces. There were no clouds over their heads—everyone inside the locker room was safe. I had to get Marissa off the field and away from whatever was about to happen.

I found my voice even though my heart had moved to my throat.

"Get inside!" I screamed, my eyes on Marissa as I pushed through the line to get to her, a salmon swimming downstream. "You have to get inside!"

She must have heard the terror in my voice, because she didn't hesitate. She rushed forward, pulling the remaining girls with her as I held the door open and frantically shoved people through.

I saw Dwight just as Marissa crossed the threshold, a dark cloud storming over his own head. He was holding a gun.

I slammed the door shut, chest heaving as I held it closed so that no one could get out. The cloud over Marissa's head folded in on itself, the danger now on the other side of the door.

There were so many choices I could have made that night. I could have rushed the field and tried to tackle Dwight. I could have shouted to warn the crowd. I could have gone into the stands and tried to move the people with darkness thrumming over their heads out of the way.

I could have, I could have, I could have.

Instead, I held the locker room door with white-knuckled fierceness, my eyes never leaving the space above Marissa's head. Even when we heard the first pop of gunfire. Even when we heard the shouts and screams and the *thump*ing of shoes against the metal stands as people fled for the exits.

That day, I chose Marissa.

That day, I learned that choices are like dominoes, each one piling on top of the next until there's nothing left but a pile of destruction.

34

THE DARKENED AUDITORIUM WAS FILLED WITH SHOUTS. Onstage, the video had gone dark but it was clear from the frantic shadows bouncing around the auditorium that no one had control of the situation.

It shook something awake inside of me. I had to get out of there before the houselights came on. I had to get away before anyone saw me.

I heaved myself against the exit and into the hallway. By the backstage entrance, a cluster of dance team girls were talking animatedly. Marissa was one of them. Her head snapped up and we made eye contact. There were tears staining her cheeks.

She'd seen the video. She knew.

Run, I thought. *Get out. Head to the back of the school, away from the auditorium.*

I ducked my head and ran, winding through the hallways until I reached a bathroom. At my back, I thought I heard Marissa call my name, but I didn't stop. Instead, I threw myself into one of the stalls and pressed my fingers into my eyes like I could press everything back inside. My whole body shook from cold, but at the same time I was sweating. Outside, the rain pummeled the building like fists beating against a wall.

Behind my eyelids, the horrible words from the projection screen glowed bright.

SHE COULD HAVE STOPPED HIM.
SHE DIDN'T.

Now everyone in school knew that I had a hand in what happened at the game. They'd probably think I was an accomplice—why else would I have kept my connection to Dwight a secret all this time? If things were reversed, it's the same conclusion I would have come to.

People are afraid of the things they don't understand.

My stalker warned me, and I didn't listen. I'd assumed that if I kept my family safe and kept myself surrounded by people everything would be okay. It never occurred to me that if I didn't confess, they'd do it for me.

I thought of Will's confident voice telling me that if I confessed, I'd get arrested. That my silence made me culpable.

The restroom door creaked opened. Footsteps *thunk*ed toward my stall.

"Whitney?" Marissa's voice echoed off the tile. "Whitney, I know you're in here. I can see your shoes." She tapped on the door. "Come on, you can't hide in here forever."

Couldn't I?

I sighed and undid the lock, letting the stall door swing wide. Marissa looked like something a tornado blew in—eyes wild, hair coming loose from her bun.

"Is it true?" she said, her voice low. Her eyes were wet. "Did you know what Dwight was going to do? Could you have stopped it from happening? Is that why you've been acting so weird?"

I swallowed, unsure what I was supposed to say. Unsure how I was supposed to explain it all. The pressure behind my eyes was hot and pulsing.

Marissa looked around the bathroom to make sure we were alone.

"I was right, wasn't I? You pulled me into the locker room *before* any shots were fired. You *knew*."

I paused, then nodded. My tongue felt like sandpaper. When I spoke, my voice didn't sound like my own.

"I was trying to keep you safe."

"What were you doing with him in that picture? Were you *friends* with him?"

"No— I followed him. I thought he was going to hurt himself. I was trying to talk him out of doing anything stupid before the police could arrive. Someone must have taken a picture of us while we were up there on that roof. He was saying all this stuff about getting back at people for laughing at him, but I didn't think he meant it. I didn't think he would actually *shoot* anyone. I swear."

"So then how did you know to pull me into the locker room?"

I shook my head. A tear broke free and slid down my cheek, and the dam inside me threatened to burst. My next sentence was a whisper.

"Would you believe me if I told you I know things like that sometimes?"

Marissa grunted and wiped her nose with the back of her hand. "Of course I would."

She walked toward the mirror and tried to smooth the fly-away curls back into her bun. Her reflection looked at me with red-rimmed eyes.

"When we were younger I told myself it was all just a coincidence. Right time, right place, that kind of thing. But deep down I knew better. There was something different about you. You could . . . I don't know, see when people were in trouble? It happened too many times for me *not* to know."

I closed my eyes. Outside, the rain drummed. A continuous thrum seemed to come from every corner of the room—the storm against the building, my pulse inside my ears, a steady *drip, drip, drip* from one of the faucets.

Gams's warnings rang in my ears. Outside, thunder broke the sky.

Marissa bit at her cuticle, studying me. I couldn't read her expression, but I knew whatever she was thinking couldn't be good.

"Could you have stopped him?" she finally asked.

I thought about the darkness I'd seen in the stands, snapping like sails in an unseen breeze. I'd never seen more than one cloud at a time. Could I have saved all of them? Or was the darkness giving me a choice—asking me to pick and choose who got to live and who had to die?

Maybe it didn't matter, because I had chosen, hadn't I? I hadn't hesitated. Given the choice between a crowd full of strangers and my best friend, I chose my best friend.

I squeezed my eyes shut.

Maybe I'd never know if I could have saved everyone that night or just some of them, but I knew I could have made a different choice. So many clouds over so many heads, and I'd only chosen one.

"I don't know for sure, but . . ." I blinked back tears. "Yes, I think so."

"Why didn't you?" Marissa's lower lip trembled, and I

wondered if she already knew the answer. If she'd always known, and that's why she kept having flashes of me pulling her into the locker room before a shot had been fired.

"Because I chose to save you."

I'd made so many impossible choices, but she hadn't been one of them. Really, when I thought about it, saving Marissa hadn't been a choice at all.

A low guttural sound escaped her lips. Her hand was on her mouth. Her fingers shook. Her eyebrows quivered. In that moment, she seemed so small and vulnerable. People always commented about Marissa's size, but she never seemed small to me. Not like this. Not like now.

I hated that I made her feel like this.

That's when the tears broke free, sliding down my face like the rain outside. Something between a hiccup and a sob burst from me. Then a cry ripped out of me like it had claws, thick and heaving and horrible. I reached for the roll of toilet paper mounted to the wall to try to stanch the onslaught. Outside, the wind howled. When my eyes were finally clear enough to see, I saw that Marissa had moved to stand by the door.

"Why didn't you tell me?"

"I was afraid you wouldn't believe me." The words shook on the way out of my mouth.

Marissa wiped at the tears pooling in her eyes. Written on her face was more than just the terrible confession I'd made. There was the way I hadn't been there for her this summer. The lies I'd told her all these months when all she'd asked for was the truth. And the fact that she had to learn my dark secret the same way everyone else did, when she'd given me so many chances to be honest.

She swallowed, then looked at the exit.

"You should get out of here. Go out the back so no one sees you until we can think of what to do."

"We?" I studied her face, heart squeezing. "You believe me?"

"Of course I believe you." She pressed her fingers to her eyes, smudging mascara onto her cheeks. "I knew I almost died that night. I just never really knew how close I came. I . . . I need time to process. And you need to get out of here."

"I can't. I rode here with Isaac and Beau." I swallowed against the tightness in my chest. *Isaac.* He was somewhere in the audience, watching the whole thing play out. What would he think of me now? Would he even want to see me again?

Then I thought of the image of the blood-splattered boy with the dimple. The boy who looked just like Isaac. It couldn't be him, could it?

Marissa glanced at the door again, then back at me.

"Meet me at the back entrance. I'll be there as soon as I can. But you need to go now, before people flood the hallways."

I took a deep breath and nodded, my stomach fisting as Marissa pushed open the door.

Then I was alone.

35

I SAT IN THE STALL FOR A MOMENT LONGER, LISTENING to the rain beating against the roof before finally dragging myself out of the bathroom. The hallway was empty, but it wouldn't be for long. Marissa was right—I needed to get out of there, fast.

My legs walked me toward the back entrance, moving as if choreographed. Right foot, left foot. Five, six, seven, eight.

Then I heard footsteps approaching, light and familiar. A rumble of thunder boomed overhead.

"Whitney." Isaac's voice was dark. "Marissa told me to come find you. Are you okay?"

The image from the video flashed behind my eyelids: a familiar-looking boy wrapped in a blanket, covered in a spray of blood as a policeman knelt beside him.

I turned slowly, not wanting to face the truth.

He stood several feet away, his mouth a thin line. His usually ruddy cheeks were pale, his eyes flat. I thought about that night at the football game—the way his eyes kept darting around the stadium like he was looking for someone. The way his hands gripped the seat. The sheen of sweat glistening on his pale cheeks. I thought he might have been sick, but that wasn't it at all, was it? He'd been nervous. Afraid. The way you might be if you'd experienced a traumatic event at another high school game one year prior.

"You were at the game that night, weren't you?" There was

a tremor in my voice when I spoke. "You lied to me."

He looked down at the ground, then back at me. "Can we get out of the middle of the hallway? If someone comes back here and sees you . . ."

A rock settled in the pit of my stomach, but I nodded and followed him down the corridor to the back entrance of the school, where Marissa told me to wait for her. The sky visible through the glass door ahead was as dark as a bruise.

Isaac ran his fingers through his rumpled hair. His dimple folded into a tiny C.

"That was you in the video," I whispered, dragging my eyes across his face and picturing the splatters of blood the camera had captured. How hard had he scrubbed to remove it all? Did he still see it when he looked in the mirror?

He nodded and cleared his throat.

"It was the first game. The whole school was there. I remember we were losing. And I remember watching you perform at halftime—you were in the front row and kind of hard to miss. You were really good. But everything after that's kind of a blur. I don't even remember hearing the shots. I just remember all these people screaming and running and then I looked down and my friends Jack and Emerson were bleeding . . ." He looked away, Adam's apple bobbing up and down. "They were shot . . ."

He trailed off, rubbing at his eyes. They were red and bloodshot. I placed my hand on the wall to steady myself.

Why wasn't he yelling at me? Why wasn't he asking me about the video? Why wasn't he asking me if I could have stopped it all, the way Marissa had?

"Everything was different after they died," Isaac said, eyes staring off into the middle distance. "People looked at me differently. I couldn't go near the school without having a panic attack, and we didn't have the money to move." He shook his head, a bitter laugh breaking through his grimace. "I thought if I transferred here and told people I wasn't at the game, maybe I could get a fresh start. Maybe I wouldn't have to think about it all the time."

He swallowed thickly and shoved his hands into his pockets. He had barely looked at me, not that I blamed him.

"I saw you in the backyard at Beau's party," Isaac continued, "and I recognized you right away. You were the last thing I remembered seeing before . . . before everything happened. It was like seeing a ghost. I thought, *I'm never going to escape that night, am I?*"

I thought of the way he'd looked at me on the car ride to his house, like he was afraid of me. He had been afraid, hadn't he? I'd been a giant reminder of everything that happened.

He finally looked me in the eye, and it was my turn to look away. I wasn't brave enough to meet his gaze. How could he stand being close to me all these weeks? Why would he even want to be near me?

"I realized you were Constance's granddaughter on the drive to my house. I know this is going to sound ridiculous, but your grandma kind of saved me. We started talking that summer, after everything happened. Back then I was barely sleeping. I had a lot of nightmares. My parents thought I was suffering from post-traumatic stress syndrome or something. But then one day after I walked my grandpa back to his room I heard this woman call out to me. She thought I was one of the reading volunteers, and I figured, why not? Where else did

I have to go? So I started reading to her every day after I'd drop my grandpa off. And then reading turned into talking, and I don't know. She just somehow made me feel better. Like everything was going to be okay. And she told me all about you and I guess I was curious. She was a really special woman." He shook his head, then frowned at me. "When you said you were going to the game . . . I originally wanted to avoid it, but then I thought it might help. I wanted to be stronger than the memory of that night, and I thought if someone was with me . . . if *you* were with me, I could handle it. I thought you were another victim, that you were trying to move past it all, too. I didn't know that you helped that guy—"

"I didn't. Isaac, you have to believe me. I didn't know what Dwight was going to do. Not really—"

I thought of my hands gripping the locker room door shut, protecting my best friend. Were Isaac's friends two of the people with the darkness over their heads? Could I have saved them if I hadn't been so selfish?

Isaac nodded once, then motioned toward the exit. "We should get out of here. Marissa told me to take you to your house. She's going to get Beau and meet us there."

"Okay," I said cautiously, trying to gauge what was going on inside his head. Trying to gauge, on a scale of one to ten, how much he hated me.

Then I turned toward the glass door, hand reaching for the handle, and froze. Ice ran through my veins when I saw my reflection in the glass.

Because there, floating above my head, rippled a swelling cloud of darkness.

36

THE CLOUD ROILED AND PULSED, NOT QUITE REACHING my ears. It moved with my breath, swelling in and out like a living piece of me. I'd always wondered if I could see my own darkness—if it would appear for me the way it did for others, giving me a choice to save myself. A burble of hysterical laughter tickled at the back of my throat as I realized how wrong I'd been. The darkness doesn't appear out of thin air. It doesn't *find* us. The darkness rises out of us, curling outward like some dark passenger hiding deep inside our body, waiting for a chance to escape. How had I never realized it before? I watched in horror as the shadow lifted from my pores, reaching into the air with blackened fingers.

My skin prickled with cold sweat. The temperature had dropped at least fifteen degrees, but there was no AC vent to explain the sudden chill. Which meant it must be the darkness, cold as death itself. Its icy fingers tickled the top of my head, sliding down my cheeks. Is this what everyone felt, or was the cold just for me?

"Whitney?"

Isaac's voice was a puff of hot air on my neck. He placed a hand on my shoulder and said my name again, then gently pushed me toward the exit. The cloud ballooned around me, swelling in size. Everything inside me went cold and the temperature seemed to drop yet again.

I stepped backward, away from the door and Isaac.

The cloud contracted. The cold waned.

Forward, where Isaac wanted me to go, and the cloud swelled.

Backward, away from Isaac, and it shrank.

No, that can't be right. I don't understand.

"Are you okay?" Isaac's fingers stretched out hesitantly. The darkness quivered and bulged. The chill in the air shook.

The understanding started as a slow buzz at the base of my skull, then crawled down my spine, through my fingers and toes, until every part of me hummed with the truth. The horrible, horrible truth. The chill of darkness licked at my shoulders as I tried to make sense of it.

Isaac was with Gams all summer long. They'd spent hours together—he even just admitted that they spent a lot of time talking. She could have had one of her episodes when he was with her, let it spill that I'd saved Dwight or worse—*why* I'd saved Dwight. Or maybe she'd fallen asleep while he was reading to her, and he'd thumbed through her flower-covered journal out of curiosity.

That night at Lone Star when someone left the bloodlike sludge on my window—Isaac found me so easily. Even though I'd parked all the way at the back of the poorly lit parking lot, well after visiting hours. And his car was parked right next to mine the day I found the note with Gams's picture. He was even there at Gams's memorial, with easy access to my bedroom and Will's car.

And Gams. Oh God, Gams. It would have been so easy for him to sneak into her room to siphon off some of her medication—a little bit each day so she wouldn't notice. In fact he wouldn't have needed to sneak at all—the nurses would have let him right in, just like they had all summer.

He couldn't have . . . It's not possible. He wouldn't.

I spun to face him, heartbeat heavy and palms slick with sweat despite the cold covering my body. My eyes brimmed. I'd let him get close to me. I'd welcomed him into my life. Had the answer been standing in front of me this whole time?

The video—was that what he'd been building up to all along? Wanting to make sure everyone knew the truth? Wanting everyone to know that I was the girl in the photo so they'd think I had something to do with what Dwight did that night at the game?

But you did have something to do with what Dwight did. You had everything *to do with what he did—you had two chances to stop him, and both times you failed. First with your hubris. Then with your selfishness.*

My hands shook. My stomach coiled. I felt ill remembering the feel of Isaac's mouth against mine, warm and perfect, and how easily I'd fallen for him. He made me believe he cared about me. About Gams. The answer was right in front of my face, obvious as a downtown high-rise, but I'd been too distracted by my growing feelings to put the pieces together.

"It was you, wasn't it?" The words were lava spewing out of my mouth. "The notes. My windshield. Gams. It was all you."

Isaac's brow knit together and his head tilted to the side. His mouth quirked, like there were words on his tongue he couldn't quite string together.

"What?" He seemed confused, but I knew it was an act. It had all been an act.

I turned back to the window, fingers curling into fists.

Ellie Harris was just a name in a book. Kevin was just an asshole with anger issues. Isaac had been right in front of me this whole time, and I'd missed it.

The sky outside was a wicked thing, dark as the cloud thrumming above my head. In my reflection, I saw that the blackness now licked below my shoulders. And now that I knew it was there—now that I knew what to look for—I felt it sliding its cold fingers against my skin, reaching for my hands, pulling the life from me.

Which meant I didn't have much time to save myself.

Maybe I deserved whatever it was Isaac had planned for me, but Gams didn't deserve to die for it. She'd been nothing but kind to him. Which made Isaac just as much of a murderer as Dwight. And I'd be damned if I was going to let him get away with it.

I rammed my shoulder against the glass door and burst forward into the storm, rain stinging my cheeks. Isaac's fingers slid against my back, trying to grab on to me, but I was too fast for him.

"Whitney! Wait!" he called, voice cracking in surprise.

The deluge stung my eyes. Hair clung to my cheeks in dripping cords. Water soaked my jeans, seeping through to my skin. I could hardly see through the curtain of rain, but I pushed my legs as hard as they would move in the opposite direction of the school and the monster who murdered Gams.

Behind me, I heard Isaac's feet slapping against the puddled parking lot.

He was coming after me.

37

THE YEAR BEFORE GAMS MOVED INTO LONE STAR
Assisted Living, she took me to watch her favorite modern
ballet company perform a new piece, *Summer Squall*. At first
I thought the dancers were supposed to be droplets of rain,
jerking around the stage the way wind might toss water in
a storm. But when the music reached its crescendo, actual
water began to fall from the rafters, first in a trickle, then in
a torrent, until every dancer glistened under the stage lights,
muscles slick with manufactured rain. When they spun, water
leaped off their bodies into the audience. When they landed,
circles of moisture sprayed around them, almost as if the water
itself was choreographed. They were not the storm, I realized.
They were the leaves shaking in the trees, the grass slapping in
the wind, the sky pregnant with water. They were the thirsty
earth, mouth open and hungry for the storm, twitching and
spinning as the squall raged around them. It was one of the
most beautiful dances I'd ever seen, and it was the last piece
Gams and I watched together.

I pretended I was one of the *Summer Squall* dancers as I ran
through the rain-slogged parking lot. That the water spilling
into my eyes and dripping from my hair was part of a brilliantly
choreographed number. That the *slap, slap, slap* of feet behind
me was a chorus line. That the boom of thunder was part of the
music. I was not running from my grandmother's murderer. I

was not being chased by the boy I kissed a few hours ago. The darkness hadn't risen out of me, licking cold tendrils down my cheeks. I was simply another dancer on another stage burning under another spotlight.

"Whitney! Stop!" Another clap of thunder shook the sky when Isaac yelled. I kept my eyes forward, fighting the temptation to look behind me. I did not want to see his face. I did not want to know how close he was to catching me.

Run! Fly! Gams's voice cried inside my head. I pushed harder, through the parking lot toward the school's back exit, where Mr. Gullman would be perched under the cover of a small clapboard security station.

I forced my legs forward despite the weight of rain pulling at my jeans. The small white building loomed ahead, gray in the setting sun and overcast sky. I just needed to make it there and then I could call for help. Just a little bit farther.

"Help!" I croaked once I was close enough to the window to be heard. "Mr. Gullman, call the police!"

I waited for him to stick his head out of the small window to see who was screaming, but he must not have heard me. I yelled again.

Behind me, the thud of feet faded—maybe Isaac gave up when he saw me running toward the security booth. A chill still hovered in the air around me, but there was no way to know if it was from the darkness or my rain-soaked clothes. Maybe I made the right choice running out of the school, away from Isaac, and the cloud had receded. Maybe I was safe.

Or maybe Isaac went to get his car because he knows you don't have one.

"Mr. Gullman!" I slammed my hand on the side of the small building and slid to a halt in front of the window.

My chest heaved. No one was inside.

Keep running. Head to the strip mall. You can call for help inside one of the stores.

I forced my legs to move again, turning right when I reached the street. The strip mall was a half mile ahead, next to a church. If I stuck to the side of the road, I should be safe. He wouldn't do anything to me where people could see. Right?

Cars zipped past, oblivious as they sent waves of muddy water crashing onto the sidewalk. Maybe they all assumed I was running for cover from the storm. Or maybe they couldn't even see me through the downpour and fading light.

In my head, the music from *Summer Squall* swelled. I imagined the stage, the lights, the audience, and myself at the center of the ensemble, black spandex tight against my skin. My breath was ragged in my chest.

It's the finale—the final push toward a standing ovation. Do not think. Do not stop.

Another splash sounded behind me as a car slid through a puddle, but the movement was closer and slower. Like someone pulling up beside the curb.

My heart moved to my throat, hammering beneath my skin. My legs screamed. There were too many blocks remaining between me and the strip mall. I'd never make it.

A line of trees and a grassy length of park separated me from the row of squat brick houses in the neighborhood to my right. I could run to one of the homes, ring the doorbell, and hope someone answered.

Behind me, a car door slammed. Then heavy footsteps, quick against the sidewalk. They were headed in my direction.

Out of options, I turned right toward the houses, aiming for one with a car parked in front of its walkway. I urged my legs forward in a final burst of speed, fighting against the mud sucking at my shoes and the added weight from my drenched clothes. My heartbeat stuttered in my ears.

At my back, I heard the squelching of feet. A boom of thunder. My name shouted by a familiar voice. A slice of lightning split the sky into pieces.

Then hands on my shoulders, rough as they shoved me down into the mucky ground, followed by a grunt. My face smashed into the soft earth. Stars spun in front of my eyes. I tried to push myself back up, but a knee dug into the small of my back, pinning me to the ground. The air around me turned deadly with cold.

I opened my mouth to scream, but a hand closed around my jaw, forcing something thick and cottony inside. A sharp chemical smell burned my nostrils. Every muscle in my body turned to thick, bloated blobs of useless flesh. I tried to lift an arm, a leg, but it was like trying to lift a semi with a toothpick. The edges of my vision went gray, funneling into a pinprick.

I told myself it was just the spotlight winking out, the performance ending. Time to take my bow.

Then everything went dark.

38

GRAVEL, I THOUGHT, MY FINGERS RUNNING OVER THE rocky ground beneath me. _Why am I lying in gravel?_

My head throbbed like I'd rammed it against a wall. Rain fell in a wet drizzle, plastering matted hair to my cheeks. A thick half circle of black rimmed each of my fingernails, like I'd been digging in mud.

". . . the hell are we supposed to do now?" I heard a familiar voice say. "We can't just take her back and act like nothing happened. She's seen you."

"I'm sorry!" a man yelled, the exasperation clear in his voice. "They look exactly alike. They even have the same damn haircut. How was I supposed to know I grabbed the wrong girl? I told you this whole thing has gone too far. This whole plan—"

"I have it under control! Or at least I did until you messed everything up."

I lifted my head toward the sound of the arguing voices, the movement taking more effort than it should have.

I blinked, the scene around me taking shape. The sun had sunk below the horizon. The dark sky loomed large overhead, threaded with jagged shadows of the downtown Dallas skyline. Wind whipped at my cheeks. Gravel and soot crunched under my hands.

That's when it clicked. I was on a rooftop.

No, not _a_ rooftop. _The_ rooftop. The same one that haunted my nightmares. The same one the photo had captured.

My stomach heaved.

The last few hours came back to me in a terrifying blur. I raked my eyes away from the buildings and met a dark, hollow stare.

"Mr. Bower?" My voice came out in a croak.

A hat covered his usually well-groomed hair, the brim pulled forward to shield his face from the drizzle.

I searched the roof, looking for the source of the second voice. That's when I saw Mrs. B and Penny.

Mrs. B leaned against the door labeled ROOF ACCESS, a raincoat wrapped tightly around her thin form and her hair pulled up into a slick bun. Next to her Penny sat in a crumpled mound, hands bound in front of her with a thin coil of rope. Rain beaded on her pale skin, or maybe it was sweat. She looked at me with wide, pleading eyes. The terror on her face must have matched my own.

"Mrs. B?" I looked back and forth from her to her husband, trying to make sense of it.

Mrs. B's usually kind face tilted into cyanide as she glanced at her husband. The pit in my stomach widened.

The darkness I'd seen hovering above my reflection hadn't swelled because I was going outside with *Isaac*. The darkness had swelled because I was going outside *period*, where Mr. Bower was waiting for me. Isaac never had anything to do with it.

Isaac. My heart seized at how quickly I was willing to pin the blame on him.

Penny whimpered and tried to stand, but her feet slipped and she stumbled to her knees. She would have face-planted had Mrs. B not reached out an arm to steady her.

"It's okay, dear," Mrs. B said. She clutched Penny's arm with a gloved hand. "This will all be over soon." She turned toward her husband. "Peter, will you get over here and take care of this, please?"

Mr. Bower wrung his hands together nervously, then pulled a knife from the folds of his trench coat and closed the distance to Penny.

Penny scrambled backward, emitting a sharp whine when she saw the glint of metal. I tried to stand, but slipped, still too weak. It was like all my limbs had been replaced with noodles.

"Please," Penny whispered, lower lip quivering. "Please, let me go."

"Penny!" I shouted, unsure what else to do. But then I noticed the space above her head—nothing but empty gray sky. There was no danger to save her from. Mr. Bower seemed too nervous—he looked like he was going to be sick.

Mr. Bower wedged the knife under the rope binding Penny's wrists, then yanked upward. Penny fell backward.

"No one's going to hurt you, Penny," Mrs. B said, tilting her head to examine Penny's face. "You're only here because my idiot husband can't tell one blonde from the next."

"They look exactly alike!" Mr. Bower shouted, kicking at the ground like a child. A spray of tiny rocks flew in my direction. "I thought she was Whitney! I told you this whole plan was ridiculous."

Penny rubbed at her wrists, looking back and forth between me and Mrs. B. She was dressed in the same sopping wet warm-ups I'd seen her wearing outside of the school. I thought of her running away from the building, hair plastered to her head from the rain. Had Mr. Bower seen her running and grabbed her, thinking she was me?

"You were the one leaving me the notes," I said to Mr. Bower.

"No." Mrs. B took a few steps toward me, leveling her narrowed eyes. "That was me."

Her limp was mostly gone despite the boot still encasing her foot. Her cheeks looked sharp in the darkness, like something you'd grind a blade against. Then she gave me a smile so eerie it took me back more than a year, to the first time on the roof when Dwight told me how he wanted to get back at everyone who'd ever laughed at him.

"Did I ever tell you about my sister?"

Her words rattled something loose inside my brain, and I remembered the day she'd asked if the team could use *Red* for competition season. She'd shown me a picture of her and a nearly identical girl, both dressed in sequined blue costumes and tap shoes. The realization hit me like a slap.

"Ellie Harris," I whispered, the name clicking into place.

"Harris was my maiden name." Mrs. B tipped her head to the side, waiting for me to connect the dots.

I thought of Gams and the confession she'd made that day in her room when she'd had the episode.

If I hadn't saved him . . . if I'd just ignored the darkness, that little girl would still be alive.

She'd been trying to warn me, and I hadn't listened. Not really.

"What happened to your sister?" I asked, even though I already knew the answer. Even though I didn't want to hear her say it. I squeezed my eyes shut, like that could somehow block out the truth.

"She died, Whitney. Because of your grandmother. The same way all those people died because of you."

39

MRS. B'S WORDS WERE SHARDS OF GLASS SCATTERED across a highway after a head-on collision. The rain seemed to come from everywhere at once. It turned Mrs. B's dark hair jet-black and made her skin glisten with moisture. A few strands had loosened from her bun and dripped onto her shoulders.

"Ellie and I were only a year apart," Mrs. B said, smoothing her wet hair behind her ear. "We did everything together. When she died, I was devastated. I didn't think I could carry on without her. But then your grandma showed up at our house a few weeks after the funeral and offered to tutor me, free of charge, as a way to help take my mind off things. She said she was worried about me because I'd stopped going to classes. She said I had real talent and she didn't want to see it go to waste." She scoffed and shook her head. "Ellie was the real talent—we all knew that. But still, my parents thought it was a good idea. They thought it would help me. So they said yes."

I thought of the blue sequined costume in the photo Mrs. B had shown me—it was a classic Gams choice.

"I spent all my free time at Constance's studio. When I wasn't in a class, she would tutor me, helping me work on my turnout or perfect my turns. As I got older, she let me choreograph and even teach some of the classes. She said I was her protégé, and I believed her. We all did. And she was right—dancing did take my mind off things. It didn't make me stop missing my sister, but it gave me something to focus on other than how much I missed her. All these years, I thought Constance was my savior. My hero. I wanted to be just like her. But it turns out she's a monster, just like you. It turns out my entire life has been a lie."

Mrs. B's eyes were cold as she spoke. Behind her, Penny watched with rapt attention.

"What happened to your sister?" Penny asked. She was still pressed against the wall, a few feet from Mr. Bower.

Mrs. B gave a sad smile and shook her head.

"A man hit her with his car when she was crossing the street. Witnesses say he plowed right into her—didn't even slow down as he ran a red light. His blood alcohol was well above the legal limit. Everyone thought it was just the act of a sad, drunk man who'd lost control of his car. But it was the middle of the day. There was no way he didn't see her. No way he couldn't have at least tried to slow down or swerve to miss her."

"You think he did it on purpose," I said, thinking about Gams's face that day in her room.

History repeats itself.

"I *know* he did it on purpose," she said, stepping closer so that she was standing directly over me. "You know I lied to you when I said I hadn't been to visit Constance in a while. I went to see her nearly every week. She was like a second mother to me." She shook her head and squeezed her eyes shut. "I would tell her about my students, get her advice on choreography—normal stuff. And then, after last year's tragedy, I would talk to her about my recovery. About the nightmares I had. About my devastation when I learned that I'd never dance again—how dance, the thing that had saved me all those years ago, was taken from me by that boy. Or so I'd thought." She wiped at her cheeks and looked up at the sky. "Constance always listened. Always seemed to know exactly what to say to make me feel better. Until a few months ago when she told me she had something she needed to tell me. Something she needed to confess."

She paused, waiting for me to say something, but my mouth felt like it was filled with sand. I closed my eyes, and when I opened them again she was bending down close enough for me to see the thick layer of makeup circling her eyes, attempting to hide the shadows.

"She told me she saved the man who killed my sister. He was planning to hurt himself, but your grandmother talked him out of it. Even after he told her that he thought about hurting other people. Even after he told her that he probably *would* hurt someone if he didn't do something to stop himself. Still, Constance—your *Gams*—saved him. And a few days later, my sister died. Constance didn't take me under her wing because she thought I had talent, or because she wanted to help me, or even because she liked me. She did it to clear her own conscience. She did it because it was her fault my sister died."

I swallowed. The rain had stopped but the air was still thick with moisture. I couldn't seem to get enough air in my lungs.

"Constance could have stopped with her confession right there—she didn't have to tell me the rest. But it was like something took over her body and she couldn't stop talking—I don't even think she knew I was in the room anymore. She started saying all this ridiculous stuff about dark clouds floating over people's heads and you and Dwight and history repeating itself. At first, I thought it was just nonsensical babble, but she was so *insistent*. And I thought back to you breaking formation the night of the shooting, and as bizarre as it all sounded, something clicked. Then I noticed her journal sticking out of her mattress. Why keep your journal hidden if there wasn't something in it that you didn't want people to see? So I read it. Some of her entries dated back years ago, long before she started having her episodes, so I figured there had to be some truth to what she was saying. That, and it all connected back to everything she'd confessed—about my sister, about the dark clouds. Even about you and Dwight. Your family didn't just ruin my life once, but twice."

Tears slid down my cheeks as I thought about Gams spilling her secrets to Mrs. B. It must have been so hard holding on to something so awful for that long. No wonder she told me to ignore the darkness—no wonder she was so adamant that I leave it alone. And then when I saved Dwight and it happened all over again . . . she'd tried to warn me, but I didn't listen.

"Do you know what it's like to find out your entire life has been a lie? To find out the woman you admired most in the world—the woman you loved like a second mother—ruined your life? And then to learn that her granddaughter was passing on her legacy of destruction." Mrs. B's face contorted in a look of disgust.

"You didn't have to kill her," I whispered, tears sliding down my cheeks.

She let out a bitter laugh, then held out her hand toward her husband. "Give me the book."

Mr. Bower reached into his pocket and pulled out the pink ballerina-covered notebook where I recorded the names of people I saved throughout the years. Mrs. B snatched it and held it up. The pages were limp with rainwater.

"Do you know there are almost two hundred names in this book? Two hundred people that you've saved over the years." She shook her head.

My heart gave a tight squeeze. There was a time when I took pride in every name I added, when I treasured writing down my victories like I was a hero to be celebrated. I never thought about the consequences until that night, and here was Mrs. B, yet another example of the domino effects of my impossible choices.

"In all the time I've known you, you've never missed a step, never flubbed a turn, never fallen out of a line, and yet you broke formation that night at the football game. You saw something in the stands. You knew what was about to happen, and you saved your best friend over all those other people, didn't you?" Her finger tapped the book. "That's why Marissa's name is the only one listed from that night. And why her name comes just after Dwight's, because you saved him that day on the roof. The same way your grandma saved that man."

I looked past Mrs. B to where Penny crouched on the ground, rubbing her red wrists. Her face looked stricken. Next to her, Mr. Bower paced. The rain splattered against the graveled roof, blending with my thudding pulse.

My stomach heaved. I was going to be sick.

"Your grandmother had a list just like the one you have in your book. There aren't many names in it, but that can't be the only journal your grandmother kept over the years. If you've saved two hundred people, how many people do you think Constance *saved* in her lifetime, Whitney?" The word *saved* dripped from her mouth like venom. "A hundred? A thousand? And if that's the case, how many other lives have you ruined? My sister can't be the only person hurt. I can't be the only person left permanently damaged by your need to decide who gets to live and die. How many others are there?"

I shook my head as more tears slid down my cheeks, the truth of her words slicing deep.

"You have no idea, do you?" She shook her head, disgusted. "You could have ruined a thousand lives and you'd never know. Neither would Constance. All your family ever does is take and destroy. You don't think about anyone else but yourselves."

I swallowed, wanting to deny it, but the words were lodged in my throat. Because she wasn't wrong—the evidence of the pain we'd caused was standing right in front of me. The decisions I'd made could have ripple effects for years to come, like a butterfly beating its wings in one part of the world and causing a tsunami somewhere else.

But what about the good people I'd saved? Like Isaac. And Marissa. And Jenny. Like the countless other people I'd given second chances to who hadn't gone on to hurt anyone. They had friends and families who would have been devastated by their losses if I hadn't intervened.

Didn't they deserve a second chance?

"You're wrong," I said, my teeth gritted. "They weren't all bad. Most of them were good people."

"How do you know that?" Mrs. B shook her head, mouth twisting in disgust. "You know what's most disturbing of all? There are other names after Dwight's, which means that even after what he did last year—even after you witnessed all the pain you caused—you continued to save people. You just keep on doing it, not caring about the consequences."

I glanced at Penny, trying to gauge her reaction. Did she believe Mrs. B? Her hands were unbound. She could get away—she could go for help . . . but her face was impossible to read. She sat stone-still, eyes fixed on Mrs. B as if in a trance.

Come on, Penny. Do something.

I had to keep Mrs. B talking.

"Why leave me all of the pictures and warnings? Why not just confront me and get it all over with?"

Mrs. B shook her head. "The idea of a girl who sees clouds when someone's in danger? That's the stuff of comic books and fairy tales. Even after everything your grandmother told me, it still seemed too far-fetched to be true." She gave a snort of disgust. "I wanted to make sure the things she said about you weren't nonsense. I wanted proof. So I decided to test you.

"It was too crowded in the hallway for me to get close enough to see your reaction when you saw the picture I left in your locker. But when you saw your car in the parking lot of Constance's nursing home, the way you reacted . . . you *knew* it was a cloud on your windshield. And when you saw the photo of Dwight on the roof—you threw it away like it had burned you. Because it *was* you in the picture. You were the girl who'd been photographed with him. Why would you act like that if it wasn't all true? And why wouldn't you tell someone if you didn't have something to hide?

"Then with your brother . . . it was the most bizarre thing to watch. How did you know to keep him off the freeway unless you could see the danger he was in?"

"You could have *killed* him," I said, seething, my fists

clenching. "He had nothing to do with any of this."

"But I didn't kill him, did I? Because you saved him. Because you saw a cloud hovering over his head." Mrs. B tilted her head to the side, studying my reaction.

People are afraid of the things they don't understand.

"Did you mean to kill Gams, or was that one of your tests, too?" I wasn't sure which answer was worse, but I didn't need to hear the words to know the truth. The hate was written all over Mrs. B's face.

"I told you, someone had to stop her. Someone had to make her pay for what she'd done. And I wanted to make sure you found her the same way I found my sister. It's a horrible thing seeing someone you love like that, isn't it? It's the kind of thing that haunts you for the rest of your life." Mrs. B wiped at the corner of her eye.

I blinked and saw Gams sprawled across her bed, lips parted. I could only imagine what horrible image Mrs. B had to relive from the day her sister died. It was the kind of thing I wouldn't wish on anyone.

"And the video?" I asked. "Was that your grand plan all along? Kill my grandma, out me to the entire school, and then drag me up on this roof to confront me?"

"People need to know the truth, Whitney. They deserve closure. I gave you a chance to confess on your own, but when you didn't . . ." She shrugged and looked to her husband. "I came up with a plan B."

I glanced at Penny, but her face gave nothing away. Her eyes kept darting between me, Mrs. B, and the door, like she was trying to work out an escape path.

Run, I wanted to scream at her. *Get help.*

Then Mr. Bower cleared his throat, gloved hands wringing nervously in front of him. "You need to hurry. The longer we're up here, the longer we risk being seen."

Mrs. B's eyes cut over to him, annoyance clear on her face. "If you want to leave, then leave. But I intend to finish what I started."

Ice ran through my veins. What was it that she planned to do, exactly?

Mr. Bower glanced at the exit, like he was debating what to do next. I thought of the way he followed Mrs. B around like a puppy. How Marissa thought his obsession was sweet. But the terrified look on his face said he didn't want to be here—that this hadn't been his idea.

Penny must have noticed his hesitancy, too, because suddenly she climbed to her feet as if jolted awake, her voice high and pleading.

"Let me go. Please. I won't tell anybody. I'll pretend I was never here. I swear."

Mr. Bower ran his fingers through his hair and looked to his wife, then back at Penny.

"Maybe she's telling the truth," he said, his face ghostly pale against the dark sky. "Maybe we can at least let her go?"

"Maybe," Mrs. B said. Then from the pocket of her trench coat, she pulled out a gun. The black surface glittered with rain as she pointed it at Penny. "Let's let Whitney decide."

Penny's mouth made a little O, mirroring the barrel. A rumble of thunder shook the building. Somewhere below a car alarm sounded.

"I'm going to give you another chance to save someone's life,

Whitney. Another chance to do the right thing, and hopefully this time you'll make the right choice. That's more than generous, don't you think?" Mrs. B smiled at me, her teeth flashing white against the black sky. "If you do as I say, Penny will walk off this roof unharmed. She'll go back to being captain of the dance team as if this day never happened, and it will all be thanks to you. Do you want to be a hero, Whitney? Do you want a chance to undo your wrongs and make the right choice this time around?"

"You wouldn't hurt Penny—" I started, but as soon as the sentence was out of my mouth I realized how wrong I was. Because a small black cloud had begun to form over Penny's head. It pulsed above her, blending with the darkened sky, and I knew that what Mrs. B said was true. She was giving me a choice. A chance to save Penny. And if I didn't do what she said, Penny would die.

Penny's eyes were wide and terrified. She trembled so hard it was a miracle she could hold herself upright. I wondered if she was feeling the chill from the cloud roiling above her head the same way I had earlier.

I swallowed, thinking about all the things Penny had done to me over the years—the time she hid my solo costume, or when she tried to get me disqualified by claiming I'd stolen her choreography. These last few years we'd been nothing but rivals, but we'd also been friends once. And no matter what she'd done to me, she didn't deserve this. No one did.

My life or Penny's. Another impossible choice.

"What do I have to do?" I asked.

"Simple," Mrs. B answered. "All you have to do is jump."

40

I CLOSED MY EYES AS A GUST OF WIND WHIPPED AGAINST me. It wasn't cold like the wind had been the first time, with Dwight, but it felt just as biting.

"If you jump, Penny lives. If you don't, Penny dies. It's your choice."

Penny's eyes were glued to the black mass of metal pointed at her forehead. Thunder rumbled overhead.

"No one will believe that I just jumped. They'll know that something happened." I tried to make my voice sound confident, but I couldn't hide the tremor.

"Are you sure about that, Whitney? You quit the dance team out of the blue. Your grandma died. And thanks to me telling Principal O'Connell that I saw you steal the flowers from the dance team lockers, everyone knows you've been acting erratic lately. And let's not forget the video." Mrs. B's smile was almost smug as she laid it all out for me like a perfectly choreographed routine. "Now that everyone knows you were the girl in the photo, would it be such a stretch to believe that you took your own life on the same roof where it all began? That the guilt you'd been carrying finally led you to act out in the worst possible way? I don't think so."

I thought of the video. Out of context, the picture looked pretty damning. And it was also time-stamped, so anyone could see that it had taken place a few days before the shooting. Without knowing the full context, some people might even believe the video was a confession. Not to mention the fact that I'd had plenty of chances to tell the police I was the girl in the photo. It was like Mrs. B said—why keep it a secret unless I had something to hide?

But if that was the case—

"You said I have a choice—me or Penny—but your plan all along was to make it look like I jumped."

Mrs. B shrugged. "Two lives or one. It's up to you."

I glanced back at Penny. Would they really just let her walk away from all this and trust her not to tell anyone? And what would happen if she did get away from this unscathed—would she spend the rest of her life replaying tonight over and over again in her head, the same way I replayed that day with Dwight? The guilt had become a living thing, crawling and gnashing inside of me until it was the only thing I felt anymore. Guilt was a monster no one should have to live with. Not even Penny.

I stepped toward the edge of the building and brushed the dripping strands of hair from my face to get a clearer view of the seven-story drop below. The rain-slicked street shone in the meager moonlight. Awnings beat and snapped against the wind. A few cars skated through the wet streets, but otherwise the path was clear. I was standing in almost the same spot as when the photo was taken last year—maybe someone was watching now, wondering why there was a girl standing alone on the ledge. The rest of them were too far back from the edge to be visible the way Dwight and I were that day, plus it was too dark. But the Bowers probably already knew that. Mrs. B had probably planned that, too.

I turned back toward Penny's stricken face, eyeing the

pulsing cloud of darkness rising over her head.

"You're lying," I said to Mrs. B. "You aren't going to let Penny out of this alive. It doesn't matter if I jump or you push me—she's seen too much."

A strangled sound came from the back of Penny's throat. Her cheeks were pale against the night sky. Her gold hair had gone dark with rain. From this angle, under the barely there moon, I finally saw why everyone called us the Twins. We really did look alike.

"That's not true. It's your choice, Whitney. But you have to make it now."

Behind Mrs. B, Mr. Bower paced. I wondered how long he'd been going along with his wife's plan—if he'd helped, or he'd just let his love for her drag him along until he didn't know how to turn back.

"You don't have to do this," I said to him, hoping he was listening. Then I caught Penny's gaze and held it, hoping she could see what I was doing. Hoping she understood what to do next.

"I know what it's like to live with someone's death on your conscience. It consumes you," I told her. "I don't want that for you, Penny. I don't want that for either of us. Do you understand?"

Penny nodded once, a movement so small you would have missed it if you hadn't been paying attention.

No one knew death the way I did. I'd seen it whisper over heads, unfurl its black fingers, and slide over bodies until they were nothing but shadows. I knew its quiet, its softness, and even its elegance. Maybe it wasn't a curse, but a gift that enabled me to give people another chance at life. There was no way to know what someone would do with that second chance, but maybe that wasn't the point. Maybe my only role was to give people the opportunity to keep living and let them choose what comes next for themselves.

If that was the case, then the darkness wasn't an ending, but a beginning. Like a curtain rising.

I pictured Gams's smiling face, grinning back at me from the audience as I took center stage. The spotlight shone down on me, the path clear. I heard her voice, thick and rich with hope: *You need to be brave, dear.*

I would be brave for Gams. I would be brave for myself. I would be brave for all those people I should have saved at the game that night.

I looked to Mrs. B and narrowed my eyes. That's when I saw there was a matching cloud forming over her head.

Because there was a different choice I could make.

I took one final quivering breath, then I charged for Mrs. B just as Penny swung her fist toward Mr. Bower's face.

At the same moment, the door to the roof burst open.

41

"WHITNEY!" ISAAC SHOUTED, LAUNCHING HIMSELF ONTO the rooftop along with two police officers. Marissa rushed through the open door a second later, her wild curls whipping around her face.

Mrs. B's head snapped in their direction as my body connected with hers, knocking her to the ground. The gun skittered across the roof. Behind her, Mr. Bower let out a howl as he tried to push Penny off him. Penny's arms lashed out, slapping and clawing at whatever parts of Mr. Bower she could reach.

Mrs. B and I both scrabbled for the gun. With the boot on her foot, I should have been faster. But my legs were still unsteady from whatever it was Mr. Bower had used to knock me out. I reached for the gun at the same moment as Mrs. B, both of our hands sliding against the slick surface. Her fingers wrapped around the barrel and she yanked it toward her, then pulled herself into a seated position. Above her, the thick black cloud pulsed.

"You don't have to do this," I told her. "You have a choice."

Rain stung my eyes. Above me, I felt the cold of my own darkness thrumming, sliding down my cheeks.

"You can see it, can't you?" Mrs. B's voice was filled with a mixture of awe and contempt as she searched my face. "You see one of your clouds above me."

For a moment, I thought she was going to relent—that maybe

she'd changed her mind. But then she snapped the back of her left hand across my cheek and her diamond ring connected hard with my skin. The blow sent me flailing backward.

"She has a gun!" I heard someone shout. Mrs. B lifted the pistol from her lap.

"Mrs. B, stop. Please!" I screamed.

Behind her, one of the police officers raised their weapon. I didn't think. I didn't have time. Instead I dived for Mrs. B, both hands reaching for her outstretched arms. I felt the cold bite of metal as my fingers connected with the gun. Mrs. B screamed and she jerked her hand wildly, trying to pull the weapon away from my grasp.

"Drop your weapon!" someone shouted. But she kept fighting, kept trying to pull away from me, and my fingers kept slipping against the rain-slicked surface of the pistol.

I grabbed for it again, but Mrs. B's nails found my skin and she pushed me, hard. I fell backward but so did she, and there was something about the angle her hand had on the gun— something about the way she held it, like her fingers were tangled in the trigger and she couldn't quite get them free. The cloud above her head swelled.

"Mrs. B!" I shouted, just as the air exploded with a gunshot. Just as I realized that her hand was poised on the trigger when she fell and landed on the pistol.

The blackness encased her until she was nothing but a blacked-out smudge against the rooftop. Then Mrs. B's body went still.

There was a blur of shouts and movement. I squeezed my eyes shut, trying to will the image away.

When I finally opened them again I saw Mrs. B's crumpled

body, a circle of blood pooling around her, pouring out like a dark, inky cloud. The darkness that had once warned of danger retreated, sliding up her sides and folding in on itself until there was nothing left but Mrs. B's lifeless body.

Mr. Bower ran to his wife and crouched beside her. A series of low moans burbled from his throat. Behind him, Penny stood as rigid as one of the high-rises, another soundless O on her lips.

Isaac and Marissa ran toward me.

"Whitney!" Marissa shouted, but Isaac reached me first, crushing me into a tight hug before I could say a word.

"Thank God," he said into my hair. "I was afraid we'd be too late."

"I found Isaac in the parking lot and then we saw that asshole shove you into his SUV," Marissa said, arms crossed tight over her chest. She was still wearing the white dress from the performance. It was soaked with rain and caked with mud. "We called the police and tried to catch up with him, but it was raining so hard we lost track of him when he got on the highway."

"It was Marissa's idea to check the roof. Because of the video." Isaac searched my face, then he squeezed me in another hug. "I'm so glad you're not hurt."

I squeezed him back.

"Isaac, I'm so sorry. For a moment I thought . . . I didn't realize . . ."

"Shhh. It's okay. You're okay. That's all that matters. Everything's going to be all right."

I nodded, then tipped my head toward the sky and let the rain sting my cheeks, hoping that he was right.

42

SIX MONTHS LATER

"FIVE MINUTES," I SHOUTED, FIGHTING TO BE HEARD OVER the excited titters filling our dressing room. "We need to be lined up by the stage in five minutes!"

A flurry of white fabric darted around the room as the girls hurried to make last-minute adjustments to their costumes. Something poked into my bun.

"You have a loose hair," Penny said, pressing another bobby pin into the hairpiece donning the crown of my head. My scalp felt like a pin cushion. "How's mine?" She turned so I could examine her updo. Her red dress belled outward. As usual, not so much as a hair was out of place.

"Perfect as always," I told her.

When she turned to look at me, there was a sad smile on her face. Her eyes skated across the room, watching the rest of the girls as they adjusted flyaways, reapplied lipstick, and reviewed the choreography one last time. Most days Penny hid it well, but I recognized the cloud that sometimes passed across her face, and I did my best to remind her that what happened wasn't her fault. That there was nothing she could have done to save Mrs. B.

"Is it weird that I miss her?" she asked.

I looked at Mrs. Cardell seated in the corner reading a book. She'd graciously volunteered to take over as our dance coach, but she was really nothing more than a glorified chaperone. Mrs. B would have been pacing the room, giving one of her motivational speeches as she inspected teeth for lipstick and adjusted costumes. Without her voice booming orders and words of encouragement, the room felt smaller.

I didn't think I could ever bring myself to forgive Mrs. B for what she did to Gams, but there were days when I found myself wishing things could have been different. Wishing that I'd been able to save her.

"No. It's not weird."

After she'd recovered from her shock, it was Penny who'd taken charge and explained everything to the police. She told them how Mr. Bower had grabbed her from the parking lot. How he'd panicked when he realized that he had the wrong girl and went back to get me. Penny's voice only wavered once, when she told them how they'd given me a choice—to save Penny, or to jump—but otherwise she was the picture of bravery. Even when they handcuffed the sobbing Mr. Bower and forced him into the back of the police car. Even when they carried Mrs. B's body away. Even when they drove us to the station for more questioning and our parents arrived, their faces ashen and terrified.

She didn't tell them about the darkness. She didn't tell them about the things Mrs. B said Gams and I could do. All she said was that Mrs. B learned that I was the girl in the photo and she wanted revenge. Later, I would show Penny the book I'd managed to slip into the waistband of my jeans before the police found it. I would explain what Mrs. B was talking about when she mentioned the things I saw. And I would learn that the scratches on Penny's car were nothing but a coincidence— marks left by a parking lot fender bender.

Penny surprised me—she didn't scream or tell me there was something wrong with me. Instead, she hugged me, her eyes wet.

"Thank you," she had said. "I know it was Marissa you pulled to safety, but I was on the field with her. Several of us were. If you hadn't yelled for us to get inside and held the doors closed to keep us safe, who knows what would have happened? You saved more people than just Marissa that night. You saved me, too."

I'd never thought about it that way—I'd been so focused on Marissa, so focused on the darkness I'd seen swelling above her head—that I hadn't thought about the other girls who were still on the field, some of them with darkness rising above them, when I started shouting. I hadn't thought about how Penny was just ahead of Marissa in the line, still making her way toward the locker room.

That night, I saved my team. And they, in turn, ended up saving me.

The police brought me in for questioning after learning that I was the girl in the photo. Like Will predicted, my many months of silence were extremely suspicious. That, coupled with the fact that I hadn't stuck around when the police arrived on the roof that day with Dwight, made many believe I'd had something more to do with the tragedy than I was saying. Until Penny came forward. She told the story of a girl who'd bravely pulled the team to safety, shoving girls inside the locker room and barricading the door with her own body.

Then one by one the other girls who'd been there that night came forward, each repeating their versions of the story and recalling the way I'd clung to the door to keep them safe.

If anyone remembered the order of events—that the shots were fired *after* I'd pulled them all inside—no one said anything. Not even Marissa, who reached out to the dance team alumni who'd been there that night to ask them to provide additional witness statements. Even Missy Allen, last year's captain who'd been furious at me for breaking formation, made the drive down from Lubbock to provide an in-person statement. In the end, the police didn't have enough evidence to charge me with anything. And it was hard to believe that the person who'd saved an entire dance team could have been involved in the events that unfolded outside of the locker room.

During my interview at the police station, I told them what Dwight said about Kevin and other kids at school bullying him. Somehow the news got out, which set off a ripple effect of other kids coming forward with their own stories. It turned out that Dwight hadn't been the only person Kevin harassed over the years. Including Penny. He was the reason she'd been crying outside the school the night of the vigil. They'd had a fight and broken up, and while she'd never told me outright, I had a feeling she'd seen the same anger from him that I'd experienced those last couple of weeks. Because of the school's zero tolerance policy and the number of people who'd come forward, Kevin was kicked off the football team and suspended. I'd heard rumors that he'd transferred to a private school in another district, not that I thought much about Kevin. These days, the only guy who occupied my thoughts was Isaac.

I've also spent a lot of time reflecting on my ballerina-covered notebook and the two hundred names listed inside. Yes, choices are like dominoes. But they don't always end in the worst possible outcome. Sometimes, they lead to good. Sometimes, the people we help go on to help others, and that can create a tidal wave all its own. Gams and I had become so fixated on the bad things that could happen because of the darkness that we'd lost sight of the good. For the people we saved, the darkness wasn't a curse. It was a gift. Maybe it was time I started to think of it that way, too.

Now I reached out and squeezed Penny's hand.

"Mrs. B loved this routine," Penny said, smiling at the memory. "She always thought it would win us a national title."

"Here's hoping." I pretended to hold a giant trophy in my hand and mimed waving at a crowd. Penny laughed.

"Look at you two," Marissa said, wedging herself between us. "I can barely tell you apart. It's eerie. Are you sure you weren't part of some weird cloning experiment? Or accidentally separated at the hospital when you were born?"

Penny rolled her eyes and smoothed her dress against her legs. "You're just lucky I'm feeling charitable enough to share the lead with you."

Marissa spun around so that her red dress flared around her. "Like you had a say in the matter. It's Whitney's dance. I have to say, it's still weird seeing you two working together so well."

I gave Marissa a pointed glare, silently begging her not to poke the sleeping Penny-bear. Penny was trying hard to be more amicable these days, and when I proposed the idea of having all three of us wear the red dress she hadn't completely thrown up on me. She'd relented. Eventually.

"I just think the choreography works better with three people," I'd explained, like it was my plan all along. I didn't tell her the truth—that the piece was about second chances. That the darkness had given all three of us a second chance, and so it only made sense that we dance the part together.

Marissa gave me a wide grin, then bounced back over to the mirror to inspect her hair. Over the last few months, we'd spent a lot of time talking. I told her about everything that happened with the darkness, starting with that first time I'd seen a rain cloud hovering over a man's head on a crowded downtown street and ending with that night at the game, when I'd chosen Marissa. But I was also doing a lot of listening. These days, I was trying to be a better friend. The kind of friend you can lean on when you need them most. The kind of friend that Marissa deserved. I wasn't perfect, but I was trying to be better. And according to Marissa, that was a good place to start.

There was a tap on my shoulder and I spun to find Mom standing behind me holding an enormous bouquet.

"I just wanted to wish you luck." She handed me the flowers. I breathed in their sweet smell and pulled her into a hug.

"Thanks, Mom."

"I'm so proud of you." She stepped back to take in my long red dress, bun, and stage makeup. "Gams would be, too. You look just like her."

I glanced in the mirror—a mini version of Gams stared back at me. It made my heart squeeze in the best way possible.

My relationship with Mom was another thing I was working on. After we came home from the police station, we had a long talk. It helped that Will made the drive up from Austin, determined to stand by my side while I told Mom the truth about Gams, our family, and the things we could do. Having Will there made it easier to tell Mom the truth, but to her credit she didn't argue or try to convince me that the things I saw weren't real. At least not outwardly. This time, she listened. And that was all I'd ever really wanted from her.

"I'm supposed to tell you the flowers are from Will, too. He's saving us seats."

"Line up!" Penny shouted, clapping her hands to get everyone's attention. Mom jumped, then gave me a final hug before scurrying out of the dressing room to take her seat.

The team scuttled into the hallway, white dresses billowing as they took their places.

We walked in silence toward the stage, feet marching in unison and heads held high the way Mrs. B had taught us.

Intimidation is half the battle, she used to say. *Make the other teams think you are stars before you even hit the stage.*

Another team stood in the wings ahead of us. They whispered nervously when they saw us take our places behind them. Onstage, another group glittered in black sequins, red lips grinning for the judges as they executed a series of turns. A girl in the front row fell out of her triple pirouette.

Penny turned back to the team. "Do *not* screw up," she hissed, eyes settling on a few of the freshmen as she spoke. She may have softened over the last few months, but Penny would always be Penny.

The audience cheered when the routine ended. The next team took their places on the stage. I took the opportunity to peer out from the curtain at the audience. It was a packed house, bodies jammed into almost every seat. The contemporary section of competition always drew a crowd.

Mom, Will, and Isaac were seated next to each other at the back of the auditorium and waved. They were easy to spot thanks to Beau, who waved a hand-painted sign with the ferocity of a hurricane. It read SHAKE IT, CHICKEN NUGGET! in black and gold block letters. Next to them sat Colton Wilkens, Penny's boyfriend of nearly two months. He was only a junior, but Penny seemed to enjoy having a younger man to boss around. That, and he was quickly becoming the rising star on the football team after he'd replaced Kevin, which gave him just enough clout for Penny.

Sometimes I wondered what would have happened if everything had shifted by just a few minutes. Maybe Isaac would have caught up to me and been able to stop me from running toward the strip mall. Maybe Mr. Bower never would have attacked me, and Mrs. B would still be alive. But if there's one thing I've learned, it's that the past will become a prison if you let it. There are no time machines. There are no do-overs. The best thing to do is keep moving forward. And somewhere along the way find the courage to forgive your mistakes. Gams never got the chance to forgive herself, so it was my job to make sure her legacy lived on.

You have to be brave, I heard Gams say. And I would be brave. From now on, I would always be brave for Gams. And for myself. And for all the people who deserved a second chance.

I was about to step back in line when I caught sight of movement in the third row. A small snarl of gray was rising above a man's head. He looked to be in his midforties, with dark skin and a neatly trimmed beard lining a square jaw. He could be somebody's father, or partner—he could be a good man who would go on to do good things. These days I tried to focus on the positive ripple effects that could come after I saved someone instead of imagining the bad. I made a mental note of his seat—third in from the aisle. As soon as we finished, I'd find him. I'd give him the second chance the darkness wanted him to have. I'd use my gift to do something good.

"You ready?" Marissa whispered when the team ahead of us hit their ending pose. I nodded and looked up at the beam of light shining down from the rafters.

The audience cheered. I heard Beau and Isaac the loudest, their voices carrying when it was announced who would be performing next. I imagined Gams was in the audience somewhere, her voice joining with the din.

"I'm ready," I said to Marissa. Then I took a deep breath and led us onto the stage, the rest of the team behind me. Marissa took her place on my right, Penny on my left. I counted us down and we all hit our opening positions, the air thick with the nervous excitement that always preceded a performance. The spotlight shone so bright I couldn't see the faces peering up from the audience, but I felt them watching. And somewhere, I knew that Gams was watching, too.

The music began, and so did I.

LETTER FROM THE AUTHOR

THE IDEA FOR *THE DARKNESS RISES* FIRST CAME TO ME about a decade ago. I was cleaning my apartment when, out of nowhere, a sentence popped into my head—*I was seven the first time I saw the darkness*. Years later, that line would become the first sentence of chapter two, but it began as the catalyst for Whitney's story.

Around the same time, the media was filled with news about gun violence. There had been yet another school shooting, and surrounding that tragic event was news of other shootings around the country. It struck me one day as I was listening to a podcast and the subject of gun control came up—I was becoming numb. The constant barrage of news about shootings had started to fade into the background because I was so accustomed to hearing about it. Somehow, I realized, gun violence—and more specifically, mass shootings and shootings taking place at schools—had become *normal* to me. How could the shooting of innocent people all over the country feel *normal*, let alone shootings involving children? It was a horrible, horrible thought. One that wouldn't stop haunting me.

In many ways, Whitney's guilt mirrors my own at having let myself become hardened to the violence around me.

Throughout the story, Whitney grapples with her shame about what happened at the football game and the different choices she could have made that night. It's not until nearly the end of the story, when she's watching Marissa's tribute routine at the anniversary vigil, that Whitney realizes how much bigger the issue is. She calls it an epidemic. But even as she has this realization, she can't shake her own guilt over what happened that day, at least not yet. What she fails to see in that moment is the bigger picture—if Whitney was the sole cause of her school's tragedy, how is it possible that so many similar events have taken place around the country?

At the time I write this there have been 2,032 school shootings in the United States since 1970.[1] Those numbers have spiked alarmingly in recent years—there were three hundred shootings in 2022 alone according to the K–12 School Shooting Database. I fear these statistics will only rise if we all allow ourselves to become numb.

I could tell you that gun violence is a uniquely American epidemic—that the US has at least fifty-seven times more school shootings than other countries.[2] I could tell you that in 2020 firearms became the leading cause of death among children and teens in the US.[3] I could tell you that I'm afraid that without stricter gun regulation those numbers will climb. But those are only statistics and my personal opinions, and the reality is that each of us must find a way to come to terms with this epidemic. Just know, no matter your political views, that you have a voice. Write to your congressperson with your concerns. Consider donating to or volunteering with organizations dedicated to preventing gun violence. When you turn eighteen, put your voice into action by voting for the candidates that you believe reflect your values and ambitions for this country. And not just every four years when it's time to vote for the next president, but in every election, especially those involving your local community leaders, where people like you are fighting every day to make a difference. All I ask is that you don't become numb. It's when we close our eyes that we lose any hope of making things better. When we become numb, we all lose.

[1] Naval Postgraduate School's Center for Homeland Defense and Security
[2] CNN.com/2018/05/21/us/school-shooting-us-versus-world-trnd/index.html
[3] USAToday.com/story/news/nation/2022/05/24/texas-school-shooting-gunfire-school-grounds-historic-highs/9915334002/?gnt-cfr=1

RESOURCES

Resources and programs dedicated to preventing gun violence or bullying:

Everytown for Gun Safety
Everytown.org
646-324-8250

Moms Demand Action
MomsDemandAction.org

Pacer Center's Teens Against Bullying
PacerTeensAgainstBullying.org

Safe School Ambassadors
Community-Matters.org/safe-school-ambassadors

The Sandy Hook Promise
SandyHookPromise.org

Stop Bullying
StopBullying.gov

United Against Gun Violence | Brady
BradyUnited.org

Mental health resources:

Coalition to Support Grieving Students
GrievingStudents.org
877-536-2722

The Dougy Center, the National Grief Center for Children & Families
Dougy.org
503-775-5683
Help@Dougy.org

National Alliance on Mental Illness
NAMI.org/Find-Support
800-950-6264

The National Child Traumatic Stress Network
NCTSN.org

PTSD Alliance
PTSDAlliance.org
888-436-6306

Suicide Prevention Resource Center
SPRC.org
Call or text 988

Teen Lifeline
Teenlifeline.org
1-800-248-8336

ACKNOWLEDGMENTS

I AM FORTUNATE TO HAVE AN AMAZING TEAM OF TALENTED people who helped turn *The Darkness Rises* from a pile of words into a real, live book. To say it takes a village is an understatement. First and foremost, thank you to my amazing agent, Joanna MacKenzie. How lucky am I to have you in my corner? Thank you for pulling my first book out of the slush pile and seeing it for what it could be. And thank you for your advice, expert editorial eye, and support at every step of this wild journey. Your advocacy, council, and partnership have meant the world to me.

To Liza Kaplan: you will forever have my gratitude for making my childhood dream a reality. Thank you for having such faith in my work, and for the countless hours you spent making my stories better. I am a better writer because of you.

To Kelsey Murphy and Want Chyi: you elevated *The Darkness Rises* to new heights and pushed me to make it a better, more emotional story—thank you. I'm so proud of where it landed thanks to your stewardship. Thank you for embracing me and this book with open arms.

To the phenomenal team at Viking and Penguin, including Ken Wright, Tamar Brazis, Gaby Corzo, Krista Ahlberg, Sola Akinlana, Abigail Powers, Lucia Baez, Kate Renner, Ellice Lee, Jaleesa Davis, Lisa Schwartz, Alex Garber, Felicity Vallence, Shannon Spann, James Akinaka, Bri Lockhart, Emily Romero, Christina Colangelo, and no doubt countless others—thank you! Thank you also to Jessica Jenkins for the stunning cover artwork.

Thank you to the team at Kaye Publicity—Kaitlyn Kennedy, Hailey Dezort, Dana Kaye, and Ellie Imbody—for helping to get this book into more readers' hands. Your support and advocacy know no bounds.

To the Panama Math and Science Club, past and present—Sally

Engelfried, Rose Hayes, Annemarie O'Brien, Keely Parrack, Lisa Ramee, Kath Rothschild, and Lydia Steiner. You are seriously the best critique group in the history of critique groups, and I will fight anyone who tries to challenge me on that front. Thank you, thank you, thank you for your wisdom and support all these years. And for reading *The Darkness Rises* multiple times during the revision process. I hope we write and publish a million books together. (With those little Trader Joe's cheese thingies as fuel along the way, obviously.)

Thank you to the SCBWI for creating a space for kid lit authors to learn and grow. Special shout-out to the team who organizes the Green Gulch retreat. So much of this story was written there—thank you for organizing an amazing event in such a beautiful setting.

To the friends who've supported me along the way, including the Dirty Thumbs, the Texans, and the Whartons, thank you! I am so fortunate to have so many brilliant, funny, and talented humans in my corner. I seriously don't know what I would do without you. Special shout-out to Melanie Chase and Gabe Martinez for the writing retreat brainstorms in Timber Cove and to Gabe for the headshot.

Thank you to my mom and brother, Mike, for your love and support and for reading to me when I was little. Special shout-out to Mom for passing down your love of books to me and now Sierra. Stories, it seems, run in the family. Thank you. And to my dad—we miss you terribly. Thank you for every opportunity you gave me.

To my husband, Jay—thank you for being the best partner I could ask for. There is no one I would rather spend time with—whether it's traveling the world or sitting in the living room doing nothing. Thank you for your endless support in the best of times and the worst of times. Forever with you will be easy.

To my daughter, Sierra. You have changed me for the better. There is nothing that brings me more joy than watching you discover the world. I can't wait to see who you become.

And finally, to anyone who picks up this book and decides to read: thank you.